# TENEMENT GIRL

*A Selection of Recent Titles by Anne Douglas*

CATHERINE'S LAND
AS THE YEARS GO BY
BRIDGE OF HOPE
THE BUTTERFLY GIRLS
GINGER STREET
A HIGHLAND ENGAGEMENT
THE ROAD TO THE SANDS
THE EDINBURGH BRIDE
THE GIRL FROM WISH LANE *
A SONG IN THE AIR *
THE KILT MAKER *
STARLIGHT *
THE MELODY GIRLS *
THE WARDEN'S DAUGHTERS *
PRIMROSE SQUARE *
THE HANDKERCHIEF TREE *
TENEMENT GIRL *

* *available from Severn House*

# TENEMENT GIRL

## Anne Douglas

**Severn House Large Print**
London & New York

This first large print edition published 2017
in Great Britain and the USA by
SEVERN HOUSE PUBLISHERS LTD of
19 Cedar Road, Sutton, Surrey, England, SM2 5DA.
First world regular print edition published 2013 by
Severn House Publishers Ltd.

British Library Cataloguing in Publication Data
*A CIP catalogue record for this title is available from the British Library.*

ISBN-13: 9780727894809

Severn House Publishers support the Forest Stewardship Council™
[FSC™], the leading international forest certification organisation. All
our titles that are printed on FSC certified paper carry the FSC logo.

Typeset by Palimpsest Book Production Ltd.,
Falkirk, Stirlingshire, Scotland.
Printed and bound in Great Britain by
T J International, Padstow, Cornwall.

# One

Lindy Gillan's stepmother had found her out
– again.

Not with her fingers in the till of the corner
shop where she worked as Myra's assistant. No,
no, nothing like that. Just agreeing to a bit of
extra credit for certain customers, that was all.
And you'd need a heart of stone to say no,
wouldn't you, if you thought the bairns had
nothing to eat? This being 1935 with Scotland,
like everywhere else, in the grip of a depression
and so many folk without jobs.

Not that Lindy thought Aunt Myra, as she called
her stepmother, had a heart of stone. Not really.
She had to think of making a profit in Murchie's
Provisions, which she managed for a lady-owner
they never saw, or the shop would fail and then
where would they be? Lindy and Myra would be
out of work and Scott Street – that dark, sloping
row of tenements in Edinburgh's Old Town –
would lose its one bright spot. For that was the
way most folk saw Murchie's, even if Lindy
herself daydreamed of one day getting away.

Was that what was called a pipe dream? She
smiled as she saw it was six o'clock and time to
pull down the blind over the door that said
'Closed', scarcely listening to Aunt Myra droning
on in the background. She'd heard it all before,
or something very similar.

1

This time it seemed that Myra – a bony woman in her forties with stringy blonde hair and narrow green eyes – had come back from the post office in time to see Aggie Andrews leaving the shop with a great stuffed shopping bag. And had guessed at once what Lindy had been up to. Now, didn't she know very well that Aggie had had her credit stopped when she'd never paid off a penny? So what was Lindy thinking of, then?

Standing at the shop counter, Aggie Andrews' tick book in her hand, her eyes fixed on her stepdaughter's long, slender back, Myra was beginning to get annoyed.

'Lindy, are you listening to me?'

'Sure I am, Aunt Myra.'

Lindy, opening wide her dark blue eyes as though amazed at her stepmother doubting her, moved back to the counter.

She had known Myra all her life; from the age of three, anyway, when her father, George, had married her; his first wife, Janie, died when Lindy was born. Struan, her brother, was two at the time, and for those first years before Myra came, their grandmother, George's mother, looked after them while George was away at the war. But then Grandma died and next thing they knew they had a stepmother, who wasn't too bad, did her best, but oh dear, she was a bit on the sharp side, they had to admit. Neither Lindy nor Struan let her fault finding and occasional lectures upset them, though.

'It's water off a duck's back for you two,' George would sometimes say admiringly, but then he was so easy-going himself, it was the same for him.

All in all they made the best of things, living across the road from Murchie's at number nineteen, Scott Street, a tenement packed with tenants they had learned to put up with, trying not to worry too much about the future – though lately of course the threat of unemployment was always with them. Struan, now twenty-two, had joined his father at Bayne's Brewery, hoping they'd both be all right – folk still drank, eh? While Lindy, at twenty, had her daydreams, and who could blame her? She was such a beautiful girl, everyone said, something good would be sure to happen to her.

Beautiful? Well, it wasn't for her to say, but Lindy thought perhaps she was. When she looked in the mirror and saw her heart-shaped face, her perfectly straight nose, her glossy dark hair she kept fashionably short (always saying she'd rather die than not have a good cut), she was inclined to hope that one day she would be lucky. You never knew, did you? On the other hand, being a beauty in Scott Street was not such a good start. Had to work pretty hard to believe the dreams, if you thought of that. Lindy still believed them, anyway.

'What was I thinking of?' she repeated on that bleak January evening when she was longing to put on her coat and go home. 'I suppose I was thinking of Aggie's bairns, that's all. Aggie said she could manage a few days with what I let her have. A few onions and potatoes, a cabbage, ham, and two loaves of bread. No' much, eh?'

'No' much?' cried Myra. 'It's a lot. Added to what she already owes, she's never going to pay for it.'

'I did write it down in her book,' Lindy said calmly. 'No fiddling. And as soon as her Tam gets a few days' work, she's promised to pay something off. You have to think of the bairns, eh?'

'Think I don't? I lie awake worrying about the bairns. But if I let people keep on having ticks, you know what'll happen.' Myra leaped to her feet. 'Och, we'll away home. The men'll be back any minute and I've the stew to heat up – no rest for the wicked. Get your coat, Lindy.'

Having locked the door of the shop they stood for a moment peering at the street, where the wet road glittered in the weak light of the gas lamps.

'Let's cross,' Myra muttered. 'Take care, now.'

Together they gingerly crossed the street and into the comparative warmth of number nineteen, where they had no stairs to climb, being on the ground floor. No men had arrived when they let themselves in, and only a sleepy ginger cat greeted them as they hurried about, stoking up the range, moving the kettle, putting on pans.

'Mind now, Gingerboy!' Myra cried, moving the cat from her feet, and Lindy, setting out his milk, thought: I'm glad I did give Aggie credit, anyway, whatever Aunt Myra says. Now I can think of all her family having something to eat when we're having our stew.

4

# Two

Scott Street, running between the High Street and the Cowgate, was not, unlike some Old Town streets, a place that had gone down in the world, for most would agree that it had never been up. While the ceilings of its houses were high and their windows long, the street had been built for ordinary folk, the aim being to house as many families as possible, which meant that each floor had two or three flats, some consisting of only one room, some being a little pricier with two, and a few superior ones with three.

The Gillans were lucky – they had one with three: a pleasant living room with a box bed in one corner and two proper bedrooms. No bathroom, of course, but their own WC, which was luxury indeed compared with the lot of the poor souls in the single-room flats, who had to use the one on the stairhead.

'Better than in the old days, anyhow,' some would say. 'When folk just used to shout "Gardyloo!" and throw their dirty water and slops out of the window!'

Thank heavens number nineteen didn't go that far back, Lindy would think, and was pleased enough that she was living in 1935. But that didn't stop her adding a smart house to her wish list of clothes that she hadn't had to run up on

5

Myra's sewing machine. All part of getting away, wasn't it?

Having been brought up at number nineteen Lindy knew all the tenants, old and new, and could have reeled off their names from top to bottom, but only two were special – Jemima Kerry and Neil MacLauren. Jemima lived with her widowed mother on the second floor, and worked as live-in lady's maid to a Mrs Dalrymple in the New Town, while Neil was one of five brothers whose parents lived at the top. He worked as a printer but had ambitions to be a writer, thought by most at number nineteen to be a bit of a laugh.

Jemima, small with ginger hair and hazel eyes, was twenty-four and rather on the plain side. 'Aye, no' married yet,' she would sigh, then laugh for she didn't care, only loved her job and was good at it, and could hold Lindy in thrall with her stories of life 'upstairs': the parties and dances, the splendid meals, the beautiful clothes and the daughter's presentation to the King at Holyrood.

Oh, my, it was like hearing about people from another planet, and yet there was Jemima, in contact with them every day! And she was so clever, too, at dressmaking, or making alterations, snipping here, snipping there, to create something new, or else styling Lindy's hair, advising her on make-up – she was a real tonic to have around. If only she could spend more time at number nineteen! But she was limited to her half days or the occasional Sunday, and then, of course, her mother wanted to see something of her. Still, she did what she could to fit Lindy in, although there was always Neil wanting to see Lindy, too, he being what Myra called her admirer.

He might be now, but at one time he'd been no more than one of the boys she knew at school – fair-haired, handsome, but not one to be interested in. It was only lately that they had begun to go out together, to take pleasure in each other's company, though without actually falling in love.

This suited Lindy, for she didn't want to be involved. Becoming involved could end up being married, and then what? You were in the family way. When she thought of that, she thought of her mother and shivered, for her father had said his poor Janie was no more than a bairn herself when she died. How frightened she must have been when she realized what she was facing! To be so young and know you were going to die. Quick, quick, think of something else, Lindy always told herself when she reached that point. Neil, perhaps? Yes, dear, handsome Neil. And on that miserable winter evening, it was Neil who came tapping at the Gillans' door.

Tall and straight-shouldered, he was wearing a trilby hat and a long black overcoat that was slightly too small – bought at a second-hand shop, Myra guessed when she answered the door, or it might have belonged to one of his brothers. Those MacLaurens were always swapping each other's clothes, seemingly just taking whatever came to hand. Still, he was a good-looking lad – nice regular features, light grey eyes – Lindy could do worse.

7

'Wanting Lindy?' she asked, standing aside for him to come in, at which he took off his hat.

'Yes, please.'

His glance went from George Gillan, sitting with the evening paper by the stove, to Struan, rising from the table, lighting a cigarette, and he nodded as they exchanged smiles.

'Hope you've finished your tea?' he asked.

'Aye,' returned Myra, 'but we've no' washed up.'

'Oh, I'm sorry!' cried Lindy, appearing from her little room, already wearing her coat and a dark blue pull-on hat. 'It's just that we're going to the pictures, Aunt Myra. Promise I'll do it all tomorrow, eh?'

'Promises, promises!'

'Well, how about Struan taking a turn?'

'How about it?' cried Struan, leaping up and jabbing out his cigarette in a saucer. 'I'm off to the pub!'

'And you've been working with beer all day?' said Myra. 'I wonder you don't get tired of the smell.'

'I never get tired of the smell.' Struan laughed. 'You no' coming, Dad?'

George, in his forties, with a broad face and light brown hair – looks his son had inherited – shook his head. 'Och, no. It's me for the evening paper. Maybe I'll give Myra a hand first.'

'That'll be the day,' snapped Myra, looking pleased all the same. 'Well, I'd best clear away. Lindy, if you're going, you'd better hurry or you might miss the beginning of the film. What is it, anyway?'

'It's an old one – *Flying Down to Rio*.' Lindy's eyes were sparkling. 'Got Fred Astaire and Ginger Rogers in it – their first film together. Now I want to see *Top Hat* – that's their new one, coming soon.'

'I don't know what you're talking about,' George remarked cheerfully as he lit his pipe. 'But have a good time, eh?'

'Aye, off you go with William Shakespeare here!' Struan cried, grinning, at which Lindy frowned and told him to stop his teasing, while Neil flushed scarlet as he replaced his hat.

'Come on,' he muttered to Lindy. 'Goodnight, Mr and Mrs Gillan. We won't be late back.'

'Aye, we don't like Lindy to be too late,' Myra told him.

George said comfortably, 'Och, she'll be all right with Neil.'

'I'll be all right anyway!' cried Lindy.

Outside, facing the night wind in Scott Street, she took Neil's arm.

'Now don't you go simmering over Struan! He just likes to get a rise out of you. Take no notice, is my advice.'

'He maddens me,' Neil answered, scowling. 'He's like a lot o' folk. Because I want to be a writer, they think I'm a great jessie. If he wasn't your brother I'd show him what I can do!'

'Oh, that's silly talk, eh? Why do fellows always think they can solve everything by fighting? We're supposed to be having a good time, instead of worrying about Struan.'

Neil's face cleared and his smile as he glanced down at Lindy was tender.

'Sorry, Lindy, you're right. Let's forget about Struan and think about Ginger and Fred. That's what you'd like, eh?'

'I suppose you'd rather have gone to a cowboy picture? Indians whooping and everybody firing guns?'

'I don't mind what I see, Lindy. Just like being with you.'

'Snap!' she cried, laughing, as they began to hurry to beat the wind and finished up at the cinema, out of breath, rosy-faced, but warmer and in better humour. There was no queue – what a relief – which meant they could go straight in to their one-shilling seats and settle down to escape the outside world for an hour or two. At least, Lindy could. Neil was not the type ever to put his thoughts aside.


# Three

Outside the cinema, the picture show over, the air was chill, though for January it could have been worse.

'Now, where's the snow?' asked Neil. 'Think we'll be let off this year?'

'H'm?' murmured Lindy, who was still far away in Rio, watching in her mind's eye Ginger Rogers skilfully following Fred Astaire's steps, floating so beautifully in her diaphanous dress. Lindy would have given the earth to have one just like it. What was Neil talking about? Snow? Couldn't

10

imagine snow in Rio, could you? Would she ever see somewhere like that?

'I was wondering, Lindy, did you ever finish that book I lent you?' Neil was asking as Lindy pulled on her hat and took his arm in an effort to find shelter against him. 'You know the one I mean? *Love on the Dole*, by Walter Greenwood?'

'Oh, yes. *Love on the Dole*. I did finish it, Neil. Awful sad, though, wasn't it?'

'It's meant to be,' he said eagerly. 'The story of a family in the Depression? What else could it be? Bet it made you feel you'd like to see a change, eh? In the way folk have to live?'

'Plenty of folk in tenements live like that all the time. They don't have to be in a depression.'

'My very point!' Even in the poor light afforded by the street lamps, Lindy could see the excitement in Neil's eyes. Next thing, she thought, he'll be telling me about his writing, sure to be something just as good as *Love on the Dole*, poor laddie. But already she was returning to Ginger's dress and Ginger's shoes and her beautiful hair that looked blonde, not red, because of the black and white photography. One day, it was said, most of the films would be in colour, not just Walt Disney's cartoons. Now, that would be something to look forward to!

'What I'm planning to do is write about ordinary people, too, though mine'll be Scots,' Neil was continuing, pausing to look back to see if there was a tram on the horizon. 'Won't be a copy of Walter Greenwood's book, of course, though that is a bestseller, but something on those

11

lines. I mean, too many books today are written about middle-class folk by middle-class writers. And they don't seem real, eh? Wouldn't you agree?'

'I'm sure,' Lindy murmured hastily. 'Neil, I see the tram. Let's get to the stop.'

On the tram, which they managed to catch, she thought she should talk of Neil's writing, making the mistake of trying to be more down to earth than he himself could ever be, while he sat folding his ticket and frowning.

'I mean, the nice thing is that you've got a good job anyway, Neil, haven't you? Printing – that needs training and they'll always want people like you who can do it, eh? So, you can do your writing in your spare time but you'll still have your –' She hesitated, and he looked at her coldly.

'My what? My proper job? Is that what you were going to say? As though writing couldn't be a proper job?'

'I wasn't saying that—'

'Look, I know exactly what you were saying, Lindy. It's what folk say all the time. So let's close this conversation, eh?'

'Oh, Neil, I never meant to upset you. I do think you'll be a full-time writer one day, honestly, I do!'

'OK, OK, let's leave it. But one day, I promise you, I'm going to see my books set up in print by somebody who's no' me, because I'll be the author and he'll be the printer. And one day, you're going to escape from Murchie's Provisions and do what you want to do. We're both going

12

to fly away from what we've got now, that's the thing to remember.'

'Oh, I do,' she said fervently. 'I remember it all the time.'

Walking from the tram stop towards Scott Street, they linked arms again, relieved that their little skirmish had been settled and that they could end the evening on their usual cheerful note. That's it for me, though, Lindy privately decided. No more giving advice to Neil, or even commenting on what he wanted to do. Strange though some thought their friendship to be, she valued it too much to risk losing it.

'Here we are,' said Neil, breaking their relaxed silence. 'Dear old number nineteen on the horizon.'

'You coming into our place for a minute?' asked Lindy.

'I don't think so, thanks. Better get home.'

'Struan won't be there – he'll still be with his pals.'

'I don't care whether he's there or not.' Neil pressed Lindy's arm in his. 'It's your stepmother I don't particularly want to see. Always looks at me as though I should be putting the ring on your finger.'

'Och, no! She'd never be thinking that. She knows we're just friends.' Lindy tried to search Neil's face, but couldn't quite read his eyes. 'That's the whole point for us, eh? We aren't ready for marriage?'

'Exactly right. If we're going places, we need to be free. I've seen too many fellows sink under the strain of having to keep a wife and family,

13

all their old ideas thrown out, all their dreams dead.'

'I know, I know! Folk rush into marriage, think it's grand and then you see 'em and everything's changed – there's no money, there's bairns to feed . . .' Lindy paused. 'And some don't even get that far.'

'You're thinking of your mother?' Neil asked softly. 'That was a tragedy.'

'Happens, Neil.' She began to walk towards the door of number nineteen. 'Come on, let's get in before the pubs close. You know what it's like then.'

'Wait, I just want to be sure, before we go in, that you do like being with me, Lindy?'

'Why, you know I do. We get on so well and you're so patient. Look how you go to the films I like and take me dancing when you're bored stiff with it!'

'And you do feel that we have something special between us?'

'I do.' She smiled. 'Don't know what it is, but it's there.'

'I'd say it was an affinity. Even if we have different interests, we're happy together. We feel right, somehow. Isn't that true?'

'Oh, it is! It's true.'

They gazed at each other with serious eyes until Lindy turned away.

Neil caught her arm. 'You've forgotten something, Lindy.'

'Oh, yes.' She relaxed into laughter and raised her face to his. 'The goodnight kiss.'

For some moments after their brief kiss, they

14

remained close until they moved again – the special friends – and continued down the long, dark street to the door of number nineteen, where they let themselves in.

# Four

Though the days of that winter were milder than usual they were still long, still dreary. Surely this was the worst time of the whole year, thought Lindy, struggling to find something to cheer her, but could see no beam of light in the darkness – unless you counted the talk of King George's Silver Jubilee, but that wasn't to come until May.

Meanwhile, the papers were full of Hitler and Mussolini and the threat of conflict in Europe, as well as a farming catastrophe in America where land turned to dust and families were going hungry and, of course, the ever-deepening Depression at home. No let up there.

Much as she would have liked to move on, when she read the papers Lindy decided that she must put up with the job she'd got until the situation improved. At least there were wages every week and there was no talk of being laid off, like so many workers. Yes, all seemed well, until one March morning Myra announced she'd had a message from Mrs Fielding, the owner of Murchie's Provisions. Seemingly, she was worried about the drop in the shop's takings.

15

'What's new?' asked Lindy, who was busy sorting out shelves. 'Takings have been down since we got into the slump. No' surprising, is it? Folk still like to come to the shop but they haven't the money to spend like they did.'

'Aye, but Mrs Fielding says there might have to be cutbacks.'

'Cutbacks?' Lindy was staring at her step-mother. 'What cutbacks?'

'Ssh, keep your voice down, there's customers in the shop.' Myra moved closer to Lindy. 'What she means is I might have to manage on my own.'

'Without me?' Lindy's voice was suddenly husky. 'You mean she'd give me the sack?'

'She said she'd wait to see how things go. I asked if maybe you could go part time—'

'Wouldn't want that. I couldn't manage!'

'Yes, well, she said no, anyway – it wouldn't be enough of a saving. But no need to worry yet. She's leaving things as they are for now.'

'So I've just got this hanging over my head, have I?' As she returned to her work, Lindy's eyes were mutinous. 'Looking forward to being on the dole?'

Myra turned away, tossing her head. 'What about that young man of yours? Neil's a nice fellow and he's got a good, steady job, too. You could get wed.'

'We have no plans to marry, Aunt Myra. And if we did, some married women still work. You, for instance.'

But Myra, stalking off to serve someone at the counter, made no reply, and Lindy was left to her thoughts. Better look in the evening paper, she decided, see if there were any jobs going, but she knew there were usually only domestic vacancies which she would definitely not consider. Besides, she hadn't the experience to apply, even if she wanted to, so what was her future? A wry smile twisted her perfect mouth. Talk about *Love on the Dole*! She couldn't face it. No, no, she wasn't going to end up there. Something would come up – it would have to. She'd just have to bide her time and be patient.

A week passed, during which she gradually got used to living on a knife edge, enjoying sympathy from Neil and even her father and Struan, though she knew a woman's work problems were never as important in their eyes as a man's. They had their own worries, of course, for no job was safe, and even if the brewery seemed to be doing well, who knew how long that would last? All anyone could do was hope for the best.

Alone in the shop one evening as closing time drew near, Lindy's eyes were on the clock. Myra had left early to prepare fish for tea and the last customers had hurried home through steadily falling rain, which meant that all Lindy had to do was put out the lights and lock the door after her when she left – as soon as those clock hands reached six.

'Come on, come on,' she whispered, standing at the counter, swinging her keys, and was about to fetch her coat when the shop bell pinged and the door opened.

Oh, no, she groaned, a customer! At this hour? She'd soon sort out whoever it was – but then she saw that the customer was a stranger, a young

17

man, tall, broad-shouldered, wearing a damp raincoat and cap. For a moment he hesitated, then, taking off his cap and shaking it, approached the counter.

'Hello,' he said, smiling. 'What a night, eh?'

His voice was deep and pleasant, his face not handsome but open and friendly, his hair sticking to his brow, a warm chestnut brown. Almost at once Lindy found herself smiling back, though latecomers such as he generally irritated her beyond measure.

'It is,' she agreed as the rain dashed loudly at the shop window. 'Can I help you?'

'Just hoping you could let me have some milk. I'm on my way home and suddenly remembered I'm completely out.'

'Oh, dear, I'm afraid we've none left.' She was genuinely sorry. 'We don't keep a lot because most folk get it delivered.'

'There's nowhere else I could try?'

'Well, there's a dairy on the High Street, but I'm pretty sure they'll be closed by now.'

He sighed, then gave a rueful smile. 'Oh, I can do without for once – all my own fault. Thanks, anyway.'

'No trouble. I'm sorry I couldn't help.'

'I expect I'm keeping you, am I?' His eyes, golden brown, were fixed on Lindy's face. 'Shouldn't you be closing, too?'

'At six, but no need to worry; it's only that now.'

'Still, you'll want to get home.' He replaced his wet cap. 'Goodnight, then, and thanks again.'

'We do have tinned milks, if they'd be any

18

good?' she suggested, and he paused to think, finally shaking his head.

'Not to worry, I can manage for tonight. I'll be back where I work tomorrow.'

She walked with him to the door. 'I'll see you out, then. Looks like it's still raining.'

'I'm afraid so – probably set in for the night. I'd better get going.'

He was, however, still lingering, his gaze never leaving Lindy.

'Goodnight, then.' She held the door wide open. 'Sorry again about the milk.'

'That's all right.' He moved slowly out into the rain, turning back to smile. 'Goodnight to you.'

Quietly she closed the door on the last sight of him and began to switch off the shop lights, still thinking of his smile, his generous mouth, the way his eyes had stayed with her until the very last 'Goodnight'.

What a pity, she thought, putting on her coat, that he was probably out of his area. No doubt she'd never see him again. As she did last-minute checks and prepared to leave, keys and umbrella at the ready, she wondered why should she mind about that? About not seeing him again? Well, she didn't, of course. They were – what? Ships that passed in the night.

'Goodnight, ship!' she called under her breath, as she ran home through the rain. And all through the evening, told herself it was true, they would never meet again.

# Five

In fact, she saw him again only two days later. It was just after five o'clock when she looked up from packing Mrs MacLauren's basket to see him standing in the doorway, and her heart gave a little jump. This time, because there had been no rain, he was wearing a tweed jacket instead of a raincoat, and his cap was already in his hand as his eyes went straight to her.

'That's you, then, Mrs MacLauren,' she murmured, handing over the basket to Neil's tall, angular mother. 'Sorry we've none of the cheese you wanted. It's due in any day.'

'Och, nae bother, Lindy. My lot's lucky to get any cheese at all and that's a fact.' Mrs MacLauren shook her head. 'When you think o' some folk having to live on bread and marge?'

'Very true,' said Lindy, her eyes on the young man in the doorway and biting her lip as she saw Myra moving purposefully across the shop to speak to him. 'Goodbye, Mrs MacLauren. Can you manage all right?'

'Aye, thanks. Never bought much. You seeing Neil tonight?'

'At the weekend.'

'That's grand. 'Bye, then.'

As Mrs MacLauren left the shop Lindy darted round the counter and sped across the floor towards the chestnut-haired young man, just beating Myra by a fraction. 'It's all right, Aunt Myra, this gentleman came in the other night – I think I can help him.'

'The other night?' Myra exclaimed. 'Why, where was I, then?'

'You'd left early.'

Lindy was smiling at the young man, who was himself smiling with relief that she had come to him.

'Was it milk you were wanting again?' she asked, willing Myra to move away, which she eventually did, though she still looked back with some suspicion.

'Er, no, thanks. I just thought, as I was passing again, I might pick up a few things – groceries, I mean.' Looking round at the shelves as though for inspiration, he added quickly, 'Everything looks so nice. I'm sure I can find what I want.'

'I can get them for you, anyway. Have you a basket or anything?'

He grinned. 'Never thought of it.'

'I'll give you a carrier, then. This way, sir.'

'Sir?' He laughed. 'My name's Roderick Connor, always known as Rod.'

'I'm Lindsay Gillan, always known as Lindy.'

'I'm very glad to meet you, Miss Gillan. Suppose I'd better be formal. Lead on to the provisions, then.'

Weaving between the customers, watched from the counter by Myra, Lindy, followed by Mr Connor, made her way round the shelves, suggesting items – tea, sugar, tins of beans and soup, packets of macaroni and rice, tomatoes,

21

cauliflower, a few potatoes. In the end she needed a second carrier.

'If you don't mind me asking, who's going to cook all these things?' she asked, smiling. 'You don't do the cooking yourself, do you?'

'Certainly do, when I'm at home. There's no one else.'

'I see.' Lindy, without asking herself why, felt instantly pleased to learn that when he was at home he was alone. Where was he, when he was not at home? 'Very few men know the first thing about cooking.'

'Necessity is a fine thing, Miss Gillan.' He looked at the bulging carriers Lindy was holding. 'Here, let me take those to the till.'

'No, no, I'll take them. Over here, Mr Connor.'

Aware that customers were watching with interest and her stepmother too, Lindy led the way to the till at the counter, where she rapidly rang up the purchases to a total that was more than customers normally paid at Murchie's Provisions.

'I'm afraid it comes to rather a lot,' she said in hushed tones, her eyes widening.

'Oh? What's the damage, then?'

'Seven shillings and fourpence.'

'That's all right, I need to stock up and I'd be spending the money at my local shop, so why not here?' Rod took a handful of coins from his trouser pocket and counted them. 'I think I've got it in change. That right, Miss Gillan?'

'Quite right, Mr Connor.'

No problems for him with paying, she was thinking. No need for him to take out a book for his 'tick'. Must have a good job, then? Certainly he was not on the dole.

As she passed his carriers over to him, their hands lightly touched and his brown eyes brightened.

'Miss Gillan,' he whispered, leaning towards her, 'would you consider—'

'Everything all right, sir?' came Myra's voice as she appeared at Lindy's side and fixed her new customer with a long, steady stare.

'Oh, excellent,' he answered quickly. 'The shop seems extremely well stocked – that's what I noticed the other day.'

'And why you came back?' Myra's smile was so wry, Lindy sighed. Oh, Rod Connor, did you think you could fool my stepmother, then?

'Yes, as I say,' he was floundering, 'I thought it'd be good to shop here.'

'Even when you're no' from these parts?'

'I'm from Leith.'

'Leith?' She raised her eyebrows. 'You'll need to get the tram, then. Or else the train.'

'It's all right, I've got the car today.'

There was a silence. Myra and Lindy stared. He had a car? No one in Scott Street had a car. No one who shopped at Murchie's Provisions had ever come by car.

'Oh, well, then, no need to worry about carrying anything, eh?' asked Myra. Her eyes so sharp, she was studying Rod closely. 'Must make life easier.'

'In some ways, yes.' Under her scrutiny he moved uneasily. 'Better be going now, I think. Thanks very much for your help.'

23

His gaze was on Lindy, but it was Myra who said, 'Thank you, sir.'

And then there was nothing else for him to do but put his cap over his rich brown hair, pick up his carrier bags and make for the door, conscious of eyes watching, but no one followed him. Until he set down his bags to open the door and then Lindy was swiftly at his side.

'Can be stiff, this door,' she murmured.

'If I look in for some milk tomorrow, will you be here?' he asked, glancing back at Myra at the counter.

'Sure to be.'

'Till tomorrow, then?'

'Tomorrow.'

'Lindy,' said Myra, when the door had closed on the new customer and Lindy was back at the counter.

'Yes, Aunt Myra?'

'I really don't think it's a good idea for you to be getting off with that young man you don't know.'

'Getting off?'

'Well, don't tell me he came in here for groceries when he lives in Leith! What man buys groceries, anyway? He came in here to pick you up.'

'He did not! And he has to buy groceries. He lives alone.'

'My, my, you've soon found out all about him, eh? What would Neil say if he could see you dancing attendance on a stranger?'

Lindy turned aside, flushing. 'I'd better go and help old Mrs Knox,' she muttered. 'She can never read the prices.'

'Well, if that young man comes in here again you be careful, is what I'm saying,' Myra said in a hissing whisper. 'I'm responsible for you, you know. You're no' twenty-one yet.'

'Don't I know it!' answered Lindy.

The following day when Rod came in, supposedly for milk, it was arranged, under the very eyes of Myra, again watching from the counter, that Lindy would meet him on Wednesday afternoon, half day closing for the shop, though how Rod could get an afternoon free she didn't know and didn't ask. It was agreed that they should not meet outside number nineteen, though she told him that was where she lived, but at the Canongate Kirk, from where they would set off on their walk. At Rod's suggestion, this was to be up Arthur's Seat, the famous dead volcano, an Edinburgh landmark which neither of them had climbed for years.

'Be sure to wear sensible shoes,' Rod warned. 'Don't want you taking any risks, Lindy. Would you mind if I called you that?'

'Oh, please do, then I can call you Rod. But don't worry, I won't be in my high heels. I'm really looking forward to doing the climb again.'

'So am I!' chimed Rod, before bravely taking his milk to the counter, where Myra coldly accepted his money and slammed the till drawer shut with an almighty bang. But she said no more to Lindy, who wouldn't have listened, anyway.

# Six

They were lucky. For their walk up Arthur's Seat the weather was again fine – blue sky, bright sunlight, even a breeze rather than a roaring wind. Of course, it was cold – it was only March, after all – but neither of them minded that. In fact, Lindy rather liked it – it made her cheeks look pink.

Pink cheeks, blue eyes, dark hair escaping from her pull-on hat, she knew she was looking her best as she ran up to greet Rod, who had arrived at the historic Canongate Kirk before her – and if she hadn't known it, his eyes would have told her the same.

'Oh, it's wonderful!' he cried, gazing at her. 'Wonderful to see you.'

'And you!'

She meant it. As her eyes went over him, today wearing a waterproof jacket, she was struck by his ease of manner, so different from Neil's, who for one reason or another always seemed to be on edge. But as soon as she'd thought that she felt guilty. She shouldn't be comparing Rod with Neil, especially when she hadn't told Neil about Rod when they'd met on Sunday. They were just good friends, so she might have done – but then she hadn't.

'All set?' she asked Rod swiftly.

'All set.'

26

She hesitated, looking along the Canongate, now just a thoroughfare stretching from the High Street to Holyrood but once an ancient burgh in its own right, only merging with Edinburgh in the nineteenth century. Being so steeped in history but also full of modern shops, it was always crammed with tourists and city people, and a favourite haunt of Lindy's, being close to her own home.

'You didn't bring your car, then?' she asked, turning back to Rod.

'No, I thought we'd just be walking today.' They had begun to make their way down the Canongate towards Holyrood, striding out well in their sensible shoes. 'Actually it's not my car, it's my father's.'

'Your father's? But you said you were on your own!'

'I mostly am, when I'm at home. Dad's away a lot at sea. He's a ship's engineer.'

'Oh, what a thrilling job! Always away, seeing new places!' Lindy's eyes were shining. 'Are you an engineer too?'

'Me? No.' He shook his head. 'Sore point, that, with Dad. He wanted me to follow in his footsteps but I hadn't got the same idea. In the end he accepted me for what I am and we get on well.' Rod laughed. 'When we see each other, that is.'

'So, what do you do?'

'You might be disappointed when I tell you. I work for the council. Not exactly pen pushing, though. I run a hostel for homeless men and I also do occasional work elsewhere.' Rod

27

hesitated, glancing at her with some diffidence. 'At the city workhouses, as a matter of fact.'

'Workhouses?' Lindy's eyes lost their shine. 'It's what folk dread, to finish up in the workhouse. If they get evicted, I mean, and have nowhere to go.'

'I told you that you'd be disappointed,' Rod said lightly as they crossed the road and began to skirt the railings of the Palace of Holyroodhouse, not pausing to look through the grand gates at the King's official residence. 'I know it's not what everyone would want to do.'

'I'm no' disappointed!' she cried. 'I think it's a wonderful thing to do work like that – helping others. And I bet you do a good job at the workhouses. Won't be your fault folk don't want to go to 'em.'

'You really think that?' He reached to touch her hand for a moment. 'I'm glad. Well, I do what I can, mainly checking that things are running smoothly – admin work, you might say.' He lowered his voice. 'Only wish I could do more.'

'And how about the hostel? What's it like to work there?'

'Difficult, but I think it's worthwhile. It's true that if you don't keep your head the fellows can sometimes drive you mad – sometimes because of wanting the drink and, of course, you can't let 'em have it, which means trouble. But you just have to keep calm. As I say, do what you can.'

'You must be a special sort of person to work there,' Lindy declared. 'I couldn't do it. Never in a million years!'

'Now, why d'you say that?' he cried. 'How can you know what you can do?'

They had reached the Queen's Drive, the long, snaking road that circled Holyrood Park, and were turning to walk onwards, past Salisbury Crags, an ancient cliff of rocks, to start the climb to Arthur's Seat. Yet Rod was slowing, putting his hand for an instant on Lindy's arm.

'You can't say that,' he said firmly. 'I think you'd be very good at my sort of work. I feel that you'd have the right qualities.'

'If you knew what I liked, you'd never say that!'

'What do you like, then?'

'Wearing nice clothes and make-up, going dancing, going to the pictures to see Fred Astaire and Ginger Rogers . . . anything of that sort.' Her sparkling eyes searched his face. 'There, now you're the one to be disappointed, eh?'

'Of course not! Any young girl would like the things you've said. Doesn't mean that you're not someone who cares for others.'

'Doesn't mean I could earn a living doing that, either. But listen, how did you manage to get this afternoon free? Shouldn't you be working?'

'I do get days off at the hostel – I share the day-to-day running with my assistant. But today I took a day's leave. I had some time owing.'

She thought about that. A whole day's leave? Just to be with her?

'Fancy your thinking about it,' he said, watching her face.

'I was just wondering. Well, let's get on, then. I want to see the Lion's Head – isn't that what they call the summit?'

29

'Some do. I suppose it can look like a lion sometimes, though I don't always see it.'

They were gradually beginning to climb, feeling no strain yet, the slope being still gentle, and Rod felt able to go on talking, pointing out that there were a number of places in Scotland with King Arthur's name, yet there was no record of his ever having been to the country. Did he exist, anyhow?

'Folk like to think he did,' Rod finished with a smile. 'Think it's romantic, all that stuff about Camelot, Lancelot and Guinevere, the knights in shining armour.'

'I think so, too,' said Lindy firmly. 'We had a teacher once who used to tell us stories about King Arthur's Round Table and I always wished I could see it, with the lovely knights as well.'

'But all we've got is a dead volcano that some-body called Arthur's Seat!' Rod laughed. 'You get wonderful views from the top, though.'

And so they did when they'd negotiated the last ascent which was truly steep, making their breath come fast and their legs ache, before they came out on to the summit.

'We made it!' cried Rod. 'Now we're entitled to have a rest and look at the view.'

To be shared, of course, with a number of other people, mainly tourists, but they'd never expected to be alone on this, the most dramatic of Edinburgh's seven hills. At least there was still a rock free for them to use as a seat, sinking down to gaze over the city spread out below, all its familiar landmarks so clear, and in the distance the Firth of Forth and even the Ochil Hills, standing out in relief against the backdrop of blue sky.

'No wonder Robert Louis Stevenson called this "the hill of magnitude",' Rod murmured. 'I feel that's what I've climbed.'

'It's worth it,' Lindy replied. 'And I can say I've been on the Lion's Head!'

'You're glad you came, then?' he asked softly. 'Glad to be with me?'

She studied him for a moment, half smiling before replying. 'Yes, very glad. It's been grand.'

'And not over yet.' He watched as she pulled off her hat and let the breeze ruffle her short dark hair. 'I thought we might have a cup of tea somewhere. If you know a place?'

'Know a place?' Lindy laughed. 'A tea room? They're everywhere – this is tourist land, remember.'

'And Scott Street's not far away.'

'But nobody'd say that was in tourist land.'

They rose together from their rock, smiling at nearby climbers, and began to make their descent, Lindy replacing her hat and taking the hand that Rod offered.

'It's worse going down,' he murmured.

'Gets your knees,' she agreed.

'You'll find us a tea room?'

'Nae bother. I know the very place.'

By the time they'd reached the little café in the Canongate they'd let go of each other's hands, though Lindy was strangely feeling that she and Rod already knew each other quite well, even if they'd only just met. Did he feel the same? As his golden-brown eyes met hers, she thought he did.

31

# Seven

Over their tea and buttered soda scones they kept exchanging looks, except when Lindy allowed her eyes to trawl around the café, as though in search of something. Or someone.

'Are you looking for something?' Rod asked, pouring himself more tea.

'No, no.' What else could she say? 'Just looking round.'

'Think you might know someone here? It's pretty crowded.'

'Folk I know don't spend much time in tea shops. I mean, why would we? If there's one thing we've got at home, it's tea.'

'Might have seen a friend, though.' Rod took a slice of coconut cake. 'Am I the problem, somehow? I mean, that you're here with me?'

'No, of course not.'

She was opening her eyes wide. Heavens, how sharp he was! But the fact was being with him was no problem, or shouldn't be. She didn't know why she'd suddenly begun to think of Neil. When would he ever come into this tea shop? And why should she worry if he did? Still, she didn't want to get into a discussion about it.

'Look, there was something I wanted to ask you,' she said, smiling. 'Hope you won't think it nosy.'

'Lindy, you can ask me anything you like.'

32

'Well, then, I was just wondering why you're alone when you go home from the hostel. I mean, have you no brothers or sisters, or –' She had been ready to form the words 'a mother', but they did not come and she left her question hanging, her voice trailing away.

'That's easy to answer. I've never had a brother or sister. My mother couldn't have any more children after me – she was always a bit of an invalid.' Rod lowered his eyes. 'She died when I was twelve.'

'Oh, Rod, I'm sorry! Oh, that must have been awful for you – still a laddie and you lost your ma!'

So deeply touched was her heart, Lindy at once reached across the table and pressed Rod's hand. 'But who looked after you, then?'

'Well, Dad found a housekeeper – a very nice lady – and he also took a shore job for a while, to see me over the worst. When I'd grown up, Mrs Warren went on to another job but she still comes in once a week, just to do a bit of cleaning.'

'At least you knew your mother, eh?' Lindy sat back with a sigh. 'I never knew mine. She died when I was born.'

'Why, Lindy, that's terrible! Worse than what happened to me.' Rod's eyes were full of sympathy. 'So how did your father cope?'

'First, our gran looked after us – me and my brother, Struan, who's a bit older than me – while Dad went to work at the brewery. And then he married again. That was my stepmother you saw in the shop the other day.'

Rod's jaw didn't drop but he seemed stunned.

33

'The one I was talking to? Help, I never dreamed she was connected to you! Was I all right? Was I polite? She looked –' He hesitated. 'Well, as though she could be rather – what's the word?'

'Tough? Och, she's all right. A bit keen to make us all do what she wants, but she's no' like the wicked stepmothers in the fairy stories. She's been a great help to Dad.' Lindy was looking at the clock at the back of the café. 'Rod, it's been grand seeing you, but I think I'd better go back now.'

'Oh? So soon?' He glanced at his wrist watch. 'But I suppose you're right, our afternoon is over. I had the crazy idea we might have . . .'

'What?'

'Well, gone on somewhere else, you know, for the evening. But that wouldn't have done, would it? I mean, your stepmother, your father – they don't know me. They might not have approved of your being out with me so long.' He laughed a little. 'We don't even know each other, do we?'

'I feel I do know you,' Lindy said earnestly. 'But I did tell Aunt Myra – that's what I call my stepmother – that we were just going out for the afternoon.'

'And that's what we've done,' Rod said cheerfully. 'I'll pay up and we'll go.'

'I want to thank you very much, Rod, for a lovely tea and a lovely afternoon.'

'It's meant a lot to me,' he murmured as they rose from their table. 'I'm the one who should be thanking you.'

Making their way up the Canongate towards the High Street, he seemed as though he would speak but never managed it, until finally he drew Lindy to a halt.

'Maybe you'll guess what I want to say,' he said hurriedly. 'I'd just like to ask – is there anyone . . . anyone special for you? Lord, I can't seem to talk straight! What I'm asking is have you what they call a "young man"?'

'I'll be honest, Rod,' she answered at once, relieved to be putting it into words. 'There is someone. He's no' my young man, but he is a very good friend. He lives in the same tenement and I've known him for years. We go out together, to the pictures and that. He wants to be a writer.'

'I see. I knew there'd be someone. I expect there are fellows queuing up to see you all the time, aren't there? But this writer chap – he's only a friend?'

'A very good friend, Rod.'

For a moment they stood still, oblivious of others passing by, until finally they walked on, Rod's brow furrowed, Lindy looking at him and then looking away.

'I don't understand that at all,' Rod said shortly. 'He's just a good friend? Why, for God's sake? Why is that all he wants from you?'

'It's always been like that between us. I suppose it's because we know each other so well.'

'Well, it's got me stumped. On the other hand, does it mean there's hope for me? That you might come out with me again?'

'I'd like to, Rod,' she said quickly. 'I don't think my friend would mind.'

'Lindy, that's terrific!' He grasped her hand and

35

squeezed it hard. 'Can we fix it up now? Our next meeting?'

'When would be best? Will it be difficult for you, being at the hostel?'

'I'll manage it, come what may. Trouble is my free time's pretty limited. As I said, I do have an assistant, but I still have to sleep at the hostel four nights a week. That cuts down on evenings out, and I only get one Sunday off in four.'

'Help!' cried Lindy. 'You're worse off than me!'

'I still have some free evenings, though, and I have next Sunday off – how about that?'

At the look on Lindy's face, he sighed. 'I see – that's the writer's day, isn't it?'

'We did say we might go for a walk this Sunday.'

'Well, there's next Tuesday evening?'

'Tuesday would be grand.'

'Really? Thank the Lord, then.' His face was all smiles. 'Where would you like to go?'

'Oh, I don't know. I love going out, anyway.'

'I'll see what's on. I'm willing to take you anywhere you like, except dancing. I'm no Fred Astaire.'

'No one is, except him,' she answered, laughing. 'But I don't mind where I go.'

'Leave it to me, then. Shall I call for you at your tenement? About seven?'

She hesitated, but only for a moment; it would be all right, she'd have seen Neil by then.

'Fine. If I'm no' outside, just come into the hallway. The front door's always open, and knock on the first door you see on the right. That's us.'

36

'Wonderful. Till Tuesday, then, though I'm sure to see you before.'

'Oh? Why?'

'To do some shopping, of course. And make myself known to your stepmother. Got to make her like me, you know.'

'Why, she likes you already – you're a good customer!'

Lindy, casually, was edging a little away, but Rod was quick to put his hand on her arm.

'Hey, wait a minute. Where are you off to? I want you to tell me what you're doing tonight when we might have been together.'

'What will I be doing? Darning, mending, ironing – all the chores I have to do on my time off. And maybe seeing another friend from the tenement.'

'Another friend?' He groaned. 'I'm not sure I want to know.'

'It's a girl friend,' she told him sweetly. 'Jemima Kerry, who lives up the stair. She's a lady's maid and lives in, but comes home on Wednesdays for her day off. We just like to meet, you know, and have a wee chat.'

'Jemima Kerry,' Rod repeated. 'What a relief to hear about her. I'll think of you, then, darning and mending, and having your chat. But shall I walk you home now?'

'No need!' she said quickly. 'Scott Street's just round the corner – I'll be home in no time.'

She knew he wanted to argue, but was already turning to go, her hand raised in farewell. 'See you when you come into the shop!' she called. 'And thanks again for a lovely day – I really enjoyed it!'

'Me, too,' he called back. 'Me, too!'

Already he was working out when he could revisit the Scott Street shop, while Lindy's thoughts had gone ahead to number nineteen. Would Neil be back from work now to see her coming in? Why was she worrying, anyway? He wouldn't mind about Rod, she knew he wouldn't. He and she were just good friends. Even so, she quickened her step, hoping to get back before him, so that when she did tell him about Rod she'd be looking wonderfully at ease.

'Hello, Lindy!' Jemima Kerry cried, standing in the doorway of number nineteen. 'Where've you been then to look so excited? Come away in and tell me all about it.'

# Eight

Though a little older than Lindy, Jemima had become her very close friend as soon as she'd left school, acting as something of a mentor as well as fascinating her with all her tales of upper-class life.

'Oh, my!' Lindy would say, always willing to hear more of the world that was so far away from Scott Street, thinking what a grand time the folk had who lived in it. But what was it like for Jemima? Always on the hop, stitching, pressing, brushing and curling hair, sitting up late to see her lady to bed. Lindy asked her once – how did she do it?

'Why, I love it,' Jemima told her. 'It's a hundred times better than being in service. And I get my perks – material here, bottle of scent there, beautiful hand-me-downs hardly worn – I'd never complain!'

Small and slender – some said thin – Jemima was a bundle of energy that could sweep through the tenement on her days off like a whirlwind, leaving her quiet mother quite bewildered. But Lindy was grateful to her for bringing so much colour into her life and for being so much more of a confidante than her stepmother, for it was always Jemima she turned to, rather than Myra. For instance, on her return from her afternoon out with Rod, she was desperate to talk to Jemima, not only about Rod but also about Neil.

'Oh, I've had such a nice time!' she cried, hugging Jemima, who was looking very smart in a little green costume she'd made herself with a cream silk blouse, a gift from Mrs Dalrymple, altered to her own size.

'I've met such a nice guy, Jemima, you'd never believe. He came into the shop, then asked me out, and today we went up Arthur's Seat and afterwards had tea at the Herald Café. We're going out next week, too – so, what d'you think?'

'What do I think?' Jemima's eyes were studying Lindy's flushed face and sparkling eyes. 'I think you must have had a very good time, eh? To be so full of it. Who is this fellow, then?'

'His name's Roderick Connor – Rod, he's always called. He works for the council, sort of on the social side, and he's really nice. I think he's been well educated, talks well, but he doesn't put on any style or anything. I'm sure he's very sincere.'

'H'm. Maybe.' Jemima was still considering Lindy's face. 'But you don't really know what he's like, do you? Better no' get carried away, I'd say.'

'Oh, it's all right, I know we've just met. But the thing is – all I'm worried about is—'

'So you're back!' came Myra's voice, as the front door of number nineteen opened and she strode in, burdened with carriers, her eyes fixed on Lindy. 'Now, I was wondering what time you'd come in. Hello, Jemima. Home from the nobs, eh? Lindy, open our door for me, will you, I've got ma hands full – and then you can help me with the tea. 'Bye for now, Jemima.'

'I'll see you later,' Lindy called as she opened the door for her stepmother.

'Aye, come up after your tea,' said Jemima, turning for the stairs. 'We'll have a nice chat.'

'As though you've no' been chatting your heads off already,' commented Myra, bustling into the flat to set down her bags and shoo Gingerboy out of her way. 'I'll just get the range fired up while you set the table. Then you can tell me all about your afternoon out.'

'It was grand,' Lindy answered reluctantly, aware that her stepmother was probably about to express opinions she didn't want to hear. She took a cloth from a drawer in her grandmother's old sideboard and spread it over the deal table, pretending she didn't think she needed to say any more.

'Grand, grand – aye, but what did you do?'

40

Myra asked impatiently as she finished rattling away at the range and closed the door on the fire. 'Walking, was it, or what? You were out a fair time.'

'We went up Arthur's Seat and then had tea at the Herald Café.' Lindy stooped to scratch the ears of Gingerboy, who was weaving round her legs. 'Just the usual sort of thing.'

'So now you won't want anything to eat here? And I've got some nice gammon pieces, too. Cheap offer at the butcher's.'

''Course I will want tea here. I only had one buttered scone.'

'Let's get on with things, then. If you start peeling the tatties, I'll put a pan on.'

For some moments there was silence as the usual preparations for the evening meal went ahead, until Myra said shortly, 'I think I should tell you, Lindy, that your dad and me's no' happy about you going out with this Mr Connor. Nothing against him, except we don't know him. He's just appeared out o' the blue and looks like turning your head, because here you are, going out with him and seemingly forgetting Neil. I mean, what's he going to say about all this?'

'All this?' cried Lindy. 'I've had one walk and a cup of tea with Rod Connor. Why should Neil mind? We're just good friends, anyway.'

'Now look me in the eye and say you mean that, Lindy! It's a piece o' nonsense, and you know it. Whenever is a young man going out with a lassie just a good friend? Maybe Neil's just a bit shy, hasn't got round to saying what he wants, but I bet he'll be upset over you and this

41

Rod Connor. Haven't told him yet, have you?'

'I'm going to tell him.'

'When, I'd like to know?'

'He's out at his evening class tonight, some literary course he's joined. But we'll be going out tomorrow. I'll tell him then.'

'Well, be prepared is all I can say,' Myra said with a certain gloomy satisfaction. 'Now, the men'll be in any minute – I'll make a start with the gammon.'

Needless to say, George Gillan said nothing to Lindy about Rod Connor. She'd known he wouldn't; he always left anything the least bit difficult to Myra, and that suited her, for she didn't want any arguments with her father. Couldn't imagine them, really, though Struan could stir things up when he liked and it was just as well he didn't know anything about Rod yet. He was another who'd be sure to ask, 'What about Neil?' Lindy was just hoping that when she saw Jemima again she'd be different. She'd understand.


# Nine

Running up the stairs to Jemima's brought welcome relief for Lindy from her stepmother's critical gaze. At least Myra hadn't yet told Struan about Rod, which meant he couldn't make any comments. What a relief! And as he was now out with his mates, Lindy could relax. For the time being, anyway.

'Come in, come in, dear,' Mrs Kerry cried, opening the door to Lindy's knock. 'How nice to see you. Would you like a cup of tea?'

'No, thanks, Mrs Kerry, I've just had one.'

Lindy's eyes were moving round the living room. Always so well-kept and pleasant, it seemed to her like an oasis in the desert of dreariness elsewhere in the tenement, where very little comfort was expected or provided.

Even her own home, though better than some, never looked like Mrs Kerry's, and sometimes Lindy wondered why that should be. It was not as though Jemima's mother had any more money than anybody else, or had inherited anything special. No, it must be due to the sort of gift some women had when they could make themselves look smart in a cheap little outfit simply by adding a wee scarf or a belt, or something that was different. In the same way, Mrs Kerry and Jemima, both excellent needle-women, could brighten up their flat with curtains, cushions and colourful mats, so that sometimes you'd never think you were in number nineteen at all.

She would aim to be as clever as that, Lindy decided, not so much in home-making – that was too far off to think about – but in what she wore and how she wore it. One day, yes, she would be in the sort of world where that sort of talent counted, and was cheered to find herself even thinking about it.

Not that she could stay cheered for long, when she still had to see Neil, but here was Mrs Kerry, small and neat, solemnly putting on her hat just to go up the stairs, it seemed, so that the two lassies could have their chat while she visited Mrs MacLauren.

'So nice and hard-working, Vi MacLauren, eh?' she asked from the door. 'Always appreciates a wee blether, while her boys are out, Arthur MacLauren as well, all down the pub.'

'If you want to see Mrs MacLauren, Ma, that's fine,' said Jemima, 'but we don't want to chase you away, do we, Lindy?'

'No, no,' Lindy agreed. 'You know I like to see you, Mrs Kerry.'

'Very nicely said, dear, but it's all arranged, nae bother.' Mrs Kerry gave her a pleasant smile. 'Jemima, mind you give Lindy some tea later – now, I'll away.'

'Your ma's so sweet-natured,' Lindy commented when she and Jemima were sitting together on the sofa. 'Sometimes I think my mother might've been the same. Dad never talks about her so I don't know what she was like.'

'Why, Ma remembers her, Lindy! She'll tell you about her. And I think she did once say your mother was a lovely girl in every way, and what a shame it was she was taken so young.' Jemima's look on Lindy was long and considering. 'Mind if I ask, has what happened to your ma put you off getting married yourself?'

Lindy coloured a little and was silent for some moments. 'I suppose I don't want to rush into it,' she said at last. 'Neil feels the same. He's got his reasons, I've got mine.'

'Now we're getting to Neil, eh? First, though, I think I should state the obvious – no' everyone

44

dies having a baby. You needn't be put off marrying if you meet Mr Right.'

'I'm sure Neil doesn't want to be my Mr Right,' Lindy said earnestly. 'Why, he said only the other night, "if we're going places, we need to be free". That's why I think he won't mind if I see someone else. We can still be what we are now, and that's good friends.'

'Good friends?' From her bag on the sofa Jemima took out a packet of Craven A cigarettes and a box of matches. 'Mind if I smoke, Lindy? I know you don't yourself, but I find it very soothing.'

'Smoke, then. I don't mind if your ma doesn't.'

'Never says a word.' Jemima cheerfully lit a cigarette and returned to studying Lindy.

'How about this other chap, then? The one you've just met? Is he going to be Mr Right?'

'Heavens, how can I say? I've only been out with him once!'

'You like him, though, don't you? He's the first one you've wanted to see, out of plenty that have asked – am I right?'

'He's very nice,' Lindy answered carefully. 'I mean, his job shows that. He works for the council, running a hostel for homeless men, and he looks after the workhouses as well. That shows he cares about folk.'

Jemima gave a mock shudder as she drew on her cigarette.

'He'd have to care a lot to do that sort o' work, Lindy! Be a saint, I'd say. I couldn't do it if it was the last job going.'

'Nor me. Well, all I'm saying is that he's nice,

45

I do like him, and I want to see him again. I just want Neil to understand and I think he will. Don't you agree?'

Lindy was leaning forward, her fine eyes intent on Jemima's face, her lips parted, waiting so keenly for the reply she wanted she was even ignoring the smoke from Jemima's cigarette.

But Jemima was shaking her head. 'No point asking, Lindy. I can't answer you. I just don't know what Neil will say. Might ask, though, if he happened to want to go out with some other girl, would you mind?'

'Me?' For a moment Lindy was taken aback. 'Why, I couldn't imagine it. He doesn't know any other girls.'

'But if he did meet someone, would you mind?'

'No. No, I wouldn't. I'd be surprised, that's all, but I'd still want to be his friend. I wouldn't let someone else come between us.'

Jemima shrugged. 'OK, that's you. But about Neil, I can only say again, I don't know what he'll say.'

'Oh, Jemima!' Lindy sat back, her clouded face showing her feelings. 'I've explained there's just friendship between us. I've said what I'd do. Why should he mind about Rod if he only feels friendship for me?'

'I don't think you can be sure of what he feels. He mightn't be sure himself. My advice would be, don't try to guess what he will say. Just be prepared in case it isn't what you want.'

'I think it might be.'

46

'Well, it might. Who am I to say?' Jemima laughed. 'What would I know about young men, anyway? I haven't got any!'

'Oh, that's a piece of nonsense!' Lindy cried. 'You're so attractive you could find a young man tomorrow if you wanted one!'

'Tell me where. The only men I ever see are Mrs Dalrymple's ancient butler and our cheeky footman who's all o' seventeen! Och, no' to worry. How about some tea? I've had my orders from Ma, you know.'

'I don't think I feel like any tea,' said Lindy, sighing. 'Thanks all the same.'


# Ten

Lindy and Neil were due to go dancing the following evening, though she was feeling so apprehensive she wondered if they should. Would the dance hall be the place to begin talking about Rod? Maybe they should just have a fish supper somewhere? It wouldn't cost more than the entrance fee to the hall. But then Neil would be wondering why she didn't want to go dancing, when she loved it so much . . .

In the end they did go dancing, and its familiar fascination for Lindy actually made her forget for a while what she had on her mind. In the pale pink dress Jemima had helped her make which fitted her perfectly, showing off her slender figure, she felt as near to Ginger Rogers as she possibly could, even if Ginger's fairy-tale dresses were beyond her dreams.

As for Neil, though he had no taste for dancing, he wasn't bad at it. He had mastered the art of leading and even a few variations in the steps for the quickstep and foxtrot, which always meant praise from Lindy and brought smiles to his earnest face.

When the band took its break, however, and Lindy and Neil were sitting on small chairs at the back of the hall, all of Lindy's fears returned.

'Like an ice cream?' asked Neil, mopping his brow, for the hall, filled with so many couples, was hot, but Lindy shook her head. Oddly enough, she felt cold and put a thin wrap round her bare shoulders. Even her hands were chilled as she clasped them together and finally raised her eyes to Neil's.

'Just want to talk to you about something,' she said huskily. 'While the band's away.'

'Something? What something?' Neil asked with a smile. 'You're looking very serious. Now, why would you be serious in a dance hall?'

Clearly he had no worries about whatever she wanted to talk to him about – see how he was smiling!

'Oh, I'm all right,' she answered quickly, lowering her gaze. 'There's nothing to be serious about. It's just that a young man came into the shop the other day – he's from Leith, works for the council helping the homeless – and we got talking – and – well – he asked me if I'd like to go up Arthur's Seat with him.'

Finding the courage to look up again when she

had finished speaking, she saw that Neil had stopped smiling. Stopped smiling and somehow changed. Changed from the Neil she knew to some other man, still handsome but cold, very cold, his grey eyes wintry, his face drained.

'And what did you say?' he asked. It seemed to Lindy that even his voice was different, as cold as his face.

'I – well, I said I would. I mean, it's been years since I went up Arthur's Seat.'

'You just wanted to see it again?'

'No. Well, I did, but I'll be honest, I thought it'd be nice to go with him.'

'So, when are you going?'

'Going?'

'You said you would go,' he said impatiently. 'When? When are you going up Arthur's Seat? With this fellow?'

'Oh.' She looked away. 'We went yesterday.'

Though she couldn't see him, she knew now how he would be looking. She also knew that her stepmother and Jemima had been right to try to prepare her for this, and that her own fears had been realized. Friend he might be, but Neil was not reacting like one. He was not saying, 'Fine, I'm glad you've met someone you want to go out with, because I'm only a friend and it makes no difference to us, as long as we can still be friends ourselves'. And if he had said that, she knew she would have cried, 'Oh, yes, that's what I want too, Neil! Seeing Rod Connor will make no difference to us at all!'

Suddenly she was aware that the band was back and tuning up, that people were drifting from

49

their chairs on to the floor while Neil was on his feet, looming over her. Surely they weren't going to dance again at this moment?

They weren't.

'Better get your coat,' she heard him say. 'We're leaving.'

Out in the street she thought they would be taking the tram home as usual, but when they reached the stop Neil strode straight past it and she had to run to keep up with him.

'Wait, Neil, wait!' she called. 'Aren't we taking the tram?'

He stopped and stood still until she reached him, his face still strange in its coldness as he looked down at her.

'No, we're walking,' he snapped. 'So that you can tell me what you think you're playing at, without folk on the tram listening.'

'Playing at? I'm no' playing at anything! All I've done is go out with someone who isn't you, but why should you mind?' Lindy was shaking as she faced him, her voice quite high, her eyes glittering in the lamp light. 'I've thought about it and I know I wouldn't have minded if you'd met someone else, as long as we'd stayed friends. You've always said that's what we were – just friends.'

'Special friends,' Neil said with emphasis. 'Special friends, Lindy. That means something more than ordinary friends, eh? That we had a special affinity. Means I would never have taken out some other girl. Means I've a right to mind if you decide to see some other fellow – who'll no' want to be a friend at all. I don't know him but I know what he'll want, oh, God, yes, and you say I shouldn't mind? I tell you, this news is pretty upsetting for me. Very upsetting, in fact.'

Turning on his heel he began to walk fast away again with Lindy calling and following, reaching him at last and catching his arm.

'Neil, wait, will you? Please, wait, so I can talk to you – you said you wanted me to talk.'

'Talk, then,' he grunted, slowing his pace. 'Tell me this guy isn't like every other guy – just wants to go climbing with you, just wants nice talks? Who are you trying to fool, Lindy?'

'You weren't like everybody else,' she said quietly. 'You did just want nice talks, eh? Or maybe going to the pictures, or dancing, but only as a friend? Why should I think you'd mind if someone else wanted to see me when you didn't want more?'

'Maybe I do want more, then,' he muttered after a silence, during which they walked together through the uneven streets of the Old Town, passing a few people – some the worse for drink who waved and shouted, until Neil shouted louder and they fell back in alarm.

'Hell, Lindy, I don't know what I want. I thought we didn't want romance, didn't want to be married. That was right, wasn't it? So, we could just keep on as we were, seeing each other, kissing goodnight. I thought that was what we were happy with – friendship with no strings, eh? And you never seemed to want to go out with anyone else. Until now.'

'Neil, I never dreamed –' Lindy began. 'I never thought—'

51

'That I cared for you? Well, you care for me, don't you? That's why we're special friends.'

'Yes, that's right,' she cried, her lip trembling. 'I do care for you, Neil. It's terrible to see you like this – so hurt, so wounded – and I did it, I'm responsible –'

She began to cry and he took her in his arms, his face softening, its coldness melting, his voice becoming his own again as he soothed her.

'It's all right, Lindy, it's all right, don't cry. Nothing's happened that can't be mended.'

'Mended?' she repeated, freeing herself, her hand dashing away the tears on her cheeks.

'Well, how much do you really want to see this man again? You don't know him, he doesn't know you – it'd be no hardship to part, eh? Before you get in too far?'

'You want me to do that?'

'If you want to do it, Lindy. For me.' Neil was being softly persuasive, his gaze on her intense, his hand round hers strong and warm. 'If you choose me, rather than him.'

The choice was a stark one. Between Rod, the new man she had to admit she was attracted to, was at ease with and felt she did know, in spite of what Neil said. Or Neil himself, her old, dear friend, who meant so much, who was a part of her and had been for years. Oh, God, what could she do? There was no choice at all, really. At least, only one that she could make.

Slowly she went back into Neil's arms, put her face against his and sighed deeply.

'I can't give you up,' she whispered. 'I can't let you leave me. I won't see Rod again.'

'Oh, Lindy!'

For some time they stood together quietly, until their mouths met and they kissed, at first gently, then with a strength they hadn't experienced before, which left them breathless and surprised.

'I said I didn't know what I want,' Neil whispered. 'But I know I don't want to lose you.'

When Lindy finally let herself into the flat, she found her father dozing in his chair and Myra looking up from her sewing with her usual sharpness.

'Well, you're early, then! What happened? Did you tell Neil? Did you have a row?'

Lindy took off her coat and kicked off her shoes before replying.

'I told him,' she said at last. 'He was upset but he's all right now. Quite happy.'

'Happy? With you seeing this other man?'

'Happy because I won't be seeing him.'

'Ah.' Myra rose, smiling, and folded her sewing. 'Now you're talking sense, Lindy. There was never any future in that, I'm telling you, but Neil's a nice, steady lad. You won't regret your decision.'

Making no reply Lindy glanced at her father, still sleeping, and felt like sleeping herself, just closing her eyes and shutting out all that made life difficult. Yet she knew that when she went to bed she wouldn't sleep at all.

'Like some cocoa?' asked Myra. 'I'm just going to boil the kettle. Give your dad a shake, eh? It's time he woke up.'

The last thing Lindy wanted was cocoa, but if she took it she'd stave off the time for being alone and thinking about Rod, and how she was going to tell him what she must. 'Yes, I'll have some cocoa,' she told Myra and bent to shake her father's arm. 'Come on, Dad, wakey, wakey!'

'What's that?' cried George, his eyelids jerking open. 'Who's there? Lindy, is that you? Where've you been, then? And where's Struan?'

'Don't know where Struan is but I've been out dancing, Dad. We're just going to have cocoa.'

'Cocoa . . .' He sat up, rubbing his face and shaking his head. 'Must have dropped off, eh? Have a good time, then?'

'She did,' called Myra. 'And she's told Neil she's no' seeing this other fellow, so that's that.'

'What other fellow?' asked George. 'I thought Neil was the one.'

'He is now,' Myra said with satisfaction. 'Lindy, will you pass that tin o' Marie biscuits? We'll have one with our cocoa.'

Later, in bed, it was just as Lindy had expected – she couldn't sleep. Could only think of the change in Neil; of how he'd changed from friend to – well, more than friend, in a matter of moments. She knew she'd been right in the choice she'd made – Neil meant too much to her to let him go, and now it seemed their relationship was going to be different, anyway – but, on the other hand, she wished that there hadn't been a choice to make. How was she to tell Rod that she couldn't see him any more? How to accept that that made her feel so bad? Because he wasn't the only one who was going to be upset. The truth was she wanted Rod as well as Neil, but now knew that just wasn't possible.

# Eleven

As Lindy guessed he might, Rod came into the shop on Saturday when he had time off. She had been preparing herself all morning in case he came early, but it was one o'clock when he arrived, just as Myra returned from her dinner break and Lindy was due to take hers. Couldn't be better timing, except that Myra wasn't pleased to see Rod in the shop at all and showed it, giving him a long, hard stare as he greeted her with a cautious smile, sweeping off his cap and murmuring a polite, 'Good afternoon.'

'I'll just go for my break,' Lindy said hastily. 'Shan't be long, Aunt Myra.'

'Mr Connor going with you?' Myra asked. She added pointedly, 'I expect you've things to say.'

As Rod stared Lindy gave him a beseeching look and pulled on her jacket.

'Back soon,' she murmured and made for the door, followed by Rod, when he had replaced his cap and given Myra another of his smiles, which she did not return.

'Lindy, what's going on?' he asked when they were both walking fast up Scott Street. 'What did your stepmother mean by that – that you've got things to say?'

'She shouldn't have said that; it's nothing to do with her.' Lindy's face was dark with anger. 'But she can be like that – interfering, I mean.'

'Well, if this is your time to be with me, let's forget her,' Rod said in a calming voice. 'And if this is your lunch hour, may I take you somewhere to eat?'

'Och, no, I'll have something when I get back.' Lindy slowed down and turned to look into Rod's face. 'For now, I just want to talk to you. My stepmother shouldn't have said what she did, but it's true, I've something to say.'

'And why do I think I'm not going to like it?'

Though he was smiling as he reached for her hand and turned her towards the High Street, Rod's eyes were showing his unease.

'There are cafés all over the place round here,' he said quietly. 'Let's have a sandwich and a coffee where we can have somewhere to sit.'

'I only have half an hour.'

'Not today. Your stepmother's not going to say anything today.'

'How can you know that?'

'Because she has the look of somebody who's pleased things are going her way. She won't worry if you're late back.'

'You're a mind reader?'

'Face reader. In my job you get to know a lot from the expressions on people's faces. But never mind anyone else – let's find a place to eat.'

When they'd been served with ham sandwiches and coffee in a café at the top of the High Street, Lindy's gaze on Rod was long and sad. 'Can you read my face now?' she asked in a low voice.

'I wish I couldn't. But eat something, Lindy, eh? And I will, too.'

'I'm no' hungry.'

'Got to eat,' he said firmly, and after a pause Lindy began to eat her sandwich as Rod ate his.

'Now, coffee,' he ordered.

'I could do with the coffee,' she agreed.

'To give you courage? Ah, come on, Lindy, you don't have to say anything to me. It doesn't take a mind reader to know that you're wanting to tell me we're not going to meet on Tuesday. Are we going to meet again at all?'

'I don't think so, Rod.'

Staying calm, he took a moment to drink his coffee, only the hurt in his eyes giving him away.

'The writer has spoken, has he?' he said at last, setting down his cup. 'You told him about me and he said no. Was that what happened?'

'I never thought he'd mind,' she said quickly. 'I was maybe stupid, but I thought we could stay as we were, even if I wanted to see you. After all, I have this friend, Jemima, like I said, and she doesn't mind who I see. I thought Neil should be the same.'

'Oh, Lindy, Lindy,' Rod sighed, putting a hand to his brow. 'Come on, you must've known your Neil was no Jemima! He's a man and a man can never be "just friends" with a woman.' Rod put his cup aside and raised his eyes to Lindy's. 'In your heart you knew that, didn't you? Weren't you worried about how he'd take your news?'

'I was,' she admitted. 'But I kept on thinking it'd be all right. Seemingly, I was wrong.'

'So, what the hell does this fellow really want?' Rod asked with sudden force. 'Just to keep going out with you, getting nowhere? Bit of a dog in the manger, isn't he? Stopping you seeing someone who might truly care?'

'He cares now, Rod. Things . . . have changed between us.'

At her words Rod sat very still, and for long moments there was silence between them – until a waitress came up to crash their cups and plates on to her tray.

'You folks finished? There's others want this table, you ken.'

'Sorry,' they muttered, rising quickly. 'Sorry about that.'

'Quite all right,' she answered, mollified by the sight of the tip Rod was leaving on the table. 'There's your bill, then, just pay at the desk, eh?'

'I'll walk you back to the shop,' Rod said heavily when they were in the street. 'You won't be too late.'

'There's no need for you to come with me, Rod.'

'I want to.'

At the top of Scott Street, however, he paused. 'Lindy?' he whispered.

'Yes, Rod?'

'Will you just answer me something? You say things have changed between you and Neil – is that true for you as well as him?'

'I could never let him go, I know that.'

'He threatened he would go? Not see you?'

'I had to make a choice.'

'And you chose him?' Rod looked away. 'Oh, well, then, there's no more to be said. Why didn't you tell me this before?'

'I didn't want to,' she answered softly. 'Oh,

58

Rod, let's say goodbye here, no' at the shop.' She put her hand on his arm and looked into his eyes.

'I wish we didn't have to say goodbye at all, but it's the way things have worked out, eh? Tell me you understand.'

'I'm trying to,' he said quietly, taking her hand from his arm and holding it. 'But if you should, you know, change your mind . . . have second thoughts . . . will you let me know?'

She nodded, releasing her hand, her eyes still on his. 'I didn't know you for long,' she whispered, 'but I'll never forget you, Rod, never!'

With a last, sad look, she kissed him on the cheek and ran. Ran and ran, down Scott Street to Murchie's Provisions, never looking back, while Rod stood watching, unmoving until, having seen her vanish inside, he turned slowly away. Only then did he remember he'd never told her how to contact him. She didn't have his home address, or work address, or telephone number. Should he run after her? Send a note to the shop? He shook his head. Seemed to him there was no point. She'd made her choice – the tried and trusted Neil, not him. And he couldn't see that wretched writer guy ever letting her go.

# Twelve

Days went by, then weeks, so that early spring became May and there was all the public interest of King George's Silver Jubilee – not that it affected anyone in Scott Street very much. But then came summer, with things for Lindy still seeming the same, nothing changing between herself and Neil as much as she'd thought it might.

Sometimes she asked herself, what had she expected? Neil was certainly no longer just a friend – she couldn't say that. When they went out together there was more closeness between them, more holding of hands, more passionate kisses, and she was happy enough, yet she couldn't help wondering where was it going, this relationship of theirs? They had given up discussing the future and never mentioned marriage, which in the past they'd discounted. They seemed to be content to carry on, not quite as before, but still a long way from putting into words anything definite.

Of course, when she reached the point of understanding this, Lindy had to decide what she wanted herself – and there was the problem. She had made her choice, had realized she couldn't say goodbye to Neil and had said goodbye to Rod instead, yet still couldn't be sure what her and Neil's next step should be. Marriage was the usual end to a long-standing courtship. But was she being courted?

Did she still want something else first? Hadn't Neil himself said that one day she'd be free of Murchie's Provisions and that they'd both fly away to something new? Yes, he'd said that – to fly away was what she'd always wanted and, she had to admit, still wanted. Yet there was nothing on the horizon, nothing in her life that even gave her hope that it might happen. Maybe she should just settle for Neil's love, then, for she was sure the love was there, even if it wasn't spelled out.

Back she came, full circle, to not knowing just where they were going.

Meanwhile, the recession was as deep as ever, and times just as harsh worldwide, with the added anxiety that Germany and Italy seemed to be gearing up for aggression. So far no one had been able to stop them. Where would it all end? cried the papers, and even ordinary folk who didn't usually take much notice of international problems were beginning to echo the question. Where *would* it all end?

'Know what I think?' Struan asked one evening, when tea had been cleared away and he was still sitting at the table opposite his father. 'It might be a good idea for me to join the Territorials.'

'You what?' cried George. Stung from his usual calm, he was sitting up straight, his eyes flashing with rare fire. 'Struan, are you crazy?'

'Hey, why all the fuss?' Struan was raising his eyebrows as Myra and Lindy turned from doing the washing-up at the sink to look at him. 'It's a good idea to join; it's only part time but you get paid when you turn up, and you get training for war.'

'Training for war? What are you saying?' George's placid features were suffused with colour, his eyes still showing his emotion. 'Who says there's going to be another war? After what I went through – after what we all went through – nobody in their senses would want to go through it again. I'll no' have you talking such damn' nonsense as wanting to join the TA. Let this be an end of it!'

'If it's only weekends, where's the harm?'

61

asked Myra. 'I think Struan's right – it's a good idea. Brings in extra money – what's wrong with that?'

'Maybe the brewery will tell him,' snapped George. 'Maybe they won't want their workers taking on extra duties, and with things as they are anybody who does might be the first to get the sack. You ken we're all on a knife edge, eh? Stick to what you've got, Struan, and don't be risking it.'

'Och, I'm going out,' Struan muttered, jumping to his feet. 'I was just being patriotic, eh? I mean, when you hear about the Germans rearming and Mussolini threatening Abyssinia and all that, the TA might well be needed.'

'And then there's the money,' put in Myra. 'Have to think o' that.'

'I'll have no more talk o' war in this house,' George declared and, leaving his chair, took his cap from its peg and jammed it on his head. 'Myra, I'm going out and all. I reckon I could do with a pint tonight, to clear ma head.'

'Coming with me, then?' asked Struan from the door.

'No, thanks. I don't want you spouting about Germany and all that sort o' thing. I'll go to the Falcon, see a few mates.'

'Suit yourself.' Struan shrugged. 'I'm going to knock a few billiard balls about in the Feathers, anyway. Give 'em hell. That's what I feel like.'

'Well!' Myra exclaimed as the door shut on the two men. 'All right for some, eh? Just walk out whenever they like, straight into the pub. Nowhere for us to go, is there? Mind you, your dad's usually happy to stay in. Shows he's upset.'

'He hasn't forgotten the war,' said Lindy. 'Who would, if they were in it?'

'Let's just hope there's never another.' Myra's look on Lindy was considering. 'Talking o' going out, aren't you seeing Neil tonight?'

'He's gone to his class again. I'm going to do some more on that dress I'm making.'

'If you don't mind me saying, Lindy, it should be a wedding dress you're making now. I mean, when are you and Neil going to name the day?'

'No talk of that yet, Aunt Myra.'

'No? What's the delay? He's got a good job; you've no need to wait.'

'We're happy as we are,' Lindy said firmly.

And hoped it was true.


# Thirteen

It was July and the afternoon warm when Lindy was having her tea break at the shop counter and taking the chance, while Myra served old Mrs Knox, their only customer, to look at the job adverts in the paper. Nothing, as usual.

She tossed the paper aside and crumbled a ginger biscuit. What was the point in even looking? Unless you wanted domestic service there was no hope of a move from what she had, and as no more had been said of her losing her job at Murchie's, she supposed she should be grateful she'd still got it. On the other hand, she couldn't resist seeing what was available, even

63

though she didn't actually know what she wanted, and could only be sure she'd know it when she saw it. Surely, one day, her luck would turn?

'Lindy,' she heard someone gasp, and looked up to find Jemima standing at the counter. She was wearing a linen dress and a light jacket, was carefully made up, her hair as neatly done as ever, and might have looked her usual self – except that her eyelids were red. She had obviously been crying.

'Jemima!' Lindy exclaimed. 'What's wrong? Why are you here today? It's no' your Wednesday.'

'My Wednesday.' Jemima gave a strange smile. 'My day off? Lindy, I don't need days off now, I've got no job.'

'No job?'

Lindy was speechless. People now were always losing jobs; unemployment was everywhere, but not – surely not – Jemima? So well settled with rich Mrs Dalrymple, so well-suited, so happy? Oh, it couldn't be true!

Casting a glance to where her stepmother was gossiping with Mrs Knox, Lindy came running from behind the counter to throw her arms round her friend. 'Jemima, what are you saying? You, of all people, losing your job? It's no' true, eh?'

'It's true. But that's no' the worst of it. Oh, God, no! Lindy, something awful has happened to Mrs Dalrymple, something you'll never believe. It's too terrible, too out o' the blue!'

'What? What's happened? Is she ill?'

'No, no, she's no' ill.' Jemima dropped her voice and looked around the almost empty shop until she met Myra's gaze zooming in on her. She turned back to Lindy and grabbed her arm.

64

'Look, I'd better go, but can you meet me this evening? Call for me and we'll go out, eh?'

'Yes, I'll call for you, but tell me, quick – what's happened to Mrs Dalrymple?'

'She's lost all her money.' Jemima's voice was so low, so hesitant, it was clear she could hardly bring herself to get the words out. 'Pretty much everything, Lindy. Look, I'll away. See you tonight.'

As the shop door closed on Jemima, Myra moved swiftly from her customer to the counter. 'Lindy, what's up with Jemima? What's she doing here when she should be at work?'

'I don't know the details, Aunt Myra, but she came to tell me she's lost her job.'

'Lost her job? Never!'

Myra's eyes were alive with interest, but even though she served Mrs Knox as quickly as possible and returned to Lindy to find out more, Lindy merely repeated that she hadn't got all the details yet and might know more after she'd seen Jemima that evening. Now was not the time, she'd decided, to discuss Mrs Dalrymple's misfortune, though probably it would all come out later. In the meantime, Myra would just have to wait.

'Be sure to tell me what you find out,' she instructed when it was time that evening for Lindy to run up to Mrs Kerry's flat. 'I'm dying to hear why Jemima got the sack.'

'It was nothing to do with her, Aunt Myra.'

'Well, just find out what you can, eh?'

'If it's no' confidential,' Lindy warned coldly.

'Why, if Jemima can tell you, she can tell me!' Myra cried. 'I'm an old friend of her ma's, remember!'

Without replying Lindy hurried on up the stairs. As though she had time to worry about Myra's nosiness. All her thoughts were with poor Jemima – and, of course, Mrs Dalrymple.

'Oh, Lindy, there you are,' cried Jemima, opening her door. 'I'm all ready, so let's away. Ma's lying down – she's so worried about what's happened she's got a headache.'

'I'm no' surprised; she must be that upset for you.'

'Aye.' Jemima sniffed as she closed the flat door behind her. 'It's all been such a shock and I'm just trying to work out now what to do next. But let's go to the park, shall we? Then I can tell you all that's been happening.'

The summer evening was so balmy, so beautifully different from the windy chill Edinburgh could present, and the High Street and Canongate were, in spite of the recession, crowded with visitors. Maybe not spending much, some just strolling around or window shopping, but certainly enjoying themselves; unlike Jemima, so borne down by the bolt from the blue that had hit her almost as hard as her employer. Yet, as Lindy hurried with her down to Holyrood Park, she had the feeling that after the first shock her friend was rallying, not only coming to terms with what had happened, but trying to find something that would help. How on earth could she possibly help, though? It sounded as though only money was going to save the Dalrymples, and where was that going to come from?

The royal park, that stretched so far from the Palace of Holyroodhouse, was itself full of visitors, but such was its size it appeared to be not at all crowded, which suited Lindy and Jemima as they found a place to sit, and sank down together.

'Now for a cigarette,' Jemima murmured, lighting up. 'Oh, that's grand! You won't have one, Lindy?'

'No, thanks.'

Lindy was gazing across the park to Arthur's Seat, remembering Rod, as she so often did, without the need of a reminder of their day together. It still surprised her that that was really all they'd had together, just that one day, for it seemed as if they'd had so much more.

And might, in fact, have had a future, she sometimes allowed herself to think, but she always stopped herself there, for the truth was she'd made her decision and to dwell on what might have been with Rod would not be fair to Neil. He was the one who was real, who was part of her life. Rod was – well, hadn't she thought of him once as a ship that passed in the night? Now was not the time to think of him anyway, and, turning her dark blue eyes on Jemima, she waited for her to speak.

# Fourteen

'It's all so awful, I can hardly talk about it,' Jemima began, her voice low again as she watched the smoke from her cigarette rise. 'In fact, it's so bad Mrs Dalrymple's in a nursing home – she just can't face it.'

'Oh, that sounds bad. A nursing home?'

'Aye, it's paid for by friends, you ken – she's got no relatives and couldn't afford much herself.'

'So where did her money go?'

'Might as well say, like my cigarette, up in smoke.' Jemima shook her head drearily. 'Seemingly, Mrs Dalrymple never knew anything about finance, so when she was left her husband's money she put it all into the care of a family friend. He was a lawyer, very respected, knew all about investments, so Mr Keith told me. He's the butler, or was, till he got the sack like the rest of us.'

'Are investments something to do with stocks and shares?' asked Lindy.

'Well, I'm no' sure, but I think when you invest you put money into shares – a company, or something, and then you expect to get more money back than you put in. Unless there's a crash, like in America, and then you might lose everything. But Mr Dalrymple was very canny – he never lost a penny in that crash, and if only he hadn't died, Mr Montague would never have been able to swindle Mrs Dalrymple. Which is what he did.'

'Mr Montague was the family friend?'

'Some friend!' Jemima laughed harshly and stubbed out her cigarette. 'It's all just come out, you ken, the embezzling, or whatever they call it, but he had all that cash to do what he liked with and nobody knew.'

'What a shame!' Lindy cried hotly. 'And what a rotter, eh?'

'Aye, but that's temptation for you. When they work with money, so many folk just can't resist putting their fingers in the pie.'

'To begin with everything seemed fine,' Jemima went on after a moment. 'But all the time, Mr Keith said Mr Montague was playing the market and doing badly – maybe because of the slump, but losing anyway – and at the same time was siphoning off money for himself. That's gone, too, so what it boils down to is that there's hardly anything left for Mrs Dalrymple.'

'And how was this man found out?' asked Lindy.

'Mr Keith isn't sure, but he thinks maybe Mrs Dalrymple's cheques bounced, or something, and the bank had to begin an investigation. Next thing, the police were informed and Mr Montague was arrested. Now the creditors have moved in and they'll be taking what they can get – the house, the furniture, everything. Mrs Dalrymple's already sent her jewellery to be sold.'

'Poor woman,' Lindy murmured. 'I suppose, if there's one thing as bad as never having any money, it's having it and losing it. Though I can't imagine having any money in the first place.'

'Well, we in the household never had any, that's for sure,' Jemima replied. 'But we did have jobs and now they're gone. Miss Rosemary's having to write us all references because her ma's no' up to it.'

'And what's going to happen to Miss Rosemary, then? Has she any money of her own?'

'Some, no' much. There's a trust fund her dad left, but that can't be touched till she's twenty-five.'

'But she'll have friends to help out, like her ma?'

Jemima shook her head. 'A few friends have stuck by her but most, she says, just melted away when they heard what had happened. Anyway, she's very independent and doesn't want help from friends. Wants to manage by herself if she can.' Jemima's eyes had suddenly begun to brighten. 'She has asked me, though, if I can advise.'

'You? What can you do?'

'Tell her how to find a cheap place to live, she said, where she can just take refuge – that's what she called it, refuge – until she can get a job and make a new life.' Jemima laid her hand on Lindy's. 'And you know what I'm going to do? Get her into that wee flat that's empty next to ours. Couldn't be better, could it? Just where we can be handy to show her the ropes. And it's dirt cheap into the bargain – just what she's looking for!'

Lindy's eyes on Jemima's were enormous. 'Are you crazy, Jemima? There's no way you can bring someone like her to number nineteen! It would be impossible.'

'Why? It's what she wants – she's said so. Somewhere cheap, where she can just lie low till she's got a job.' Jemima's eyes were narrowing as she stood up and brushed down her skirt. 'Anyway, where we live, it's no' so bad. Ma and me, we've done our best, and we can make that other flat nice as well. I think you're being a bit unfair, Lindy.'

'Oh, I didn't mean that your flat wasn't nice!' Lindy said hurriedly. 'It is, it's lovely, much better than anywhere else in the house. All I'm saying

70

is that number nineteen is no' the sort of place this Miss Rosemary is used to, and it might be too much of a shock.'

'You're thinking of the neighbours and the noise, eh?'

'And Saturday nights and the drink. Fights and black eyes. No' to mention whose turn it is to clean the stair. Can you see your Miss Rosemary cleaning the stair?'

'Och, no one will expect her to do that! Anyway, Ma and me, we're going do what we can. Cooking and that sort o' thing.'

'Cooking?' Lindy shook her head in disbelief. 'Look, I'm sorry for the lassie, but if she says she wants to be independent why no' let her try it? Why try to look after her all the time?'

'Why not? I've nothing else to do,' Jemima answered bitterly.

# Fifteen

Concerned though she was about losing her job, Jemima's spirits rose as soon as it was confirmed that Miss Rosemary had secured the empty flat at number nineteen and the way lay clear for the spring-cleaning work to begin. First would come the washing and scrubbing of the walls and floors, she told Lindy, with painting and wallpapering to follow, and then some curtain-making and maybe a cushion or two before the furniture came over. Miss Rosemary, it appeared, had been able to salvage a few pieces of furniture from the creditors – at a cost, of course – which was a piece of nonsense. Her ma's own furniture, eh?

'Still, I think she'll find it comfortable enough here,' Jemima finished with pride. 'There's no bathroom, but she's got a hip bath coming with the furniture, so she'll manage, eh?'

'Oh, yes, she'll be fine,' agreed Lindy, wondering if it was true. 'How long is all this going to take, though?'

'Couple of weeks. When Ma and me get going we don't waste time, and we want to be quick. I know Miss Rosemary's dying to get into her own place.'

'Where is she now?' asked Lindy.

'With one o' the friends who's stayed true, but the thing is, she's so sympathetic Miss Rosemary says it's driving her crazy. It's her poor ma that's the invalid, no' her.'

'And how is Mrs Dalrymple, then?'

'A bit better, but staying where she is for the time being. Miss Rosemary visits regularly.'

'Tell me this,' said Lindy, after a pause, 'are you going to keep on calling this lassie "Miss Rosemary" when she's living here?'

Jemima's look was shocked. 'Why, what else should I call her?'

'Well, things are different now. You aren't working for her mother any more. You're equals, eh?'

'Equals? She's still Mrs Dalrymple's daughter, Lindy. Losing money hasn't changed the way things are.'

'So what are the rest of us going to call her, then?'

'I couldn't say. Miss Dalrymple, maybe?'

'And I'll be Miss Gillan?' Lindy laughed. 'Come on, Jemima, this girl's in a different world now, whatever you say. But I'll have to admit, I'm longing to see her. When will she be coming?'

'As soon as we've finished the flat,' Jemima answered eagerly. 'And we're starting tomorrow!'

Naturally, as she was Jemima's ex-employer's daughter, all in number nineteen were taking great interest in the pending arrival of the new tenant. Fallen on hard times, so Jemima said, but my, wasn't Jemima knocking doors out o' windows, then, getting a place ready for her? And how much was it all going to cost? Who was paying? If it was Jemima, would the young lady be able to pay her back?

'If she's short she can always sell some o' that furniture she's had sent over,' remarked Myra with a sniff. 'I saw it coming in. Everything mahogany, with such a polish you could see your face in it, and the prettiest wee dressing table decked out in frilled material and all! Anybody would think that girl was still in Heriot Row, eh?'

'I believe she had to pay something to get that furniture from the creditors,' Lindy told her. 'So Jemima said. Must've felt fed up about that. Her ma's own furniture!'

'H'm, well, I'd be sympathetic if it wasn't for Jemima making such a fuss. I mean, you'd think it was royalty coming here, no less.'

'And that's true,' Lindy commented afterwards to Neil. 'Anyone would think it was some princess coming the way Jemima's been going on. I do feel sorry for her Rosemary, but she's no' as badly off as some, eh?'

'You can say that again,' said Neil earnestly. 'I've no sympathy with that sort at all. I mean, how'd they get their money in the first place? Investments? Stocks and shares? All completely immoral. There's no work involved, no production, no creation. Why should we shed tears if they lose money? Let 'em see how the rest of us have to live.'

'To be fair, Neil, the lassie can't be blamed for the way her folks live, eh? I mean, you've no choice where you're born. And then Jemima says her dad wasn't one o' the idle rich – he did have a job.'

'Oh, yes? Worked his fingers to the bone, did he? Doing what?'

'I'm no' sure. Merchant banker, I think.'

'Merchant banker?' Neil exploded into laughter. 'Oh, what a struggle he'd have to live, doing that! Look, let's waste no more time talking about this Rosemary. Just remember, she's no better than anybody else, so don't go thinking she is.'

'As if I would!' cried Lindy, adding to herself, but she's sure to have better clothes.

# Sixteen

On an August evening – too nice to go to the pictures, really – Lindy and Neil were about to saunter out from number nineteen to see *Top Hat* when Jemima caught them at the door.

74

'Lindy, Neil – wait! Don't go yet, she's here! Miss Rosemary. I've seen the taxi!'

'Taxi?' Neil repeated, putting his head out of the door. 'Oh, sure, it's there. I can see a lassie getting out.'

'We never knew she was coming tonight,' Lindy exclaimed. 'Aunt Myra will be furious – she's out to her whist drive!'

'Let me through, Miss Rosemary will be looking for me!' cried Jemima, her face flushing, her eyes bright. 'But don't go yet, I want to introduce you.'

'Prepare to curtsy,' Neil whispered, grinning, but Lindy, highly excited, shushed him with her finger to her mouth as Jemima came hurrying back, followed by the taxi driver, who was carrying two leather suitcases and a hatbox. Behind him, looking everywhere with interest, was a tall, willowy young blonde woman, dressed in a pale blue dress and jacket. Miss Rosemary had arrived.

'Jemima, where shall the driver put the luggage?' she asked, her clear, clipped voice sounding English rather than Scottish, and adding with a smile to Lindy and Neil, 'I'm sorry, am I in your way?'

'No, no,' Lindy hastily replied, while Neil, standing to one side, was silent until Jemima, hovering, made polite introductions and then asked the driver just to leave the cases in the hallway.

'There's still two to come,' he told her, making a great show of breathing hard with effort. 'I'll have to go back for 'em.'

75

'I'll get them,' Neil offered suddenly. 'I can take 'em up the stair.'

'Fine by me,' said the driver. 'That'll be one and six, miss, if you don't mind.'

'Oh, certainly,' replied Miss Rosemary, opening her narrow leather bag and taking a half crown from her purse. 'Thank you so much for your trouble, driver. You've been most helpful.'

'That's quite all right, miss,' he replied, giving her a puzzled look she probably didn't notice but which the others in the hallway understood very well. He would almost certainly be thinking what the hell was someone like this particular fare doing in somewhere like number nineteen? And with luggage and all? Well, not his job to stand wondering. Touching his cap he departed, followed by Neil, who swiftly returned with a suitcase in either hand.

For a long moment he gazed at the new tenant, joined by Lindy, whose eyes had scarcely left Rosemary since she'd stepped through the door, and who had already been wishing she could sell her soul for a pair of her beautiful soft leather shoes. But how amazing was it that Jemima's Miss Rosemary should be exactly as she'd expected her to be? So distinctive, so elegant, so absolutely self-assured, she couldn't be mistaken for anything but 'a lady', from the sort of background that was as far from the tenants of number nineteen as the moon. And then, of course, she was so pretty.

Maybe not beautiful was Lindy's rather relieved opinion – her high-bridged nose being too long for that – but her hair was golden, her eyes a clear

76

blue, and she was so tall and slender and held herself so well it had to be admitted that she was a 'stunner'. Heaven knew what the folk of number nineteen would make of her – even Neil seemed to have been struck dumb – but it was very likely that she wouldn't stay long. Not once she'd seen the way life really was in the tenement.

'Want these up the stair?' Neil asked, finding his voice at last and turning to Jemima.

'Yes, at the flat, please – and I'll bring the other two.'

'Oh, let me!' cried Miss Rosemary. 'You're all being too kind.'

'You take the hatbox,' Lindy told her. 'I'll help Jemima. But then we have to be away.'

Up the stairs went the luggage, meeting only Aggie Andrews coming down with a bag of washing, her shadowed eyes like saucers.

'Miss Rosemary, this is Mrs Andrews,' Jemima murmured. 'Just on her way down to the basement where we do our washing. Your turn for the copper tonight, eh, Aggie? This is Miss Dalrymple – she's a new tenant, moving in next to Ma and me.'

'Aye, I know, you've done her place up, eh?' murmured Aggie, sidling away. 'Pleased to meet you, miss. Hope you'll be happy.'

'Why, thank you!' Miss Rosemary called after her as she took off down the stairs. 'Jemima, how nice everyone is! I'm sure I'll settle in well.'

'Here you are then,' said Lindy, setting down her load at the door of the flat next to Jemima's. 'Neil and me have to go now, but we hope you'll be happy, too, Miss Dalrymple.'

77

'Oh, please, call me Rosemary! But thank you both so much. I do hope I haven't kept you.'

Rosemary? Not Miss Rosemary? Lindy glanced quickly at Jemima, whose mouth was slightly open, but then she took Neil's arm and, calling, 'Nae bother, only too glad to help,' made him hurry away with her.

'Shouldn't we carry the luggage into the flat?' he asked, turning to look back. 'It's heavy stuff, eh?'

'For heaven's sake, Neil, they can manage! Didn't I bring one of the cases up myself?'

'Yes. All right, then.' Neil said no more, remaining silent all the way to the tram stop, though Lindy had plenty to say.

'So that's the famous Miss Rosemary, eh? Well, she's certainly a lovely girl and beautifully dressed. Did you notice her dress and jacket? And her shoes? What wouldn't I give for them, eh? But I suppose you'll be saying the money she's spent could have gone to feed a family, and that's quite true. Can still admire really good quality things, though – I mean, there's a place for them too, do you no' think?'

'Here's our tram,' said Neil.

# Seventeen

' "Heaven, I'm in heaven!" ' cried Lindy, dancing along the pavement on the way home from the cinema while Neil slowly followed. 'Oh, isn't

"Cheek to Cheek" a wonderful song, Neil? Weren't they marvellous, dancing to it – Fred and Ginger? I honestly think *Top Hat* is one of the best pictures ever, don't you agree?'

'How can I talk to you when you're so far ahead?' Neil called. 'And it's no' dark yet. Everybody can see you dancing.'

'I don't care, I feel like dancing. But, OK, I'll walk with you – if that'll make you talk, anyway.' She waited for him, then put her arm in his. 'You've scarcely said a word all evening.'

'We were supposed to be watching a picture.'

'But even in the intermission you were like a wet weekend. Now don't be telling me you didn't enjoy *Top Hat*?'

'Oh, yes, I enjoyed the dancing – terrific. But the story was silly. Same old thing, I thought.'

'Who cares about the story? You don't go to see Fred and Ginger for the story, Neil!'

'I'm a writer, I care about it.' Neil shrugged. 'Reckon I could do a lot better than that scriptwriter, anyway.'

'Sure you could.'

For some time they walked without speaking and at the tram stop, the evening being so fine and still so light, they decided to give it a miss and keep going.

'I wish you felt like me,' Lindy said suddenly. 'I mean, about the picture. To see something like that – so good, so perfect, really – makes me feel good, too. Takes me right out of myself, sends me flying, just like you said we would one day.' She stared up at his handsome profile and sighed. 'But you don't feel like that, eh?'

'Suppose I don't.' Neil turned his head to look at her. 'I'm glad it made you happy, anyway. I like to see you happy.'

She smiled. 'That's nice, Neil, thank you. But let's talk about you know who, eh? If I hadn't been full of the picture, I'd have been talking about her already.'

'Who? Who'd you mean?'

'Come on, Neil – Miss Rosemary, of course! Isn't she just like you expected? Though I must admit I never expected her to ask us to call her Rosemary – made Jemima stare, I can tell you!'

'I think it's a sign that she's no' what I expected,' Neil said slowly. 'You were right, in fact – she shouldn't be blamed because of her background. It's nothing to do with her that she's been so privileged, and you can tell that by the way she treated us, eh? Couldn't have been more friendly, could she? No hint of playing the grand lady or anything like that. I was – well, let's say I had to revise my opinion.'

'My, you're certainly talking enough now,' Lindy remarked. 'Heavens, what a flow – and all praise.'

'Oh, I wouldn't say that. I don't know her well enough to be sure what she's like – I'm only going on how she was this evening. And then, you have to remember that she's facing a real crisis in her life, something we haven't had to do, and she's taken it very well. Moved out of the life she knows to something quite different, and not shown bitterness or self-pity, or anything. It is something to admire, Lindy.'

'Oh, yes, I agree. Thing is, I wouldn't say folk

80

like us have never had to face a crisis in our lives, Neil. Some live that way all the time, if it's a question of finding where the next meal's coming from.'

'As though you needed to tell me that!' he cried. 'I was talking of you and me – our families being so lucky to be still in work and have food on the table.'

'And knowing that could change any time, Neil. If Dad lost his job and the shop was closed – and it could close, there's no' much turnover these days – we'd be in crisis, too. I reckon Miss Rosemary doesn't really know yet what hardship is – and might never know, come to that. What's the betting an admirer will come riding up on a great white horse and carry her off to riches?'

'You think so?' asked Neil quickly.

'Och, who knows? I'm just guessing. Come on, here's number nineteen looming ahead. Let's have a cup of tea with Dad and Aunt Myra. Poor old Myra will be dying to hear about Rosemary.'

'I don't think I'll come in tonight, thanks, Lindy. I want to do some writing before bed. But it's been a grand evening, eh?'

'Grand,' she agreed, though her gaze on him was doubtful. 'Don't forget our goodnight kiss, though.'

'As though I would!' he cried with enthusiasm.

But the kiss, when it came, might have been described as short and sweet – not quite the same as their kisses of late. What was on his mind? Lindy wondered, as they parted at the stairs. The writing he was planning to do? Or what they'd been talking about? He certainly seemed a long way away from her.

'Is that you, Lindy?' came her stepmother's voice. 'Come away in and tell me all about Miss Dalrymple, then!'

# Eighteen

If Lindy had thought Miss Rosemary would move out of number nineteen as soon as she'd seen the dark side, she was mistaken. Far from being upset by the way her neighbours behaved, particularly on Saturday nights, she seemed fascinated by it, and when Mrs Kerry tried to apologize and said Rosemary must be horrified, she told her, no, no, it was the way some people were – she must try to understand.

'Most folk here lead hard lives,' Lindy explained, when she and Rosemary had joined Jemima and her mother one evening in Mrs Kerry's flat. 'Men as well as women, and the way the men relax and let off steam is to go to the pub – then you see what happens.'

'How can one blame them?' Rosemary asked. 'I'm just beginning to understand what their lives must be like – it's no wonder they want to escape. But then, as you say, the women's lives are hard, too, and they just seem to stay at home.'

'And take what's coming sometimes.' Lindy sighed. 'I don't blame the chaps going out to the pub, but why knock their wives about when they get back?'

'Very few do that here,' Jemima said quickly.

82

'And it's just the drink, you see. They're good lads, really.'

'Is poor Aggie's husband one of them?' asked Rosemary diffidently.

The other women exchanged glances.

'You saw her black eye the other day?' Jemima asked reluctantly. 'Aye, I'm afraid the drink does seem to have a bad effect on her Tam. He's always sorry afterwards.'

'I should think he is!' cried Lindy. 'Should be ashamed of himself, hitting a woman. My dad would never do that, drink or no drink.'

'It's a real shame he's that way,' Mrs Kerry ventured quietly. 'Like Jemima says, he's no' a bad lad at all.' She turned to Rosemary. 'But has it upset you, dear, seeing poor Aggie? That's the last thing we want to happen, to have you upset when you've troubles of your own.'

'Oh, please don't worry about me, Mrs Kerry!' Rosemary replied hastily. 'Things have worked out so well for me, personally, I can't thank everyone enough for their kindness. All the work you did on the flat, Jemima, and the cooking you've done for me, Mrs Kerry, it's been amazing. I really feel I should learn to do some cooking myself – perhaps you could teach me a few simple dishes?'

'Oh, no, dear!' Mrs Kerry cried in alarm. 'I'd get that flustered, eh? I could never teach anyone.'

'Never even taught me,' Jemima said, smiling. 'But no one would expect you to do anything, Miss Rosemary. Don't you worry about it.'

'I did say no need to call me "miss",' Rosemary said reproachfully. 'And I don't see why I shouldn't be expected to do anything. I mean, I

83

haven't even done any washing yet in your basement – you've done it all, Jemima. And then there are the stairs. Am I not supposed to take a turn? I saw a lady sweeping them yesterday but when I offered to help, she said' – Rosemary laughed – 'nae bother!'

Everyone laughed with her, but Lindy was thinking that the words perfectly summed up the attitude of those in number nineteen when it came to expecting the new tenant to do anything. 'Nae bother', 'that's all right', 'no trouble', 'don't worry about it'.

It seemed to have been readily understood that Rosemary, in spite of her wish to be the same as everyone else, was far from being the same; was, in fact, some sort of fairy tale being dropped into the tenement as though by a spell. And who could expect a fairy-tale being to sweep the stairs, or take a turn for the copper in the basement to do her own washing?

Rather teasingly, Lindy asked Struan if he wasn't interested in taking out such a pretty girl as Rosemary, to which he'd snorted in derision.

'Me take out *Miss* Rosemary? Are you joking? How could I afford to take somebody like her anywhere? I can scarcely afford beer for myself, never mind taking her to the North British Hotel, or the Caledonian or somewhere!'

'She'd never expect that, Struan. She knows you're no' one of her rich crowd.'

'Well, I'd feel a fool, asking her out for a cheap seat at the pictures and a fish supper to follow. Neil's brothers were saying the same. Lovely girl, no' for us.'

'I'd say they were all absolutely wrong,' Neil himself declared next evening when she told him of her conversation with her brother on the way to their usual dance hall. 'Rosemary would never expect to be wined and dined by anyone from Scott Street, but it wouldn't stop her wanting to go out with a fellow because of that.'

'You think so?'

'Sure I do. I told my brothers the same. If she was really attracted to someone she'd be happy to go out with him whoever he was.'

Lindy was looking dubious. 'I don't know if you're right. Going out with someone here could be the start of something that wouldn't do for her, Neil. I mean, treating us all as friends is one thing, but getting really involved with a chap from a different background . . . that'd never be the same.'

Neil shook his head. 'Lindy, you're wrong. I've talked to Rosemary. She's no snob. I think when she marries it'll be for love, no' money or background.'

'For love *and* money, I'd say. These society folk marry each other.' Lindy laughed. 'When did you ever hear of a debutante marrying somebody from a tenement?'

'Usually they don't meet people from tenements.' Neil hesitated. 'The difference with Rosemary is that she has.'

Lindy stopped laughing, her dark blue eyes on Neil's face suddenly searching – for what she wasn't sure, maybe nothing. Probably nothing, in fact.

'Think she's found anyone?' she asked, forcing herself to speak lightly. 'In our tenement?'

'I don't know. How would I know?'

'Oh, you'd know, all right. You know what they say – love and a cold can't be hid.'

'Haven't seen either.'

'Nor me.' Lindy was trying to relax. 'I expect Rosemary's too busy to fall in love. She's got to find a job. When she does she'll be away, you know. She isn't here to stay.'

'Hasn't done much so far about finding a job. What could she do, anyway?'

'I've no idea. What sort o' thing do debutantes do? Arrange flowers, go dancing, have cocktails?'

'Doesn't sound much like work to me. Might take Rosemary quite a while to find anything, then.'

'Might. Meanwhile, she seems to be happy here.'

'That shows what she's like,' Neil said eagerly. 'She's settled so well. Got some character, eh?'

With her looks she doesn't need character, Lindy thought, then felt a little ashamed. It was true what Neil said. Rosemary was a person of character, and nice-natured with it. If only folk were not so obsessed with her . . . As they moved on to the floor for a quickstep it came to her, worryingly, that by 'folk' she had meant Neil. No, that was a piece of nonsense! He was just interested, the way they all were. Only to be expected.

'When are we going out again?' she asked as they arrived home after a pleasant enough evening. 'Tomorrow, Sunday, as usual?'

'Aye, tomorrow. Go for one of our walks, eh?'

'I thought we might go somewhere different. Take the bus to Cramond or Swanston, maybe?'

'Think I'd rather stay local this time, Lindy, so I get back early. I've some reading to do for this course I've taken on.'

'Thought that had finished?'

'New session starts this month.'

'Oh, well, where'd you want to go, then?'

'We can decide when we meet. I'll call for you about two, all right?'

'Fine. See you then.'

They kissed, only briefly, which did not surprise Lindy – lately, all their kisses seemed to have been brief. Now, that wasn't to be expected, was it? She decided not to think about it. Neil had things on his mind: his writing, his course; he'd sort himself out sometime. Meanwhile, she had Aunt Myra to face, for the usual chat.

'That you, Lindy?' cried the familiar voice.

'Who else, Aunt Myra?' called Lindy.


# Nineteen

On Sunday afternoon Lindy was alone in the flat waiting for Neil, who was late. Glancing at the clock she saw it was showing ten minutes after two, which meant he was not very late, then, but still . . .

'Shouldn't be late at all, should he, Gingerboy?' she asked the ginger cat, who had stalked in from her wee bedroom, where he often slept for hours.

Naturally he only gave her a scornful look, then went to see what was in his saucer.

'Want some more milk?'

She bent to pour him a little from a jug in the scullery, then straightened up to smooth the skirt of her vivid green dress that she was wearing for the first time, having put the last stitch into its hem the night before.

For some reason she had felt it important to get it finished for today's outing with Neil, had wanted to make sure that she was looking her best, even if a little different, in something new. Not that he'd take much notice, he not being one to worry about appearances, only putting on the first thing that came to hand himself. Still, she would feel better if she looked right. More confident about their afternoon together, for there had been something in Neil's eyes as he'd said goodnight last evening that worried her just a little. She couldn't say what it was, but was rather afraid that she might soon find out.

Suddenly, with a rush of relief, she heard his voice just outside the flat door. He was here at last. But at the door she paused. Who was with him? Whose was that other voice, answering his? Light, charming, quite familiar. Lindy knew it well.

'Hello, Rosemary!' she cried, opening her door. 'Hello, Neil.'

They were standing together, smiling at her, Rosemary in one of her favourite pink outfits with matching hat, and Neil – Neil was in a brand-new sports jacket. Lindy couldn't believe it, couldn't take her eyes off him. Neil, not in some aged coat belonging to one of his brothers, but a handsome tweed jacket, so stiff and pristine it had to be new? Where had he got it from? Where had he found the money to buy it? His shirt looked new, too, and his tie, and though she had seen his flannel trousers often enough, she'd never seen them actually pressed – with a crease, for heaven's sake?

'Sorry I'm late,' he said, still smiling. 'Just bumped into Rosemary on the stair and we were chatting.'

'My fault,' Rosemary murmured. 'So sorry, Lindy. But I'll be on my way now – I'm going to visit my mother.' She held up a small carrier bag. 'With her favourite chocolates.'

'How is your mother?' Lindy asked politely, moving her gaze with an effort from Neil.

'Oh, much better! In fact, she'll be going to a friend's in Devon soon for some convalescence.'

'That's grand,' said Neil. 'But look, would you like me to get you a taxi, Rosemary? I can ring from the phone box down the street.'

'A taxi? Oh, no, I'm trying to master the trams!' Her smile was radiant. 'Goodbye, then, you two, have a lovely walk.'

And she was gone, Neil hurrying to open the outer door for her, before turning back to Lindy.

'Sorry about that, Lindy. Are you ready, then?'

'Just come in for a minute,' she answered coldly. 'I'll get my hat.'

'So, where's your folks?' he asked, stooping in the living room to scratch behind Gingerboy's ears while Lindy put on her straw hat.

'It was such a nice afternoon, they've gone to the Botanic Gardens. Maybe we could go too?'

'And meet half of Edinburgh?' Neil hesitated. 'The truth is, Lindy, I want to talk to you.'

Alarm bells ringing, she raised her eyebrows. 'First, Neil, I'd like to know where you got that sports jacket.'

He looked down at it, shrugging. 'I bought it, of course. Saved up for it.'

'Without a word to me? You know I'd have liked to help you choose it.'

'Sorry, didn't think. Just felt it was time I had something decent to wear.'

'And you got a new shirt and tie as well, and pressed your trousers. What's going on, Neil?'

'What d'you mean, what's going on? Can't I look respectable for once?' His eyes flashing, he suddenly drew up a chair at the table and sat down, putting his hand to his brow. When he took it away his eyes had changed, become dark, with a look of hurt Lindy had never seen in them before.

'Och, you're right to ask,' he said in a low voice. 'I wanted to look good for her.'

There was a long silence broken only by Gingerboy's mewing as he wove round Lindy's legs, while she took off her hat and threw it to one side. The clock struck the half hour but neither Lindy nor Neil looked at it and, after a moment, Gingerboy departed back to Lindy's bedroom as she sank slowly into a chair.

'You said you wanted to talk, and I want you to. I want to hear exactly what you've got to say.'

'Lindy, I'm sorry. I'm more sorry than I can tell you—'

'Don't tell me about being sorry. Tell me about her.'

90

He had lowered his sad eyes, was staring at a button on his new jacket, and for a little while seemed unable to speak. Finally he looked up, met Lindy's stormy gaze and put his hand again to his brow. 'I'd never expected it, never knew what it was. I mean, I'd read about it and all that, but it'd never happened to me, you see, and until it's happened you don't know what it's like, can't even guess—'

'What are you talking about?' cried Lindy, leaning forward, her lovely face so strained it seemed for a moment not hers. 'Tell me what you're talking about!'

'Falling in love,' he answered quietly. 'Falling in love at first sight.'

'At first sight?' She sat back, turning pale. 'You fell in love with her, with Rosemary, at first sight?'

'From the moment she walked through the door after the taxi driver with her luggage.' As though in wonder at his own words, Neil was shaking his head. 'I didn't know it at the time, but that night I couldn't get her out of my mind. I kept seeing her face, hearing her voice, and it came to me – it was just like all the books say, and the poetry and stuff that I never thought would apply to me. I thought I'd gone mad, was dreaming or something, but it's just gone on the same. I see her everywhere, think about her all the time, and I know that's how it's going to be for me, Lindy. She's the one. I've found her; I'll never let her go.'

'No,' Lindy wailed, 'no, Neil, you're wrong. She isn't the one for you. How could she be? This is the sort of thing that hits folk and then goes. Passes. It's no' real, no' the same as what we've got, Neil. Can't you see that?'

'Oh, Lindy!' He tried to take her hand but she snatched it away and he sat, wincing, in his chair until he could bring himself to speak again.

'Lindy, what we've got is different. It's special, and we're true friends, but we've known each other all our lives, and maybe that's too long. You're so beautiful, any man would want you, but we . . . I guess we just know each other too well.'

'Yet you made me give up Rod Connor,' she said quietly. 'To think of me with another man, you said, was very upsetting – maybe we were more than good friends, you said, maybe you did want more. And I thought you were so much a part of my life I could never let you go, so I said goodbye to Rod and we were fine, better than before. Until Rosemary Dalrymple walked into our lives and now she's all you can think of . . . Is that no' true, Neil?'

'Oh, God, Lindy, I wish it wasn't, but it is. I'm hers, I have to be, I canna live without her, there's no more that I can say—'

'Does she even know?' Lindy asked, her voice so cold he seemed to shudder.

'Nothing's been said, but she knows, all right,' he brought out slowly after a moment or two. 'Women always know these things, eh? Every time she looks at me, she'll see what I feel.'

'And you think she feels the same?'

'You think she might not? Because of the differences in our lives?' Neil stood up, his face mask-like in its seriousness. 'I told you, she's no snob.

92

She'll know me for what I am; she'll see that I can make her happy.'

'But you've never said anything to her?' Lindy had also got to her feet, her face as serious as Neil's. 'Better speak to her, then, so you'll know where you stand.'

'I intend to, but I had to speak to you first, Lindy. It's been worrying me for days because I didn't want to hurt you.'

'Didn't you? That's nice to know.' She walked swiftly to the front door and held it open. 'Better go now, Neil. Sorry about our walk.'

'Look, let's still go out, Lindy, and have tea somewhere. We can still be friends, you know, no need to part—'

'Oh, no, Neil,' Lindy said decisively. 'We can't still be friends, because we were special friends and now we're not. You've put Rosemary in my place – that's changed everything.'

'Lindy, that isn't true!' he cried, then lowered his eyes and turned aside. 'I told you, this happened – I didn't choose it – but I – I can't put it back. It's with me now, for ever.'

'Just what I said. Everything's changed. Goodbye, Neil.'

'Lindy –'

She looked away, her hand on the doorknob, and when he finally walked through, his face still set, still mask-like, she closed the door after him. Then she went to her room, took off her new green dress, changed into an old blouse and skirt and lay down next to Gingerboy on her bed, waiting for the tears to fall.

93

# Twenty

There was no hiding Lindy's red eyes from her father and Myra when they returned from their walk, and as soon as Myra saw her she was quick to pounce. Why wasn't Lindy out with Neil? Why wasn't she wearing her new dress? Why were her eyes all red?

'Have you had a row, then? Better tell us what's been happening.'

'Aye,' said George, putting his arm round his daughter. 'Tell us what's wrong, pet.'

'Neil and me have split up,' Lindy said, leaning against her father's shoulder for a moment, then pulling away and blowing her nose. 'We can't be friends any more.'

'Why, you've been friends for years!' cried Myra. 'More than friends, eh?' Her green eyes sharpening, she shook her head. 'There's more to this than you're saying, eh? Now, you tell us just what's been going on.'

'Hello, hello, any tea going?' came Struan's voice as he appeared at the door, his eyes going to the unlaid table. 'Hey, what's up, then? Are we no' eating today?'

'You know we don't have much tea on a Sunday,' Myra snapped. 'You had a big enough dinner, Struan, to last you till bedtime!'

'Are you joking? I left the lads to see what was going, and here you all are looking like

94

wet weekends.' Struan's gaze went to his sister. 'Lindy, have you been crying? What's happened?'

'She's had a falling out with Neil,' Myra told him. 'Now leave her alone, Struan, and sit down while I get the tea. What there is of it.'

'Fallen out with Neil?' Struan's face darkened. 'What's he done, then? If he's upset you, Lindy, I'll go up the stair and knock his block off! That great jessie was never right for you, anyway.'

'Oh, stop that talk o' fighting!' George ordered, taking his chair by the range. 'Neil's no' a bad lad, there's no need for you to get your dander up, Struan. This'll all be over tomorrow, eh? Lovers' quarrels never last.'

'Lover? Neil MacLauren's never been Lindy's lover! He's never appreciated her and that's the truth. Why, I saw him the other day making sheep's eyes at Miss Rosemary, and she was looking bored out of her head. He needs to be taught a lesson.'

'Talking to Miss Rosemary?' Myra asked quickly. 'Lindy, is she what the row was about? Did you catch Neil with her, like Struan says?'

'I don't want to talk about it,' Lindy said huskily. 'All I know is that it's all over between Neil and me and it's what we both want. Aunt Myra, I don't think I'll bother with tea, if you don't mind. I'm going up to see Jemima.'

'And what good can she do, then? First sign of trouble you go running up to those Kerrys.'

'Jemima's my friend. I want to tell her what's happened, that's all.'

'Suit yourself,' Myra retorted, sniffing. 'But

family's best when the bad times come, if you ask me.'

'Ah, let the lassie go,' said George. 'She knows what she wants to do, eh?'

'Well, come back down, *some*time,' Myra called, as Lindy moved to the door.

# Twenty-One

As soon as Jemima opened her door Lindy flung her arms around her.

'Oh, Jemima, it's so bad, so awful – Neil's fallen in love with Rosemary!'

Jemima drew Lindy into the flat and closed the door. 'I know,' she said sympathetically.

'You know? How? How do you know?' Lindy's great eyes searched Jemima's face. 'Did he tell you?'

'No, of course not! I could see it, plain as day, every time I saw the way he looked at her. I thought you'd have seen it, too.'

'I never saw it,' Lindy said desperately, thinking it was she who'd said to Neil, 'love and a cold can't be hid', and all the time he'd hidden his love from her, yet not from Jemima. How could that have been possible? Because she hadn't been looking, hadn't expected to see it, and so had not. How could she have been so blind?

'He talked about her a lot; he always admired her, but I didn't think – I never thought – he could be in love with her. I mean, it's crazy.'

'Well, I'm no expert, but that's what love is, eh? The sort he's got, that takes a hold of you and keeps you prisoner. Want a cup o' tea?'

'Just tea would be fine.' Lindy looked round the living room. 'But where's your ma?'

'Gone out with Mrs MacLauren. They've taken the tram to the Meadows, but I said I wouldn't go because I'm preparing for the interview.'

'Interview?'

'You remember: I've got an interview at Logie's tomorrow for a job in the alterations department. I'm taking some samples of sewing work I've done – mending, embroidery, lace and that.'

'Oh, Jemima, I'm sorry! 'Course I remember, I'm just no' thinking straight.'

'Don't worry, I understand. You've got enough on your plate to think about without anything from me. Just wait till I make the tea, and then you can tell me what happened.'

When they were sitting with their tea Jemima asked how Lindy had finally found out about Neil's love for the new tenant. Had he admitted it?

'Yes, he told me this afternoon. We were due to go for a walk, but then I saw him coming down the stair with her – with Rosemary – and he was wearing a new sports jacket and new shirt, tie and everything, and I sort of knew he'd hadn't bought them to please me. Then, in the flat, it came out – he told me he'd fallen in love with Rosemary the minute he first saw her.' Lindy looked across at Jemima, her lip trembling. 'That time when she arrived and the taxi driver had her luggage. Do you remember?'

'I remember.' Jemima pushed a plate of short-bread biscuits towards Lindy and took out her cigarettes. 'Come on, eat something. You'll feel better.'

'Feel better?' Lindy sighed, but took a biscuit anyway and crunched on it, not tasting it, not caring. 'I'm just so shocked and upset, Jemima, I don't think I'll ever feel better. It's as though I was on solid ground and suddenly it's gone. I'm falling, like you do in nightmares, only without stopping.'

'I can understand how you feel, Lindy. Neil's always been there, eh? Sort o' rock. What's happened has to be a shock for you.' Jemima lit a cigarette, her eyes thoughtful. 'The thing is, though, you two were never in love, were you? Weren't you always . . . just friends?'

'What are you trying to say?' asked Lindy, her eyes glittering. 'That I shouldn't mind if he tells me he's crazy about someone else?'

'Well, didn't you once say you'd accept it if he did go out with another girl? Didn't you say you wouldn't let someone else come between you?'

'I said that?' Lindy sat back. 'No, wait a minute, I remember now – I did say it, but that was before things changed for us. After I'd said I wouldn't see Rod it was different for us, for Neil and me. He said he couldn't stand to think of me with another man, and I said I couldn't hurt him. So . . . we became more than friends.'

'You really loved each other?'

'Well, we never put anything into words, but I felt the love was there. We neither of us were keen to get wed – but everybody does get wed, eh? I did wonder sometimes where we were going because we both – you know – wanted something better than we'd got.'

Jemima drew on her cigarette. 'Like writing for Neil? And what for you, then?'

'Och, just daydreams.' Lindy smiled a little. 'Something in the dress world, maybe? Pie in the sky? But whatever I did, I must've thought Neil would be there.'

'Has he said he actually wants to part from you, though? I bet you mean as much to him as he does to you. He probably wants to stay friends with you, as well as loving Rosemary.'

'If he does, he can forget it!' Lindy cried. 'He did sort of say we could still be friends and I told him it wasn't possible. Not now he's lost his head over her.'

Jemima sighed deeply. 'My guess is that he's going to need you again very soon, Lindy.'

'Why? Why should he?'

'Isn't it obvious? He has no hope of a relationship with Miss Rosemary. I know her background; I know what she'd have to give up to marry someone like Neil. She's a lovely girl, very kind-hearted, but she'll never do it, never. Her real life will never include him, and he's going to be broken-hearted if he thinks it will.'

Lindy was silent for some time, then she rose. 'You could be wrong about that.'

'I don't think so.'

'All right, he'll be broken-hearted, then. Maybe I should feel sorry for him.' Lindy gave a quick sob. 'But I only feel sorry for myself.'

At the door they hugged again and Lindy wished Jemima all the best for her interview next day. 'You'll walk it, Jemima! They'll be glad to have someone like you.'

'Maybe. There are so few jobs going, I expect there'll be hundreds in for it. I'll just have to do the best I can.' Jemima studied Lindy's woebegone face. 'You try to keep cheerful, eh? And, listen, are you going to get in touch with that other fellow? Rod, was he called?'

'Get in touch with Rod? How could I? Even if I could find him, what would I say? Excuse me, I've been dumped by that friend I told you about – like to take me out again some time?' Lindy shook her head. 'I couldn't do that. Besides, I don't feel ready to meet him yet. I'm only thinking of Neil.'

'I know, you will be, but don't give up on Rod. I have the feeling he was keen.'

'Who knows? Look, I'd better go. Thanks for listening to me, Jemima. You always do.'

'Things'll change for you, Lindy. They'll be good again, honest they will. You'll see!'

With a slight nod, Lindy waved and moved slowly down the stairs, but on the last step, her heart beating fast, she froze. The front door had opened and stepping lightly through came a girl in pink, smiling as though at a dear friend.

'Lindy, hello there!'

It was Rosemary.

'I'm just back from seeing Mother,' she went on. 'Oh, dear, I was so tired, I cheated – took a taxi. Bang goes my budget!'

I should speak to her, thought Lindy, I should

be polite, show nothing. But she couldn't. Couldn't say a word to the delightful girl who'd stolen Neil's heart and probably didn't even know it. Couldn't, for the life of her, pretend that all was as it had once been. Moving swiftly past Rosemary, her face averted, she reached her own door, scrabbled at the handle, and let herself in, Rosemary's voice echoing after her, 'Why, Lindy, what's wrong? Lindy!'

But Lindy, closing her door, shut her ears to the voice and felt no remorse. Felt, in fact, nothing at all.

# Twenty-Two

As soon as she'd realized Lindy was no longer speaking to her, Rosemary, desperately puzzled, approached Jemima.

'What have I done?' she asked, her blue eyes wide. 'I thought I had made a friend of Lindy, who was always so kind, but then suddenly she doesn't want to know me any more. Have you any idea why?'

'Afraid not,' Jemima said, firmly crossing her fingers as she spoke her lie. 'Why don't you ask her?'

'I'd like to, but she keeps so well out of my way I can't seem to catch her. I don't want to go to the shop, and – well – sort of confront her.'

'I'm sure it will sort itself out, Miss Rosemary,'

Jemima replied, hastily correcting herself. 'I mean, Rosemary. If you like, I'll have a word with Lindy. I want to tell her my good news, anyway.'

'Would you speak to her? That would be wonderful, I'd be so grateful.' But as she took in Jemima's words, Rosemary's eyes began to shine. 'Your good news, did you say? Oh, Jemima, you got the job at Logie's!'

In genuine delight Rosemary hugged her mother's one-time lady's maid. 'Oh, I'm so pleased for you, I can't tell you – though I knew all along you'd be successful. You'll be perfect for Logie's, absolutely perfect!'

'I'll do my best,' Jemima murmured modestly and, excusing herself, hurried round to Murchie's Provisions to tell Lindy the good news the postman had brought that morning.

At the shop there were more hugs, from Lindy and even Myra, with cries of 'Congratulations!' and 'I told you so, I said you'd walk it!', and smiles from customers, glad to hear good news for a change. And getting a job, especially at a grand store like Logie's, was certainly that.

'Oh, I'm so pleased for you,' Lindy told Jemima earnestly when the customers had returned to shopping and Myra was ringing up her till. 'It's a real ray of sunshine, eh? I couldn't be happier. When do you start?'

'Next week,' Jemima replied. 'They're really keen to have me – there's a grand wedding coming up, lots to do and they're short-handed, so they'd like me to start as soon as possible.' Jemima gave a sigh of satisfaction, then said she'd better begin shopping herself – she had a list somewhere.

'First,' she whispered, 'I think I should tell you, Lindy, that Rosemary's very upset you're giving her the cold shoulder and wants to know why. Seemingly, she's no idea.'

'No idea,' Lindy repeated, her smile fading. 'So he hasn't told her.'

'Probably hasn't found the courage yet.'

'Was full enough of that when I last saw him.'

'Ah, but when it comes to the crunch, if she gives the wrong answer, that's all his dreams over. So he's putting it off.' Jemima hesitated. 'You haven't seen him, I don't suppose?'

'No, and I don't want to.' Lindy, seeing Myra looking her way from the counter, began to return to her work of unpacking a box of tinned goods. 'But it's really horrible, Jemima, making sure he's no' coming down the stair when I leave the flat, or walking down the street when I leave the house. I feel like a criminal, and it's no' my fault!'

'I wouldn't try to avoid him, or Rosemary. Just be polite if you see them and avoid unpleasantness. That's what I'd do.'

'Easier said than done!' cried Lindy.

All the same, as the days went by it became more and more worrying to her, always having to be on the lookout, and she decided that if she saw Neil she would speak to him, after all. Ask him straight out if he would declare his love to Rosemary, for she was certain he hadn't yet done so. If he had, Rosemary would certainly have understood Lindy's feelings, and surely would have told Jemima. And Neil himself would either

103

have been over the moon or down in the mire, and it seemed he was neither, for Struan said he would have heard.

'Just say the word and I'll still give him what for,' he promised Lindy, who told him not to be so foolish. Violence never did any good.

'Wrong this time – it'd make me feel good,' Struan retorted. 'It's time Mr Shakespeare got taken down a peg or two.'

That might happen soon enough, thought Lindy, still willing to speak to Neil if she saw him, but such was the way of things she never did see him, on the stairs or anywhere. She did see someone else, though, on a chill, wet Saturday in October. Someone who'd come into Murchie's Provisions after a long interval; someone she'd thought she'd never see again. And it was Roderick Connor, always known as Rod.

# Twenty-Three

The way the scene was set, it was like the showing of a film she'd seen before. Myra having 'popped home' as she called it for her dinner break, Lindy was alone at the counter, listening to the rain pelting the windows, when the shop bell pinged and the door opened. She raised her eyes and stood very still. For there he was, just as she remembered him: a young man in a raincoat, a wet cap in his hand, his hair plastered to his brow and his gaze going straight to her.

Had time gone into reverse? she wondered. Was she seeing what had once been, but now was over? Or was this Rod come back to see her, as she'd never imagined he would? I must look like a ghost, she thought, for she'd felt herself turning pale but, surely, he was the ghost?

No, it was flesh and blood Rod all right, his expression, as he approached the counter, wary, his smile uncertain.

'Hello, Lindy,' he said quietly. 'I'm afraid my cap's dripping.'

'That's all right,' she answered, her own voice sounding far away.

'Never thought it would rain like this.'

'No.'

He took a step nearer the counter. 'Listen, I know I shouldn't be here, but I thought I'd see how you were – maybe do a bit of shopping –'

'It's nice to see you.'

His eyes widened. 'You don't mind?'

'No, I don't mind. You've every right to come here.'

'You mean, you can't stop me doing my shopping. But are you sure you don't mind?'

'I told you, it's nice to see you.' She hesitated. 'How've you been, then?'

'Me? Fine. Well, getting by. How about you?'

She looked down at the counter, then up again as a customer from the back of the shop came up with a cabbage and a bag of onions.

'After you, son,' she said cheerfully to Rod, who stepped back with a smile.

'Go ahead, please. I haven't got my stuff yet.'

'If you're sure? Lindy, I just want to take these

back for our dinner – says threepence on the cabbage, but it's no' that grand – can you knock a bit off?'

'Certainly, Mrs MacInnes,' Lindy said recklessly, for Myra rarely reduced anything. 'Make it tuppence, then. That'll be fivepence altogether.'

'Thanks, pet, I've the coppers here – that OK?' Mrs MacInnes, from number twenty-one, smiled from Lindy to Rod and hurried away with her vegetables, leaving Lindy to smile at Rod herself.

'What were we saying?' she asked.

'I was asking how you were?'

'Getting by is about right for me as well as you.' Her smile faltered. 'Want me to help you with your shopping, then?'

'Couldn't we go and have something to eat? Do you have a break soon?'

'When Aunt Myra comes back.'

He sighed. 'She won't want to see me.'

'I don't think she'll mind.'

'You don't? How's that?'

Lindy put her finger to her lips. 'Shh. She's coming now. I'll get my coat.'

'Hey, don't leave me –'

'It's all right. I won't be a minute.'

'Well, Mr Connor, this is a surprise!' Myra cried, her green eyes going over Rod as she arrived at the counter still in her mackintosh. 'Haven't seen you in here for some time, eh? Thought you'd forgotten us.'

'Haven't been round this part lately,' he mumbled. 'Might get a few things today – after lunch.'

'Well, if you need any help, just say. But here's Lindy.' With a smile that mystified Rod, Myra moved round to the back of the counter. 'You two going out for a bite to eat, then?'

'That's right,' Lindy said swiftly. 'See you later, Aunt Myra.'

'No hurry. There'll no' be many in today, with all this rain. Take my umbrella, Lindy – it's at the door.'

'Thanks, I will.'

'I don't believe this is happening,' Rod said when he and Lindy were facing the rain outside, he holding Myra's umbrella over both of them. 'I mean, not only you coming out with me, but your stepmother smiling as well.'

'Needn't worry about Aunt Myra. She's pleased to see you, just like me.'

'But that's what's so odd.'

'Never mind it now – where are we going, then?'

'Where we went before, in the High Street?'

'I was so miserable there,' Lindy said in a low voice, as the rain pattered on their umbrella. 'But I don't mind going back.'

'Are you miserable now?' Rod asked, bending his head close to her face.

'Sort of.'

'I see.'

As he straightened up, away from her, she pressed his arm. 'I'll tell you about it in the café.'

As the day was so cold and wet they felt like something warmer than sandwiches and ordered omelettes – ham for Rod, tomato for Lindy. That done, there was an awkward pause while their eyes met and moved away, and neither spoke.

Finally Rod leaned forward. 'You going to tell me why you're miserable?' he asked gently.

Lindy hesitated, seeking the right words for what she wanted to say. After playing with her fork for a moment she raised her eyes to Rod's. 'I think I'm feeling more let down than miserable, to be honest.'

Rod's brown eyes lost their warmth. 'Let down? Why, who's let you down? That writing fellow?'

She nodded. 'Yes. Neil.'

'I thought he was supposed to be your friend? The one you couldn't do without?'

'He was my friend, Rod. He was what you say.' Lindy's voice was low. 'At least, I thought he was.'

'I know. You chose him instead of me.'

'I did tell you why.'

'You did. He was the special one, he'd always been there; you couldn't risk losing him. Now he lets you down. So, tell me – what did he do?'

'Ham omelette, tomato omelette,' intoned the waitress, the same who'd served Lindy and Rod before, but who showed no recognition now. Why should she? They remembered their last meeting only too well, but to her they were just two more customers.

'Who wants what?' she asked, and once they'd said, dashed down their plates.

'May we have some bread, please?' Rod asked politely. 'Crusty, if you've got it.'

'It's extra for bread, and it's no' crusty, anyway,' she snapped.

'That's all right, we'll have it.'

'Hang on, then.'

'I know who's crusty,' Lindy whispered, and Rod grinned.

'I suppose it's hard work being a waitress – they're bound to get a bit crabby now and again.'

'You're so sympathetic, Rod.'

'Not towards your writing friend. If he's hurt you, Lindy, I wish I could meet him. Give him a piece of my mind, and a punch or two.'

'A punch or two? You sound like my brother.'

'Your bread!' cried the waitress, depositing a plate of rolls on the table and hurrying away.

'She's doing her best,' remarked Rod, passing the plate to Lindy. 'And if I sound like your brother, it's because he's got the right ideas about your so-called friend. You still haven't told me how he let you down.'

'I suppose it wasn't really his fault. He said he couldn't choose what happened, anyway. But then he said he couldn't put it back.'

'Put what back? For God's sake, Lindy, spell it out!'

'Falling in love. Neil fell in love with someone. At first sight.'

'Fell in love?' Rod stared. 'With someone else? Was he mad?'

'He thinks so.' Lindy smiled coldly. 'But he still hopes she's going to love him in the same way.'

'Who is she? Who is this girl he could think he loves more than you?'

Lindy sighed. 'I'd better explain, Rod. Her name is Rosemary and she's a new tenant. But no ordinary tenant.'

As briefly as she could, Lindy told Rod about

Rosemary Dalrymple and the misfortunes of her mother, Jemima's ex-employer. How Rosemary was living temporarily in the tenement and had settled better than anyone had expected, but wouldn't be staying. How Neil had not yet declared his love but was certain Rosemary would share it and want to marry him, which did seem to show that he was, if not mad, at least blind to reality.

'In a way, I think I should feel sorry for him,' Lindy finished, after the waitress had whisked away omelette plates and taken their order for apple pie. 'But I feel too upset, Rod. He's destroyed what we had; he's sort of left me dangling over a great hole, and I don't seem to want to forgive him.'

'Of course you can't forgive him!' cried Rod. 'Whatever the reason, he's let you down, just as you say. You're the one he's supposed to love, not this girl from Never-Never Land, isn't that right?'

'I don't know. Jemima thinks we were never really in love and it's true, we weren't for a long time – we were just friends, as I said. Then that seemed to change.' Lindy looked at Rod. 'After he'd made me give you up.'

'Don't remind me,' said Rod, and both were silent.

The apple pies arrived and were eaten without more talk, then Rod paid the bill and they left the café, the waitress again smiling over her tip.

'You're sure you didn't want coffee?' Rod asked Lindy in the street, busy with lunchtime traffic. She shook her head and said she must get back.

'Your stepmother said no hurry.'

'Aye, but Saturday afternoon can be busy. I should go.'

'Do I take it Neil is no longer the blue-eyed boy for her?'

'Too right. He's out of favour.'

'And I'm in?' Rod's look was serious. 'Or not? Look, I don't care about being in favour with anyone but you. You know that, don't you?'

'I don't know why you should want to be, Rod, after what I did.'

'Don't think like that, Lindy. I understood how things were for you. Neil had been a part of your life; I was someone you'd just met, didn't really know. How could you be expected to choose me over him?'

'There you go again,' she sighed. 'Being so sympathetic. Making me feel bad.'

'Come on, you've no reason to feel that.' He gave a slight smile. 'I mean, you came out with me today. Didn't send me packing.'

'I don't want to send you packing, Rod.'

He took her hand and held it. 'But?' he asked quietly. 'There is a "but", isn't there?'

She released her hand and began to walk up the street, Rod walking with her, step for step.

'It's just that I still feel a bit . . . battered, if that's the word, Rod. I want to see you, but I've – I don't know – lost all confidence.'

'Oh, Lindy, if I could lay my hands on that damned friend of yours, I'd – hell, I don't know what I'd do. You were so full of life, so much at

111

ease with yourself, weren't you? And he's made you feel rejected when that's the last thing you should ever feel. Look, what you have to do is understand that Neil's ideas don't count now. He's put himself out of your life, he doesn't matter, and now you can begin to forget him.'

Rod's eyes were shining as he put Lindy's arm into his. 'And I'm the one to help you to do that, Lindy. Will you let me? Will you give me the chance?'

She nodded, her expression clearing, her own eyes, if not shining, meeting his directly, and her hand suddenly finding its way back into his. 'Rod, you're very good to me,' she said quietly. 'I'm really grateful. If you want to see me, I want to see you.'

'You mean that? Oh, Lindy!'

They began to quicken their steps back to Murchie's Provisions, where they exchanged long, serious looks as a last chance to say goodbye before going back into Myra's realm.

'You going to help me shop?' asked Rod.

'Of course. You'll have forgotten where everything is.'

'But first tell me – when can I see you again?'

'Sunday?'

'Sunday? You mean tomorrow?' He took a long breath, only just stopping himself in time from saying aloud that Sunday, of course, was no longer the writing fellow's day. It was his day now, and he didn't have to stop himself from smiling at the thought. 'That'd be wonderful, because it's my Sunday off. At the hostel we only get one in four, so that's a bit of luck. What time shall we say?'

'Two o'clock? Come to the tenement – we're

number nineteen this street, you remember. Come into the hall and knock on our door, first on the right. I'll be waiting, anyway.'

'Why do those words sound so amazing?' Rod gave one last press to Lindy's hand, then pushed open the shop door and laughed at the sound of the bell. 'In we go!' he cried. 'Let shopping commence!'

# Twenty-Four

All Sunday morning, to everyone's dismay, Myra worked on cleaning the living room – shaking mats, washing the floor, dusting everything in sight, until even George was driven to complaint, Struan fled, and Gingerboy slept under Lindy's bed rather than on it, to be sure of being out of the way. Lindy was forced into helping Myra, though she too complained, saying if all this was being done to impress Rod Connor, he might not even come in.

'He's only coming to collect me, Aunt Myra. I don't even need to invite him into the flat.'

'Of course you should invite him in, Lindy! I thought that was why you'd asked him to call for you here.'

'No, I just thought it'd be a good place to meet. Anybody'd think he was my young man, but I've only been out with him once.'

'That's true,' George put in. 'We're no' going to be on show as future in-laws, eh?'

Myra shook her head. 'He's keen, George. He's been keen right from the start. I saw that when

I first saw him looking at Lindy in the shop, but I thought she was Neil's girl and didn't want to encourage him.'

'I was never Neil's girl,' said Lindy quietly. 'Listen, are we finished now? It all looks very nice. So let's get on with Sunday dinner, then. I want it out of the way in good time today.'

'I wish it was dinner time now,' George groaned. 'If I'd known you were going to be going through this place like a whirlwind, Myra, I'd have gone out with Struan.'

'Well, you can stop complaining,' Myra declared. 'Dinner won't be long. The meat's nearly done, as a matter o' fact, and Lindy can put the veg on, eh?'

'And you'll make the Yorkshire puddings,' said Lindy.

'Best thing I've heard all morning,' said George. 'Struan better hurry back, eh?'

When the meal was over and the washing-up done, Lindy disappeared to get ready while Myra occupied herself putting the finishing touches to the living room. A chenille cloth, not seen since Christmas, was spread over the kitchen table, and a small vase of artificial flowers placed in the centre. The cushions on the sofa were plumped up, a final brush was given to the hearth by the stove, and all newspapers and magazines were tidied away. Even a comb was run through George's hair by his wife's nimble fingers, which made Struan burst out laughing.

'Don't tell me Dad needs tidying as well?' he cried. 'How about me? How about you, Aunt Myra?'

'You're all right,' she said grudgingly, 'but I'm going to put on my good dress, like I do every Sunday – nothing special there. As for Lindy, I needn't worry about her.'

'Too right,' said Struan. 'Here she comes, dressed to kill, eh?'

'Oh, what rubbish!' said Lindy, appearing from her bedroom and laughing. 'I've only changed into a twinset and tweed skirt.'

'Look grand, anyway,' Struan told her seriously. 'Though what the minister would say to you wearing lipstick on a Sunday I'm sure I don't know.'

'As though you know anything at all about the minister!' Lindy retorted. 'We're no' kirkgoers, are we?'

But it was true – she did look lovely in the dark red twinset that seemed to enhance the fresh-ness of her complexion and her black hair, while her deep blue eyes shone with particular brilliance as they moved to check the clock.

'It's nearly two, I'll see if Rod's there,' she said quickly and hurried towards the door.

He had just that moment come into the hallway of number nineteen through the outer door that was only locked at night and, for a moment, both he and Lindy stood still, poised to greet each other but not actually moving. Then they moved closer, smiles lighting up their faces.

'Lindy!' cried Rod.

'Rod!' Her eyes went to a wrapped bunch of chrysanthemums in his arms. 'Why, what have you got there?'

He glanced down at the flowers and gave an embarrassed smile. 'These are for your step-mother. I'll be seeing her, won't I?'

'Oh, yes, if you'd like to come in while I get my hat and coat.'

'Think it's all right to give her flowers? I mean, not too obvious?'

'All right? Rod, it's a lovely thought – she'll be thrilled. I don't know when anybody I know ever had any flowers!'

'You shall have some, then. Yes, why not? I'd like to give you flowers, Lindy.'

'No, no, I don't need any. But, come on in to meet the folks, then. Even Struan's here at the minute.'

Rod, looking apprehensive, followed Lindy into the living room of the flat, where three expectant faces were turned towards him. Even Gingerboy suddenly appeared and fixed him with a yellow stare.

'This is Roderick Connor, everybody, always known as Rod,' Lindy announced. 'Rod, this is my dad, Aunt Myra you've met, and Struan, my brother.'

'How d'you do?' said Rod, standing with the flowers in his hand, half-wishing he'd never brought them, except that Myra's green eyes were already homing in on them and her lips were parting in a smile.

'Very pleased to meet you,' George said, rising from his chair, but even before he could put out his hand Myra had moved smoothly forward towards Rod.

'Nice to see you again, Mr Connor,' she

116

murmured, her eyes still on his flowers, and laughed. 'Even if it's no' in Murchie's, eh?'

'Please call me Rod,' he said quickly, and placed his flowers in her arms. 'Er, these are for you.'

'For me?' She flushed. 'How lovely! I'll just get a vase—'

'I'll get one!' cried Lindy. 'That big jug in the scullery, Aunt Myra?'

'Grand, put some water in, then. But Mr Connor – Rod – you'd no need to go giving me flowers. No' that I'm complaining!'

'Should think not!' cried Struan, leaning forward to shake Rod's hand. 'We've only had artificial flowers in here up till now. Nice to meet you, Rod. Me and Dad work at Bayne's, the brewery. Hear you're with the council, then?'

'That's right,' answered Rod, looking for Lindy and relaxing when she reappeared with a large earthenware jug, smiling at him as though to say, 'don't worry, we'll soon be on our own'.

Aloud, she told Myra she'd leave her to arrange the flowers, as she and Rod wanted to get off for their outing.

'Going walking?' asked George kindly. 'Nice day for it.'

'Or climbing?' asked Struan. 'Didn't you go up Arthur's Seat when you first met?'

'I've got the car today,' Rod said reluctantly. 'Thought we might go for a drive.'

'Car?' Struan repeated, staring. 'Never knew you had one. What sort?'

'Morris Eight.' Rod smiled. 'Not very big.'

'Big enough! My God, I'd go out in a dodgem car from the fair if I had one!'

'Struan, Struan, this is Sunday, remember!' cried Myra, looking scandalized. 'George, tell your son to stop taking the Lord's name in vain.'

'Aye, Struan, that's no way to talk on a Sunday,' George said. 'We may no' be kirkgoers, but we expect better than that.'

'Whatever will Rod think?' asked Myra, glancing at him, but he was again looking at Lindy, who had put on her coat and was adjusting her hat at the kitchen mirror.

'All set!' she called. 'Rod, let's away.'

'When do you think you'll be back?' asked Myra.

'Oh, we won't be late,' Rod assured her earnestly. 'It gets dark fairly early nowadays.'

'You'll be very welcome for a cup of tea, you know.'

'Thank you, Mrs Gillan, that's very kind, but I – well, I've brought a bit of a picnic.'

'A picnic? Oh, Rod, that'll be lovely!' cried Lindy as her family stared in astonishment. A man putting up a picnic? Who'd ever heard of such a thing?

'Fancy you doing that!' Myra exclaimed. 'You'd never catch Struan doing anything of that sort.'

'Hey, I could cut a sandwich, all right, if I wanted.' Struan grinned. 'But I'd get a lassie to do it for me, eh?'

'And when did we ever have a picnic, anyway?' asked George. 'Just hope it's no' too cold for you two.'

'Don't forget, they've got the car,' said Struan.

After an awkward little pause, Rod cleared his throat. 'It was very nice to meet you, Mrs Gillan and Mr Gillan – and you, Struan.'

'And Gingerboy,' Struan returned. 'Don't forget the cat. Listen, can I come out to see the car?'

'No,' Lindy said firmly. 'If you do that we'll be stuck for ever in Scott Street while you and Rod talk cars. Come on, Rod.'

But Rod was hesitating. 'Look, it won't take a minute to show Struan the car – it's just outside, parked at the kerb.'

'Lead me to it!' cried Struan, grinning at Lindy, who was shrugging. 'Don't often get the chance to see a private car of any sort.'

'Can you drive?' asked Rod, as the three young people left number nineteen. 'You might like a spin out some time.'

''Course I can drive! I've driven the brewery vans often enough. Do you mean it, Rod? I'll take you up on the offer any time.'

'Sure, I mean it.' Rod's voice was suddenly soft with pride as he took out his keys and opened the door of the blunt-nosed little blue car standing at the kerb. 'And here's the car itself. Not very big, as I told you, but it seats four, with a good boot for luggage, and it's in terrific condition. Got it second hand, but it's never been any trouble – had no big bills—'

'It's grand!' cried Struan, seating himself in the driving seat. 'Wow, what wouldn't I give to have something like this?'

He was so happy even Lindy hadn't the heart to tell him to move out, but in the end he leaped out himself, hurrying round to open the passenger door with a flourish and help his sister into her seat.

'Wouldn't have minded having a look at the engine,' he muttered, 'but better let you two get off, eh? Thanks, Rod, I appreciated that. See you again, eh?'

'Certainly!' cried Rod, starting his car with the handle, then jumping into the driving seat. ''Bye, Struan. Good to meet you.'

And with Struan waving and looking rather forlorn, Lindy and Rob left Scott Street in the little Morris on their first drive together.

'Have you really got a picnic?' Lindy asked. 'I can't believe it.'

'Look on the back seat, then. See a shopping basket? That's it.'

'Rod, you're a marvel!'

'Only aim to please.'

'I'm pleased, all right,' said Lindy.

## Twenty-Five

'Oh, Rod, isn't this grand?' cried Lindy, her eyes shining, her face alive with excitement as they drove towards the centre of the city. 'Everything looks different, eh? I mean, from a car? I'm only used to trams. Or my own two feet!'

'I'm glad you're enjoying being in my car, then,' Rod said, taking pleasure in her delight. 'But what we have to decide now is where you'd like to go.'

'Go? Oh, anywhere! I don't mind. What do you think, then?'

'Well, we're a bit limited, only having the afternoon.' Rod hesitated. 'I didn't dare ask you to come out for the whole day.'

'Why? I wouldn't have minded. You should have said.'

'I didn't want to rush you, Lindy. I know it's true, what you said – you've had a battering. And then your folks might not have been pleased about you spending the whole day with me.'

'You don't have to worry about my folks, Rod. I could tell Dad liked you and Aunt Myra's all for you, now.'

'Because I gave her flowers?'

Lindy was silent for a moment. 'Because your name isn't Neil,' she said at last.

'He was her favourite once, wasn't he?'

'That's all over now. Listen, where are we going, then?'

'I was thinking of North Berwick, but it might take too long. How about Aberlady? That's on the way. Don't know if you know it?'

'No, I don't remember it. I've been to North Berwick – just the once – on a school trip, so we must have passed it. Is it a village?'

'Just a village now, with golf courses to hand, but it was a busy harbour once. The merchants used to export grain and wine, so there were always customs men around trying to catch smugglers avoiding paying the duty.' Rod laughed. 'My dad used to tell me stories that my grandfather had told him – he was a fisherman on this part of the coast, but he's been dead for years. I never knew him.'

'So your folks have always been to do with the sea?'

'Yes, and you're wondering why I'm different. I do love the sea, but I suppose I've just never wanted to spend my life on it. Which was a big disappointment to my dad, as I think I told you.'

'And I told you that what you do is really worthwhile. You shouldn't apologize because you didn't go to sea, Rod.'

'No, maybe not. Well, if we've decided on Aberlady, let's make for the coast.'

'Oh, I'm so lucky,' she said quietly. 'Being given a trip like this. Thank you, Rod.'

'My pleasure, Lindy.'

Autumn sunshine was struggling through the cloud mass over Aberlady Bay when they arrived and left the car to walk on the shore. Here there were dunes and piled-up sand, mudflats and waving grasses, flocks of birds swooping and calling, and very few people. In the distance Lindy could only see two couples walking together and throwing sticks for three happy spaniels, which made her turn to Rod with a smile.

'So nice, eh? We've practically got this place to ourselves. Very different from Portobello beach, where there's never a place to put a pin sometimes.'

'I know – it's usually like this. So quiet, you can't imagine all the activity of the old days. But you can still see the merchants' granary inland, and there are a couple of small hotels, mainly for golfers.'

'I think it's beautiful.' Lindy was breathing

deeply. 'Smell the air – so fresh, so clean! When you spend all your time in a city full of smoke, you forget what fresh air's like. Sort of . . . unused.'

'Suits you,' Rod said softly, his eyes on the heightened colour of her face, the brightness of her eyes. 'Why don't you take your hat off?'

'I think I will.'

She took off her hat and laughed as the breeze sent her dark hair whirling. 'Come on, let's walk and walk! I've got my sensible shoes on!'

'And then have our picnic,' said Rod, beginning to stride away. 'I don't know about you but I always want to eat my sandwiches the minute I've arrived.'

'No sandwiches till we've been to that point in the distance, Rod. Have to earn them.'

Back from the point, they decided to have their picnic in the car, out of the breeze and the beady eyes of the gulls, Rod taking charge of opening the basket and displaying his efforts.

'First, madam, the thermos. Do you mind that I've put up coffee? I never like thermos tea.'

'Rod, anything you've done is all right by me. I'm just so amazed you did it.'

'Well, you know I look after myself. Why should I not be able to produce a few sandwiches and a thermos of coffee?'

The 'few sandwiches' turned out to be what Lindy described as a feast. There were hard-boiled eggs, tomato and lettuce sandwiches, ham sandwiches, sausage rolls, biscuits with cheese, iced buns and small chocolate cakes, all served with paper plates and napkins, and all making Lindy's eyes widen.

'Rod, this is unbelievable! Honestly, it's lovely. But so much! How are we going to eat it all? Just the two of us? There's enough for an army.'

'I suppose there does look to be rather a lot,' he said thoughtfully. 'I got carried away. But don't give me too much credit. Apart from the eggs and sandwiches it's all bought – and for God's sake, don't tell your stepmother – from my local shop. I wanted it to be a surprise and you would have been wondering what on earth I was doing, buying all this stuff.'

'Buying up the shop,' Lindy laughed, her eyes meeting his. 'Oh, Rod, you are so sweet, eh? Trying to make me forget my troubles, make me happy.'

'And are you?' he asked quietly. 'Happy?'

'I am. I think I really am.'

'Maybe just for now?'

'Who knows?' Suddenly she leaned forward and kissed his cheek. 'Rod, thank you. For today, the picnic and everything.'

Putting his hand to his cheek, he looked away. 'Like to pour the coffee? I've got two mugs somewhere.'

'Think I'll have something to eat first. But what shall it be? A boiled egg, maybe.'

'There's salt if you want it in a twist of paper in the basket.'

'Oh, no!' She laughed. 'You think of everything, eh? Are you like this with everything you do?'

'Only if I really care,' he answered seriously, and then they were both silent, beginning to eat, to enjoy the picnic, and something more that neither of them would put into words.

It was dark when they arrived back at number nineteen and Rod, switching off the car engine, turned to look at Lindy. 'Here we are, then, back home – at least, for you.'

In the light of the street lamp he could see her face, serious instead of smiling, her eyes, looking dark, fixed on him.

'I've had such a grand day, Rod – I don't know how to tell you – it's been wonderful.'

'For me, too.' He took her hand. 'Just wish it needn't end, but I suppose they'll be waiting for you.' He smiled and shrugged. 'Must keep your folks happy.'

'Rod, you needn't worry about them. They won't be waiting for me yet.'

'Maybe, but I want them to feel I'm a responsible guy, someone they can trust, and you have been out with me for quite some time.' He smoothed her hand with his. 'If we get it right this time we could have longer next time – that's the way I see it.'

'Honestly, Rod!' For a moment Lindy's lovely mouth tightened, then relaxed. 'Oh, well, you're probably right. They'll be pleased you've brought me back safe and sound, as though I was a bit of china. No, I mean it, you're right. But I did have such a grand time. I know what you mean about no' wanting it to end.'

'I haven't – you know – tried to go too fast for you?'

'Too fast? No, I've felt better today.' Taking her hand from his, Lindy fiddled with the car door handle. 'I haven't thought of Neil at all.'

'Why, Lindy, that's terrific! Best news of all.

Hang on there, I'll come round and let you out. That handle's stiff.'

On the pavement, under that same street lamp, they quietly embraced, then Rod kissed Lindy on the cheek, as she had kissed him.

'I'll come into the shop,' he whispered. 'To fix up when we can meet again. But, listen, do you want the rest of the picnic? There's a lot left, I'll never get through it.'

'Oh, Rod, I was wondering if you'd let me have it. I'd like to give it to one of the families.'

'Of course I'll let you have it!' He gave her the basket from the back of the car and they stood gazing at each other for several moments.

'Goodnight, Lindy,' Rod said at last. 'Thanks for coming today.'

'Goodnight, Rod. Thank you – for everything.'

At the door to number nineteen, she watched him return to his car and drive slowly away before she turned to go into the house – and was almost knocked down in the hall by a flying figure, running as though the furies were after him. It was Neil.

# Twenty-Six

His face wasn't his. Or, so it seemed at first to Lindy, staring at him in fright. Where was the handsome young man who'd been her

126

friend? Replaced by a white-faced, wild-eyed stranger, who scarcely seemed able to take in that it was Lindy he'd almost sent crashing to the floor. Lindy, who'd only been able to save herself and Rod's basket by the sheerest good luck.

'Neil, what is it?' she cried, holding him by the arm. 'What's happened? What's wrong?'

'Lindy?' he murmured, gazing into her face as his own face worked with emotion, and he put a hand to his brow as though he must hold it to prop up his head. 'Lindy, she's up there – she's fine; she says she isn't and she's crying, but she's all right. She's all right, Lindy, because she doesn't care. She's told me, she told me just now, and I'd brought flowers and a bottle of wine. I thought we were going to celebrate—'

'Neil, is it Rosemary you're talking about?' Lindy was still holding on to his arm. 'Is she really all right? You haven't—'

'Haven't what?' His wild eyes flamed. 'Hurt her? God, no, I haven't hurt her! I couldn't, she doesn't care, she's told me, didn't I say? Can't you see? I'm the one that's hurt!'

Flinging off Lindy's hand, he flung himself away from her and shot through the door still as though chased by unknown forces, and though Lindy at once ran after him, the street was empty. He was nowhere to be seen.

Oh, God, what do I do now? Lindy asked herself, returning to the hall and standing still, her shaking hands still holding Rod's basket. Take the picnic to Aggie, she decided, but then what? Then she must see Rosemary. See if she really

127

was all right. Only she didn't want to, didn't want to at all.

Still shaking, she mounted the stairs to Aggie's flat, hurrying past Rosemary's in case she should appear, and knocked on the door.

'Who is it?' came Aggie's voice over the sound of shrill crying. As usual, somebody wasn't happy in the Andrews' flat.

'It's only Lindy, Aggie. Come on, open up. I've got something for you.'

A moment later Aggie's pale face appeared at the door while two of her children clung to her legs and a third, the one who was crying, kept up the wails in the background.

'Will you shut up?' thundered Tam's voice. 'Or I'll give you something to cry about!'

'He's just teething, he canna help greetin',' Aggie whispered, her eyes going to the shopping basket in Lindy's hand. 'What was it you got for me, Lindy?'

'I wondered if you'd like this picnic stuff we never finished, Aggie? There's sandwiches and cheese things and some sausage rolls, iced buns – and look, little chocolate cakes. I think there'll be enough for everybody.'

'Let's see, let's see!' cried young Alex and his sister, Matty. 'Oh, Ma, see what's in the basket! Oh, can we have 'em, can we have 'em?'

'I want a choclit cake!' squealed Matty. 'Ma, can I, can I have a cholit cake? Can I?'

'Wait, wait, I'll have to see . . .'

Aggie's eyes were enormous as she took the basket from Lindy and gazed at the contents. 'Did you say it was a picnic, Lindy? Was it no' too cold for a picnic? I dinna ken, because I've never been to one, eh? But it's awful kind to give us all this. Are you sure you want to?'

'Sure I do.' Lindy pushed the basket into Aggie's arms. 'But I've got to go now. Be good, you bairns, eh?'

'We'll all say thank you!' cried Aggie. 'Thank you, Lindy!'

Waving her hand, Lindy skimmed away, anxious still not to see Rosemary, but there she was, outside her flat, waiting for Lindy on the stairs.

'Lindy, can you spare me a minute?' she asked, her voice shaky, very different from usual, just as Rosemary herself, like Neil, was different from usual. Though still as well dressed as ever, with her blonde hair as stylish, she looked as though she'd had a shock, something she couldn't handle, could only shed tears over, for there were marks of them on her porcelain cheeks, and her eyes were red.

Well, of course, Lindy knew she'd had a shock and what it had been, but hadn't expected tears. Not from Rosemary, who'd kept such a stiff upper lip over her family's misfortunes, but here she was, wanting to talk, and it could only be about Neil. 'Sorry,' she said, taking a deep breath. 'I'm just on my way home.'

'Oh, please, Lindy! I must talk to you! I know now why you haven't wanted to speak to me and I understand – I do, really, but I'd be so grateful if we could talk now.' Rosemary's eyes were pleading, filling again with tears, and Lindy, feeling she could do nothing else, sighed and knew she'd have to give in.

'Just for a few minutes, then, but first, have you thought of speaking to Jemima? She's always been a grand help to me.'

'Oh, I know, she'd be wonderful, but it's you I want to talk to, because – well, because I know I've hurt you, too. Though you must believe me, I never meant to, it's the last thing I'd do. But come in, please, come in. It's so kind of you, I do appreciate it.'

## Twenty-Seven

It was some time since Lindy had been in Rosemary's refurbished flat, but she marvelled afresh at its splendid appearance: Jemima's decoration, Rosemary's lovely pieces, the rugs and cushions, the gilt-framed pictures. What an amazing place it was, then, to find in a tenement in Scott Street! Not that it was very tidy. Seemingly, in spite of all her willingness to help, Rosemary's new life did not include any real housework, and it was well known that Jemima always rushed round with broom and dusters for Miss Rosemary's flat when she cleaned her mother's. That was only to be expected. But at least Rosemary now knew how to make a cup of tea and offered one to Lindy, who declined it, saying she really couldn't spare much time.

'So, what was it you wanted to talk to me about?' she asked, reluctantly sitting down at Rosemary's invitation. As though she didn't know! But she must let Rosemary say what she had to say.

'Oh, Lindy, I'm sure you know already. I was on the landing, I heard you with Neil in the hall – not what was said, just your voices. But you'd have seen him, seen the state he was in –' Rosemary put a lace-edged handkerchief to her eyes. 'It was so terrible. I've never seen anything like it – I mean, the change in him.'

'After you'd told him?' Lindy asked coldly. 'Told him he'd got everything wrong?'

'Told him? Yes.' Rosemary put aside her handkerchief. 'But what else could I do? I had no idea, you see, no idea at all. It came like a bolt from the blue. Hit me so hard I could barely speak.'

'But you did speak, didn't you?'

'Lindy, I had to. I couldn't let the poor boy go on believing – well, what he did believe. He'd brought flowers, you know, and a bottle of wine. He said they were for a celebration.' Rosemary dropped her voice and looked away from Lindy. 'Of our love. Can you imagine how I felt?'

'No, because you must have seen it coming, Rosemary.' Lindy's tone was flint-like, her eyes as hard. 'Women always know when a man's keen, eh? They've a way of looking, of talking – even other folk can tell. Don't tell me you've no experience of men falling for you and Neil'd be no different, even if he's a tenement lad. But you did nothing, eh? You just let him keep on going with his dreams till he got the nerve to speak and then you put the knife in. No wonder he went to pieces!'

'No, no, Lindy, I didn't know, I swear I didn't!' Rosemary cried. 'I never for a moment thought that he – honestly, I never believed . . .'

As she fell silent, understanding suddenly flowed through Lindy, who stood up abruptly and moved to Rosemary's door.

'I see,' she said quietly. 'It's true what you say – you never imagined Neil could think of loving you, because of what he was. A tenement lad, like I said. He believed two people could love each other whatever their background, but maybe he was just crazy. I said myself he was, so maybe you can't be blamed for thinking that too.' Without looking again at Rosemary, Lindy opened her door and said quietly, 'Goodnight, then.'

'Wait,' Rosemary said in a low voice. 'Wait. I can be blamed. I see it now. I can be blamed. Lindy, I blame myself.' She moved to Lindy and put her hand on her arm. 'But what can I do?'

'Don't think there's anything.'

'Do you think he'll be all right? He was so strange – I was so worried – am worried –'

'We'll just have to wait and see what happens.'

Though she would never speak of it to Rosemary, Lindy knew in her heart she was not altogether surprised by Neil's extreme reaction to Rosemary's rejection. He'd always been different from the other young men in the tenement, living on his nerves, given to fits of moodiness – maybe because he was a writer, if that was the way writers were.

To have lived in a fool's paradise over Rosemary had still been paradise for him, and when she told him it wasn't maybe it was only to be expected that he couldn't take it. Poor Neil. Lindy saw now only too clearly that he'd never been in love with her. Loved her, yes, as a dear friend, but to be caught in thrall to a woman as he was with Rosemary – no, he'd never had that kind of feeling for her, the 'girl next door', the one he'd always known. Just as well, as she'd never felt it for him. Did she feel it for Rod? Just for a moment, her heart lifted as she thought of him. How happy she was with him, how easy he made everything! But now was not the time to dwell on her own feelings and, as anxiety for Neil came back into her mind, Lindy looked at Rosemary.

'He'll be all right,' she said as confidently as she could. 'Try no' to worry. He'll have to work things out for himself, eh?'

'I suppose so,' Rosemary answered, her eyes troubled. 'But thank you for talking to me, Lindy. I'm so sorry I seem to have caused . . . so much trouble. I never meant to, but that's no excuse, I see that now. I should have done things differently, should have seen what was happening . . .'

Lindy, turning away, shook her head. There was nothing she could say to help. If only they knew where he was, what he was doing . . . Maybe gone drinking, to drown his sorrows? No, it was Sunday, most pubs would be closed. Anyway, Neil was not a drinking man. Would Struan have any ideas where Neil might go in the state he was in? If he was at home that Sunday evening Lindy decided she'd ask him, might even suggest he collected Neil's brothers and went to look for him . . . Yes, why not?

'Rosemary, I've got to go,' she said quickly.

'If my brother's in I'll ask him to help find Neil.'

'Oh, would you, Lindy?' Rosemary raised her drenched eyes. 'Would you let me know if he does?'

'I will. But you go and see Jemima, eh? She'll help, she always does. Goodnight, Rosemary.'

'Goodnight, Lindy – and thanks. All my thanks again.'

Wasting no more time, Lindy ran down the stairs home. Strange, how far away her trip with Rod seemed now, yet it was no more than a few hours in the past. Rod, though, was not far away, and even though she couldn't give herself up to thoughts of him, she knew, when this anxiety over Neil had gone, there he would be, in her mind, making her feel better. Now, though, she had to tell her family what had happened.

# Twenty-Eight

They were in the living room, Struan as well, thank God, and the kettle on the range was boiling, which meant there was going to be tea and she could do with that, could do with something. For, even though she'd seemed well, she realized she was actually quite exhausted. The toll of seeing Neil and coping with Rosemary was making itself felt, and she would have given a lot just to burst into tears and go to her bed. As though she could!

'Is that tea you're making, Aunt Myra?' she

asked with such a tremble in her voice all eyes in the room immediately focused on her, and even Gingerboy, supposed to be asleep on George's knee, gave her one of his stares, as though he realized something was wrong.

'Why, lassie, you sound weary,' said George. 'Have you tired yourself out?'

'And you're awful late back,' put in Myra. 'We wondered if you'd had a breakdown.'

'No, we never had a breakdown, we had a grand time by the sea at Aberlady, and the picnic was lovely – I've just been up to give what was left to Aggie.'

'Hey, you might have remembered me,' Struan said, frowning. 'I bet there were some sausage rolls, eh? I can just see Rod buying sausage rolls.'

'As though you don't get enough to eat here!' snapped Myra, though her eyes were still on Lindy. 'And is that where you've been, eh, all this time, talking to Aggie? She's no' usually got much to say.'

'No, I've been talking to Rosemary.' Lindy heaved a great sigh. 'And before that I saw Neil. He was like a madman, running out into the street in a terrible state because Rosemary had turned him down. And she was in a state, too, crying because she'd got such a shock, and then he was so strange, no' like himself at all, she didn't know what he'd do, but I couldn't help.'

Tears at last filled Lindy's eyes and she brushed them away. 'In fact, I blamed her – I said she should have warned him off earlier, but then I felt a bit sorry, because she did seem to care and was so worried about Neil. And so am I.'

At first there was silence after Lindy had finished speaking, with Myra glancing at George, George shaking his head, and Struan still frowning.

Myra was the first to speak. 'So, where's he gone, then – Neil?'

'We don't know. He just ran out into the street, and when I ran after him I couldn't see him.'

'Where could he go?' asked George. 'On a Sunday?'

'I thought, Struan, you might go and look for him,' Lindy said eagerly. 'Maybe get his brothers to look as well?'

'What good would that do? He's no' going to take any notice of us. Sounds as mad as a hatter, from what you say.'

'Aye, crazy,' Myra agreed, rising and moving to the range to make the tea. 'He was always different from everybody else, always likely to go off the rails. I often used to say that, eh? I used to say that very thing to his mother, poor woman.'

'I don't remember you saying that,' said Lindy. 'You thought Neil was very sensible, with a good job and just right for me.'

'He may have made folk think he was nice and sensible, but look at the way he messed you around, Lindy! And then to go and fall for Miss Rosemary? As if he had any sort o' chance there. Now if that doesn't make him sound crazy, what would?'

'I always liked Neil,' sighed George. 'I think you should go and look for him, Struan. I don't like to think of him wandering the streets.'

'What are you all afraid of?' cried Struan. 'That

he's going to throw himself off George the Fourth Bridge?'

'Plenty have,' said George. 'Or the Dean Bridge, maybe.'

'Never Neil,' Struan said firmly. 'He's too fond of himself to do that. Thinks he's going to be a great writer, eh? So he's no' going to waste it all by taking a leap.'

'Will you stop it?' Lindy cried. 'You should be trying to help, Struan, instead of acting so heartless.'

'All right, all right.' He ground out the cigarette he'd been smoking. 'I'll go up and see if the MacLauren lads are in and we'll do what we can. No one's going to call *me* heartless!'

'Sorry,' said Lindy, drinking the tea Myra gave her. 'It's just that I'm frightened Neil will do something silly, if you want to know. You didn't see him tonight. I did.'

'And all this over Miss Rosemary?' asked Myra, clicking her tongue. 'Who could believe it?'

I could, thought Lindy, but she said nothing. She felt a little better, drinking the tea and knowing that Struan was going to help. Maybe Neil would be found safe and well, not ready to jump off a bridge at all. Maybe she'd just exaggerated how he looked and he wasn't acting crazy – was just upset, which was only to be expected? Truth was, she knew she hadn't exaggerated anything, for Rosemary had been frightened by Neil's reaction too, and from the look on his face when he'd run into the street, he wasn't to be trusted to look after himself.

137

'We're away,' called Struan, putting his head round the door. 'I've got two o' the MacLauren boys; the others are out. Better go up and see their ma, Aunt Myra – she's upset. Didn't even know what had happened to Neil till I told her.'

'Oh, poor Vi! I'll go up now,' said Myra. 'But what a devil that Neil is, then, causing all this trouble!'

'Struan, I was thinking I could come with you,' Lindy suggested, jumping up. 'If we find him he might listen to me.'

'No, no, you'd only be in the way.' Struan, putting on his cap and jacket, dismissed the idea without a second's thought. 'It's dark – no place for a lassie. We'll be better on our own. See you later – don't know when we'll be back.'

'Try no' to worry, pet,' George said to Lindy when they were alone, except for Gingerboy. 'Neil will soon come to his senses, I'm sure. People get over these things, you know, it's no' the end of the world.'

'It takes time, Dad. Doesn't happen overnight.'

'No, but what I'm saying is he won't be likely to do anything daft once he's cooled down a bit.'

'I hope you're right.' Lindy's eyes went to the clock. 'Oh, it's so awful, waiting. I wonder how long they'll be?'

'Depends,' said George, 'on if they find him.'

Two hours and more went by. Myra came back, saying she'd had a job to calm Vi down – she'd been all for going out and looking for Neil herself till Myra had persuaded her otherwise. Anyway, she was calmer now and was waiting like everyone else to see if the boys had found him. In the meantime, Myra was saying she'd make some more tea and they could have some bread and cheese – she'd some chutney somewhere – when the flat door banged and Struan returned.

'No sign of him,' he announced, taking off his cap and pulling back his damp hair. 'And it's freezing out there – let me get near that range, eh?'

'No sign?' cried Lindy, rising. 'Oh, no, Struan – where'd you look?'

'Everywhere. Including the bridges, let me tell you, and he's certainly no' jumped off because nobody has tonight. He must have gone inside somewhere, but where I've no idea. What's open on a Sunday night?'

Lindy stood very still. 'I know,' she said softly. 'Churches. Did you try any churches?'

'Neil's no churchgoer, there'd be no point.'

'It'd be somewhere to go, that's all.' Lindy was already getting into her coat, pulling on a woollen hat. 'I'm going to look, anyway, and don't try to stop me.'

'Don't ask me to go out again,' cried Struan. 'I've had enough and so have the lads.'

'I'll come with you, Lindy,' said George. 'Myra, we'll no' be long. Keep the kettle on.'

'Of all the silly things!' groaned Myra. 'You'll never find that crazy laddie out there. Leave him to come home on his own, I say!'

'He might never come home,' said Lindy, now ready to leave. 'Come on, Dad, let's go.'

# Twenty-Nine

They found him in the third church they tried, a church on George the Fourth Bridge, not far from the famous jumping-off place for suicides which looked down into the Cowgate below. Lindy could hardly look at it without shuddering, but it was all right – Struan had said nobody had jumped off anywhere that night, and when she and George went into that third church, there was Neil. Sitting at the back, difficult to see in the shadows except for a white blur that was his face, but he was there and Lindy's searching gaze found him with ease. She touched her father's arm.

'There he is, Dad. There's Neil.'

'I see him,' whispered George. 'What do we do now? There's no one about but they might be locking up soon.'

'Do they ever lock up?'

'Aye, I'm sure. There's stuff to steal.'

Lindy took a step towards Neil who, if he'd seen them, made no attempt to speak.

'I think he's looking better,' said Lindy. 'I'm going to speak to him. Wait here, Dad.'

'I should be the one –'

'No, let me do this.'

Closer to the silent figure, Lindy changed her mind. Neil wasn't looking better. True, he'd lost the wildness that had so frightened her earlier,

140

but it had been replaced by a desolation she'd never seen in any face before, and was to her just as worrying. Taking a deep breath, dredging up courage, she moved to sit beside him.

'Hello, Neil. It's Lindy.'

'Think I've lost my eyesight?' He turned to look at her. 'I know who you are. Point is, what are you doing here?'

'I came to find you, with my dad. We want you to come home. Your ma's worried.'

He looked down at his hands folded in his lap. 'Ma's got no need to be worried.'

'We were all worried, Neil. We didn't know where you were – what you might do –'

'Why, what did you think I'd do?' He looked up. 'Finish it all? Give up on life? Jump off the bridge?'

'We didn't know – you were so upset. I'd never seen you so upset –'

'I'm upset, all right, but I'm no' taking a header into the Cowgate.' He shook his head. 'Looked down, though, looked down for a long time.'

'Neil, you didn't!'

'I did, I looked. I thought, suppose it's what they all think, the folk who go over – that's it, that's the way to be free. Free of pain, eh? Free of the ball and chain.'

'Ball and chain?'

'Aye, the ball and chain she's fastened round me. I'll no' say her name, I'll never say her name, but you know who I'm talking about.'

Neil's eyes, in the shadows, were dark pools dead of all emotion; the more Lindy looked into them, the less close she felt to reaching him. No longer a crazy man, he was still a stranger. The man who'd been her friend, her special friend, had left her. Moved away, where she could not follow.

'They say folk get over love,' she said hesitantly. 'If it's no' returned. That's what they say.'

'I know what they say.'

'If you could believe it –'

'I'll never believe it. It's too much to ask. Because I really thought she loved me.'

'I know,' sighed Lindy.

'Well, she must have known I thought that – women always know. But she never let on because she was just playing. I was different, eh? No' like her other guys, so I guess she was fascinated. All the time I was thinking she felt the same as me, she was just . . . playing. And that's what hurt, Lindy, that's what'll always hurt. She humiliated me.'

'No, Neil, she didn't!' Lindy cried. 'I was like you – I thought she must've known you were serious, too, but she says she didn't know and I believe her. She says it came as something out of the blue and now she feels so terrible—'

'Terrible?' Neil leaped to his feet. 'She feels terrible? That's a laugh, eh? Pity I don't feel like laughing. Look, tell your dad to take you home. You've found me, I'm no' going to do something daft, so there's no need to talk any more. Just tell Ma, though, will you, that I'm OK? It'd be good if you could do that.'

'But aren't you coming home, Neil? They'll be locking the church soon.'

'I'm never going home, Lindy. Never going

back to number nineteen.' Neil had begun to walk away, towards George further up the aisle. 'I'm going to book in somewhere tonight, a bed and breakfast place, and tomorrow I'll find somewhere to live.'

'What are you talking about?' cried Lindy, running after him. 'You have to go home, your ma's waiting – everybody's waiting—'

'Think I want to see 'em? See 'em all laughing at my crazy ideas? Who did I think I was, then, trying for Miss Rosemary?' Neil looked back, his face dark with anger. 'I'll get on better away.'

'But what about your ma? She'll be wanting to see you.'

'I'll go back after I've settled in. I'll explain and I'll see she's no' missing my money. I'll still give her something to make up for leaving.'

'That's good, Neil, that's good.' Lindy touched his arm. 'But what about me? Is this goodbye for us?'

'Thought that was what you wanted, anyway. And you've got your new fellow, isn't that so? I bet you're seeing him already, eh?'

Lindy made no answer. What could she say? Unshed tears were gathering in her eyes. She felt suddenly so weary she could have dropped down where she was and shut out the world. Except for her dad, waiting so patiently, and Rod, elsewhere, who might be waiting, too. Well, if he was waiting for a true end to her attachment to Neil, it had come. She'd seen it tonight – an ending that was not the first, but more definite than the first and harder to take. Yet it was time to take it and she would. The special friendship that had once meant so much no longer had any place in her life.

'Hello, Mr Gillan,' she heard Neil manage to say politely. 'Thanks for coming, but there was no need.'

'Just wanted to help,' George answered. 'Can we do anything?'

'Neil's going to find a place to stay tonight, Dad,' Lindy said quickly. 'He doesn't want to go back to number nineteen.'

'Is that right? Oh, well, maybe we'll see you tomorrow, Neil?'

'Sometime, anyway, Mr Gillan.'

'We'll go, Dad,' said Lindy. 'Neil will be going off to find his place.'

They left the church together, then paused to say goodnight. Or, rather, goodbye.

As a street light showed his ravaged face, Neil's empty gaze found Lindy's but did not linger. Soon, he had turned and was walking away.

'Don't forget to see Ma,' he called back.

'I won't,' said Lindy. She put her arm in her father's. 'Let's go home, Dad.'

'Aye, let's,' said George.

# Thirty

The buzz of excitement that gripped number nineteen after Neil's departure lasted for some days. Nothing so dramatic had happened since one tenant had chased another down the stairs with a knife, but that was years ago and had not involved anyone as grand as Miss Rosemary, or a fellow like Mr Neil Shakespeare, who thought himself so superior to everyone and had taken such a toss.

'Pride goes before a fall,' folk said wisely. 'Serves him right,' said others. 'Getting involved with the quality, eh?'

But then there was Vi, his poor mother, who'd taken the whole affair very badly and whose eyes seemed permanently red, while even his brothers seemed subdued and his father, Arthur, would fire up if anyone even dared to speak of what had happened.

So much sympathy came their way. It had seemed to some that the person who'd got off best and perhaps without reason was Miss Rosemary herself and, gradually, the tenants' viewpoint had begun to change. It came to be seen that Neil needed sympathy, too, having probably been led on by a society girl who should have known better. Stood to reason, eh? Would he ever have fallen in love with her if she hadn't let him? Showed what happened when somebody like her came into lives like theirs. Maybe it was time for her to go?

Jemima, of course, was furious over what was said of Rosemary. 'The very idea!' she cried to Lindy. 'Blaming Miss Rosemary for leading Neil on! As though a lady like her would ever do that!'

'I'm sure ladies do that sort of thing all the time,' Lindy answered. 'I don't believe Rosemary did, but Neil somehow got the idea that she loved him and when she said she didn't he just couldn't take it.'

'But that's his fault, no' hers,' argued Jemima. 'Of course, I'm very sorry for him, but I'm sorry for Miss Rosemary, too. She's been so upset, she scarcely puts her nose out of her flat – she's really miserable.'

'Hasn't found a job yet, then?'

Jemima put her finger to her lips. 'It's still a secret, Lindy, but she has got an iron in the fire, as they say. If anything comes of it she'll be on her way.'

Just as well, thought Lindy, then Neil might be able to visit his family without worrying, or even return to live at number nineteen. Somehow she didn't think that that was likely. At least she was free herself to look forward to meeting Rod again, which was to be for a meal the following evening, something they'd arranged practically under Myra's nose in the shop but had her blessing, anyway.

Not much used to eating out, except for fish suppers, Lindy was charmed by the little café Rod had chosen in Frederick Street and, when they'd been shown to a table, enjoyed looking around, while Rod was happy looking at her.

So full of colour in her green dress, her face flushed with excitement, her eyes sparkling, it seemed to him that she lit up the whole room, and certainly he was not the only one looking at her. It was only when he said she must tell him what had been happening at number nineteen that her light seemed to dim, her face lost its glow and she looked down at her plate.

'You were very mysterious in the shop, saying there'd been trouble but not what it was,' he went on, alert to the change in her. 'But if you don't want to talk about it, I'll understand. Shall we order first, anyway?'

'Oh, yes, let's do that,' Lindy agreed, seeming glad of the reprieve, but when the waitress had taken their order for a beef dish she raised her eyes to Rod and seemed ready to speak. 'Thing is, it's someone else's trouble, really, and I feel bad talking about it. But you're you, and I do want to tell you. I suppose you'll have guessed, anyway, that the person in trouble is Neil.'

'Neil? This is something to do with the new tenant you told me about?'

'Yes, it's everything to do with her, with Rosemary. He was so sure she felt the same as he did that when he finally got round to telling her he loved her and she said she didn't he just went to pieces.'

Remembering her scene with him, Lindy's voice cracked a little. 'Rod, I'd never seen him the way he was then. I'd just come in from our lovely day last Sunday when he came hurtling down the stairs like a madman, like someone I didn't know at all. And when he told me she'd turned him down I was so afraid because I could tell he couldn't deal with it and I didn't know what he'd do. When he ran out into the street I wanted to follow him, but he was nowhere.'

'Poor girl,' Rod whispered, touching her hand. 'What an ordeal!'

'For him, for him.'

'Yes, for him, too. So, what happened? Did he come back?'

'No.' Lindy told of how she and her father had

147

eventually found him in a church, of how he'd been calmer, but was so bitter about Rosemary he wouldn't even speak her name and had decided not to return to number nineteen. Seemingly, he was now living in some bedsit, away from his family and everyone he knew.

'Poor devil,' Rod murmured. 'You're right, he's put himself through hell. But, there, it's no good saying he shouldn't have loved her – you don't get any choice over love.'

Lindy, gazing at his thoughtful face, wanted to question him, but at that moment the waitress brought their beef and she waited a while. Only when they had finished and were studying menus again for the sweet course did she venture to ask the question in her mind. 'Rod, mind if I ask – did you – I mean, have you ever – felt like Neil yourself?'

He gave a reassuring smile. 'Me? No, thank God, I just know how it takes some people. Nearly always people like Neil – highly strung, nervy . . . poets, maybe. Isn't that how he is? A writer, anyway. Or, would-be writer.'

'Yes, that's how Neil is. He's always been like that – different from other folk. I didn't think you'd have had his sort of feelings, Rod – it was just your sympathy showing through again, eh?'

'Well, I did go out with one or two girls when I was younger but there was never anything serious, never any question of great love or anything.' Rod looked closely into Lindy's eyes. 'How about you? Was there ever anyone for you, apart from Neil?'

'No, because I never wanted anything serious,

either. Neil and me – we were happy to be just friends.' Her lower lip trembling, Lindy said quietly, 'Now that's all gone – he's gone from my life altogether.'

Rod sat back, sighing deeply. 'Is that true, Lindy?'

'It's true.'

'Are you ready yet, then, to think about me? I still don't want – you know – to press you. It's for you to say.'

She was silent for a moment, during which he studied the way her dark lashes shielded her lowered eyes, and waited. He knew he would read her answer in those fine eyes of hers when she finally looked up, and was trying not to let himself be too hopeful. Couldn't help taking confidence, though, from the way she'd seemed to want to talk to him that evening. 'You're you', she'd said, hadn't she, as though he was someone special? Was he, though? Suddenly her eyes were raised. She was looking at him at last.

'Rod,' she said quietly, 'I think of you already. There's no need to press me.'

'Really?' He put his hand to his brow, laughing a little. 'Do you mean it, Lindy? You're not still . . . getting over things? Hell, I mean, getting over Neil. Why don't I say his name?'

'I just said – he's out of my life altogether.'

'I know, but even so you might not be free of him for some time. Time is what it takes, they say.'

'I know, but things have changed for me, Rod. They changed when I saw him after Rosemary had turned him down. I stopped feeling – well, what I used to feel – and was just so sorry. So sorry for him. As though you might feel sorry for a stranger who was hurt.' Her eyes, still resting on Rod with mesmerizing effect, were full of the sadness she'd been trying to describe. 'Does that make sense?' she asked, at which he took her hand with a firm, strong grasp.

'Lindy, it does. It makes all the sense in the world. Don't you see – it means you're free. Free to move on. With me, if you want, but free, anyway.'

'Free,' she was echoing, when the waitress reappeared.

'Made up your minds?' she asked brightly.

'Minds?' Rod repeated.

'About your sweet course, sir. There's apple tart, treacle tart, trifle or ice cream with choice of sauce.' She sighed. 'Or do you just want cheese and biscuits?'

'Treacle tart, please. Lindy, how about you?'

'Oh, the same,' she said vaguely. 'I don't mind what I have.'

'Nor do I,' Rod chimed eagerly. 'At least, not when it comes to puddings.'

They were quiet walking back to number nineteen, Lindy's arm in Rod's, as though so much had been settled they scarcely needed to speak. Reaching the door of the tenement, they halted and exchanged long glances, and then, quite naturally, a long, passionate kiss on the lips. Their first real kiss, they might have said, as they separated, not to be confused with those pecks on the cheek they'd exchanged before. Was it to be the first of many? Oh, yes. But for that first time, it was something so special, something they so much wanted to remember, they did not repeat it.

'When can I see you again?' Rod asked with sudden urgency. 'I hope you'll say soon. As soon as possible.'

'All right,' she said, laughing. 'That's what I'll say. But we've both got jobs, eh? You know what my hours are.'

'And mine,' he groaned. 'I love my work at the hostel but I'm so tied, it's the devil's own job to get the time off I want. How about Friday, though? Friday evening? Maybe we could go to the pictures?'

'Oh, yes!' she cried. 'Friday, then. I'll see what's on. What do you fancy?'

'Whatever suits you. I'll come here, shall I? About seven?'

'I'll be waiting.'

They exchanged another long glance and almost embraced, but in the end just said goodnight. As Rod walked away, looking back and waving, Lindy blew him a kiss, then waved as he did before turning to go home.

If only she didn't have to see Myra, or Struan or even her father, she thought. Didn't have to say what sort of time she'd had, or what she'd had to eat, or when she was seeing Rod again. He was fast becoming her own special secret, not to be shared, yet had to be. What else could she do but talk about him to the family when she'd just been out with him? Sighing heavily, she opened the flat door.

'Hello!' she called. 'I'm back!'

'Had a good time?' asked Myra.

'Oh, yes! Wonderful time.'

And that was certainly true.

# Thirty-One

Things had changed for her, Lindy had said, over the dinner in the restaurant, and oh, how true that was, she realized afresh, when the grey days of November might have been summer because of her meetings with Rod. It was never easy to arrange being together, both having to work long hours and Rod, of course, having commitments to the hostel and the workhouses that must come first before any time off. Somehow they managed to meet, however, driving out in the evening darkness to the cinema or for a meal, coming home for rapturous goodnight kisses well away from number nineteen. And the more they met, the sweeter it seemed that, after all their earlier problems, now they had no problems at all. Were, in fact, as Rod had said, free.

Free? Well, not completely. Lindy still worried about Neil, but it was true what she'd told Rod – he was no longer part of her life, and though she would always care what happened to him, she was no longer responsible for his happiness. There was the difference from the old days.

He visited his mother, she knew, and the word around the tenement was that he was all right, going to work, getting over the shock of his rejection, even if not the pain. That would take time, of course, but there was no longer any need to worry about him. Everybody got over love affairs, eh? Maybe, one day, he'd find someone else.

As for Rosemary, though still at number nineteen, she was keeping herself very much to herself, Jemima being the only person she saw. It might not be long, though, before she moved on, Jemima again told Lindy. There was a job she was keen to get; she just had to persuade her mother that it was the right one. If it worked out she'd be finding herself another place to live.

'So her little experiment of seeing how the other half lives is coming to an end,' commented Lindy. 'Hasn't exactly been a success.'

'She's had a hard time,' Jemima replied coldly. 'No one thinks of her and what she's been through.'

'I'm sure she'll get over it. Especially now she's found herself a job, eh?'

'As a matter of fact, I found her the job. At least, I sort of suggested it.'

'You did?' Lindy stared, frowning. 'Whatever sort of job could you find for her, then?'

Jemima shook her head, enjoying her moment of mystery. 'Shh, I'll tell you all about it when it's all arranged.'

'Never found anything for me, I notice.'

'Why, you don't want anything now, do you? You've got your Rod.' Jemima smiled. 'When do we hear the wedding bells?'

'No plans for them,' Lindy answered cautiously.

'We don't really talk of the future; we're happy as we are just for the minute.'

A knowing look swam into Jemima's eyes. 'That sounds a bit too familiar. Isn't that what you used to say about Neil?'

'No!' cried Lindy. 'What I feel for Rod is quite different from what I felt for Neil!'

'So, what's holding you back? Oh, Lindy, you're no' still afraid of marriage, are you?'

'No, honestly, I'm not. I think now, if you find the right person, marriage is right, but the fact is – Rod and me – we haven't discussed it.'

'He's no' popped the question? Maybe you've put him off, talking about finding a new job?'

'As though a new job's going to turn up for me, anyway!'

'Better settle for being a bride,' said Jemima.

There were times, it was true, when Lindy thought the same. Once that first kiss with Rod had turned into loving closeness and the pleasure of passionate embraces, she'd found herself carried away by the thought of really making love, which was not something she'd ever thought much about before. Just as Neil must have found a great divide between what he'd felt for Lindy and the love that had swamped him for Rosemary, so Lindy had found being with Rod had opened up floodgates of passion in herself she'd never known could exist. No wonder folk wanted to get married, eh?

Yet both she and Rod were cautious, and it was true that, in spite of her feelings for him and her joy in being with him, there was a little bit of her that felt regret she might never, as Neil had put it, one day fly. But that was a piece of nonsense, eh? Better, as Jemima said, to settle for being a bride – if that was to be on offer, and in the meantime, enjoy what she had.

## Thirty-Two

November, 1935 brought bad news to the country. Not just the foreign stuff they knew about, but carefully expressed anxieties about the King's health, and fears that the Prince of Wales might still not be married when he came to the throne. No one wanted a bachelor king. Why didn't he get on with finding a suitable bride? There were rumours that he was seeing an American woman, and though no one really believed that, many hoped that George the Fifth would just keep going. Aye, that'd be best, eh? Always best to stick to what you knew.

'Do you think the Prince of Wales will ever marry?' Lindy asked Rod one evening when they were driving back to number nineteen after a cinema outing. There had been pictures of the Prince at some function or other on the newsreel, and she'd wondered how someone of his mature age hadn't already married and had a family.

'I mean, he's over forty, eh? I don't know anyone over that age who isn't married.'

'Oh, I expect he'll tie the knot sometime,' Rod answered, not letting his eyes stray from the road

155

ahead as there was fog about. 'It's difficult for him – he has to marry the right person.'

'I should think everybody'd want to do that!' cried Lindy, laughing.

'What I mean is, the woman he marries has to be approved by the King and all sorts of people. Maybe the ones he's wanted haven't come up to scratch.'

'Some of the papers are saying he's seeing an American woman.'

'Nothing wrong with being American, but I believe she's married already.'

'Won't be her he marries, then.'

As they turned into Scott Street and Rod stopped the car well away from number ninteen, Lindy found herself wondering at the way their talk was going. So much interest in the marriage of the Prince of Wales . . . All right, she'd started it. Maybe it was always at the back of her mind that one day there might be talk of their own marriage – hers and Rod's. That maybe, in this very car, after an evening out together, he might propose, and she would have to know what to say. Well, what would she say? Yes, oh, Rod, yes! I do love you so!

Neither of them had put their love into words, but both, she was sure, knew it was there. In their hearts. At least, she knew that about herself, and surely, when she looked at those dear golden-brown eyes of Rod's, she knew it was there too? Yet he didn't speak, didn't discuss the future – always held back. Because he wasn't sure of her? Sure of what she wanted? Thought she might not say, when he proposed, 'Yes, oh, yes!'

The truth was she wasn't sure herself that she would. She did love Rod. She did want to be married to him. But maybe not just yet.

'Penny for them?' she heard Rod whispering as he took her hands in his. 'You seem lost in a brown study, whatever that is. I've never known.'

'I was just wondering why we were talking about the Prince of Wales,' she said, which was mainly truthful.

'You mean, instead of us? Quite right. We're much more interesting.'

Rod's lips found hers and for some time they kissed with their usual heady passion, yet sooner than usual Rod drew back.

'Lindy,' he murmured, rubbing her hands which were cold, for she'd taken off her gloves, 'there's something I've been meaning to ask you –'

Meaning to ask? Her heart gave a leap. Was this it? What she'd been waiting for, preparing herself for? No sooner had she asked herself the questions, she knew it wasn't. Rod's approach was too casual, too matter of fact. If he'd been about to propose he wouldn't have been like that. She knew him too well to believe it. Relaxing, she squeezed his hands. 'What is it, then?'

'Well, there are two places I want to take you.'

'New places?'

'New to you. One is my home, in Leith.'

Ah. Lindy's eyes brightened with interest. She'd often wondered why Rod had never invited her to his home. When his father was at sea he lived in the house alone on his days away from the hostel, which meant that if he took her there they would be alone too, and wasn't that just what they wanted? Yet he'd never asked her to go there.

'Your home, Rod? That'd be wonderful. I've always wanted to see it – when can we go?'

'That's the thing, Lindy. I don't feel we can until my dad comes home, but he's due back at Christmas and we'll fix it up then.'

'Christmas? Why wait till then? Why does your dad have to be there, anyway? I don't understand.'

'Come on, you do.' In the shadows of his car, Rod was looking embarrassed. 'Whatever would your stepmother say, and your father, if I took you to my home and there were only the two of us? They wouldn't be happy, would they?'

'Why, Rod, that isn't true!' Lindy was flushing, her eyes wide with surprise. 'Aunt Myra wouldn't mind at all. Neither would my dad. They trust you, Rod. So do I!'

'I know, I know, but – well, it's the way it'd look. I don't want to upset anybody.'

'You needn't worry,' Lindy said firmly. 'And I'd like to see where you live.'

'OK, but let's leave it for now, because the other place I want to take you – I know it won't sound exciting – is where I work. I mean, the men's hostel.'

Rod had dropped Lindy's hands and was gazing at her apologetically. 'It's important to me, somehow, that you see it. Because it's a part of me, I suppose, and I'm hoping you'll be interested.'

'Of course I'll be interested,' Lindy said at once. 'Like you say, it's where you work and it's important to you. When could I come, though?'

'Any evening,' he said eagerly. 'Or a Sunday afternoon. You needn't stay long. Maybe come after the chaps have had their Sunday dinner, say half past two?'

'Next Sunday?'

'Next Sunday it is. Oh, Lindy, it's nice of you to say you'll come. I appreciate it.'

Their eyes met and they sighed as though relieved they'd got duty out of the way, and now moved readily into the best part of the evening, which was their blissful meeting of mouths and hands and murmurings of names, until it was time for Lindy's reluctant departure.

'Oh, God, Lindy,' Rod murmured, walking with her to her door. 'It's not easy, being trusted.'

'You are, though,' she told him.

'You can count on it,' he said steadily. 'Goodnight, dear Lindy. See you Sunday, then – seems a long time away.'

'Dear Rod, it's four days,' she said with a smile.

In the flat her father had already gone to bed, but Myra was still up and so was Struan, not long back from the pub. 'Needn't ask if you had a good time,' he said cheekily.

'What do you mean?' asked Lindy, glancing quickly at her stepmother.

'Come on, you've got that look, eh? Unmistakable.'

'Give over teasing her,' said Myra, setting out plates for next day's breakfast. 'Of course she's had a good time with Rod.'

'He says he might take me to see his home,' Lindy said casually as she took off her coat. 'That'd be all right, eh?'

Myra raised her eyebrows. 'See his home? Will his dad be there?'

'Only if we go at Christmas. I'm no' sure when we'll go.'

'There'd just be the two of you?' asked Struan. 'Better take me along to keep an eye on you.'

'What a thing to say!' cried Myra. 'Why, Rod's a nice lad. He'd always behave well.'

At which Struan only shrugged and gave one of his grins.

'Like I said, I don't know when we're going,' Lindy said sharply. 'Next Sunday I'm going to the hostel where he works – he'd like me to see it.'

'That homeless fellows' hostel?' cried Myra. 'Why ever should he want you there?'

'Always thought he was a bit of an odd bloke,' commented Struan, 'but I won't say a word against him, seeing as he lets me drive his car now and again.'

'And I won't say a word against him, anyway,' Lindy retorted. 'Now I'm away to my bed.'

But not, for some time, to sleep.

'A bit of an odd bloke,' Struan had said of Rod, which was so obviously untrue she might have had another argument over it, except that she wanted to get to bed and decided just to let it go. All the same she couldn't help wondering again, as she turned over and over against her pillow, why Rod held back the way he did. Strange, when he loved her, as she was sure he did. One day, surely, they would take a step forward to something?

Oh, enjoy what you have, she told herself. It

160

wasn't as though she was so very anxious to be married, was it? No, but she did want Rod to be keen for it, or at least to know why he was not.

Her last thoughts before sleep finally claimed her were to wonder what his hostel would be like, and what sort of residents she would see there. And, oh, yes, what should she wear?

# Thirty-Three

'Everything plain,' Myra advised the following Sunday afternoon as Lindy was about to get ready for her visit to the hostel. 'That jumper you're wearing now, I'd say, and that skirt would do. You don't want anything smart.'

'I was going to wear my good twinset, Aunt Myra. This jumper's ancient!'

'No, no, it'll be fine. And no lipstick, remember. You don't want to attract the sort o' men who are in that hostel.'

'That's right,' George put in. 'I don't know why Rod wants Lindy to go there, anyway.'

'He'd just like me to see where he works,' Lindy said, frowning. 'But he'll expect me to look smart, like I always do, so I'm going to wear my twinset and my lipstick. Don't forget, he'll be there. I won't be seeing the hostel fellows on my own.'

'Thank goodness for that,' Myra retorted with a shudder. 'But I've made my point, so you do as you please.'

161

'OK, Aunt Myra. I'm away to get ready.'

'I must say I'll be glad to see you back,' George sighed when Lindy appeared in her best twinset and her usual lipstick. 'Shame Rod can't come and collect you, eh?'

'Dad, he's on duty, he can't get away.'

'Well, you tell him to take good care of you, eh?'

'As though I need him to do that!' cried Lindy, buttoning on her winter coat and pulling on her woollen hat. 'Look, stop worrying. Those poor chaps in the hostel aren't going to do me any harm. See you later!'

Leaving her father and stepmother to exchange glances and shake their heads, Lindy hurried from number nineteen with some relief, taking deep breaths of the chill November air as though she'd been feeling suffocated. So much fuss made of girls doing anything the least bit different was frustrating. Especially when she thought about Struan's freedom to do whatever he liked. What an unfair world it was for women, then! No point in dwelling on that now, though – she had to find Rod's workplace off Nicolson Street that meant so much to him. When she was on the tram she'd have another look at the little sketch map he'd given her.

It was just half past two on a striking church clock when she arrived at Guthrie House, a square, modern building fitted in between two older houses. She'd thought it might have been a conversion of a nice, elegant Edinburgh house, which was the sort of place she admired, but then it was only a hostel and Rod liked it. At least the windows were clean, even if their net curtains looked as grey as the pebble-dashed walls, and the woodwork needed a coat of paint, but that was probably because money was tight. Always was. She rang the bell.

Out came Rod immediately, his face all smiles – he'd obviously been waiting at the other side of the door. 'Oh, Lindy – you made it!'

'Did you think I wouldn't?'

'No, no, I'm just sorry you had to come on your own. You know I'd have liked to bring you.'

He drew her into a wide hall with doors on either side, a wooden staircase at one end, pegs stacked with coats and caps by the entrance, and framed prints of Edinburgh on the distempered walls. Not too bad, thought Lindy, as Rod took her coat and hat and fitted them precariously on to the crowded pegs. The inside of the house was better than the outside, anyway – apart from the smell of carbolic and cooking, of course, but Lindy was already wondering when she would see Rod's clients. She had to admit, she was just the tiniest bit apprehensive.

'Well, what d'you think?' Rod asked, his eyes very bright. 'Of my hostel?'

'Oh, very nice,' she answered quickly. 'What I've seen of it.'

'Used to be a health clinic until that was moved to the infirmary and then it became a hostel. Somebody called it Guthrie House after Doctor Guthrie. Have you heard of him?'

'At school, I think. Did he work with poor bairns? Wanted 'em to have an education?'

'That's right. He started the Ragged Schools

163

and always campaigned for compulsory education back in Victorian times. In a way he was
one of the first social workers.' Rod smiled. 'I
like to think he'd approve of what we're doing
here.'

'He certainly would.' Looking around, trying
to please, Lindy murmured, 'And it's good that
you've put up pictures. Makes all the
difference.'

'The prints? Got them in a second-hand shop,
probably ripped out of a book. Framed 'em
myself.'

'Rod, you didn't! That was very clever, eh?'

'Oh, sure, I'm a genius.' He took her hands in
his. 'But it's so good to see you here, Lindy – I
hope your folks didn't disapprove? It's only to
let you see where I work.'

'That's what I told them.'

'They did object, then?'

'No. Well, they were just sort of asking, you
know, why you wanted me here. But I explained,
so it was all right.'

'Truth is, I expect they're worried about you
meeting my chaps, but there's no need, and there
aren't many around at the moment, anyway. Just
a few playing table tennis in the recreation room.'

'Where are the others, then?'

'Out, or having naps in the dormitories. You
needn't see them.'

'You don't mind them going out?'

'Of course not – they're not prisoners!' Rod
laughed. 'Actually, I see two chaps coming down
the stairs now. I'll introduce you.'

Aged perhaps thirty or so, the two men on the

stairs were respectably dressed in jackets and flannels, with caps over short, neat hair, not at all as Lindy had imagined homeless men to be. But then, they were now in Rod's care – of course they would look respectable. As they reached the foot of the stairs and advanced slowly down the hall she braced herself to smile, but though they stared they did not smile back.

'All right, Bill?' Rod asked pleasantly. 'Mungo?'

'Fine, thanks, Mr Connor,' one of the men replied. 'We're just away for a wee bit o' fresh air.'

'Good, good. This is Miss Gillan, by the way. She's just looking round.'

'Afternoon, miss.' The man who'd spoken before touched his cap then nudged his companion, who seemed not to want to speak. 'We'd best away, eh?'

'See you at teatime, then,' Rod called. 'Cold beef and pickles, remember.'

When the men had gone out, closing the front door carefully behind them, Rod smiled apologetically at Lindy. 'As you'll have gathered, those two aren't much given to conversation. We've just found 'em some new clothes – well, second hand, of course – and they've had their hair cut and a good tidy up. Should be ready to go job hunting at the end of their time here.'

'How long can they stay?'

'Well, no one can live here, but we offer more than some of the charities who only give them a bed for the night and then they have to go. We try to kit them out, get them patched up and then hope they can move on.' Rod sighed deeply.

'Trouble is, we're so strapped for cash, as you can imagine. I have to fight for every penny.'

'I bet,' said Lindy.

'Worst is, a lot of the chaps go back to the streets and we can't do much for them, but the ones who've just become homeless because they've lost their jobs – well, we do all we can to help them back to ordinary life.'

'Rod, you're wonderful! I really admire you.'

'Oh, please!' Rod's cheekbones were tinged with red. 'Come on, I'll show you our recreation room.'

As he opened one of the doors leading off from the hall, he said in a whisper, 'Don't mind if the few fellows around give you a good stare, will you? We don't get many visitors like you, Lindy.'

'I won't mind.'

'In we go, then.'

The recreation room, long and narrow with a scuffed, carpet-less floor, had an upright piano in one corner, two card tables, two sagging sofas, several wooden chairs and a wind-up gramophone – at that moment silent. The ping-pong game evidently over, three middle-aged men were sitting, smoking, on the sofas, while a fourth, rather younger, was on the floor, fiddling with a small wireless. All, as soon as Lindy walked in, fixed their eyes on her.

'Everybody OK?' asked Rod. 'This is Miss Gillan from the council, just looking round. Miss Gillan, meet Jem, Walt and Reg, and Sean on the floor.'

'Another snooper, eh?' asked Jem from his sofa. 'Thought we had one o' them round last week.'

'No one comes snooping,' Rod returned pleasantly. 'And no one came last week.'

'Take no notice o' Jem, Mr Connor,' Walt put in. 'He imagines things, eh?'

'Who says I imagine things?' cried Jem. 'I tell you, there was someone round last week asking questions.'

'Is the lassie asking questions, Jem?'

'What else is she here for?'

'Just to see that everyone is happy,' said Rod. 'I hope you are. It's what I want.'

'Aye, you're a good man, Mr Connor,' said Sean on the floor. 'We appreciate what you do. But what I want is to get some help here. This wireless doesnae work and we have tae listen to that wee gramophone. It's only got a couple o' records.'

'Aye, "Danny Boy" and "Blue Skies",' Walt chimed in. 'If I hear them again I'll go mad, eh?'

'I'll have a look at it later,' Rod said cheerfully. 'Now, if you folk are all right, we'll move on.'

'Nice to meet you,' Lindy murmured, clearing her throat.

'Likewise,' Reg and Walt said politely, and though the man called Jem remained obstinately silent, Sean on the floor added: 'Come and look round again soon, eh?'

'Wasn't too bad, was it?' asked Rod when they were back in the hall. 'I'm afraid Jem isn't very friendly. He suffers from depression – he's had a broken marriage.'

'I'm sorry about that.'

'His reason for going on the street.' Rod's face was still rather red. 'Listen, I hope you didn't

167

mind that I had to tell a little white lie there, saying you were from the council? If I'd said you were my friend I'd never have heard the last of it.'

'Hey, I'm feeling quite proud,' Lindy answered, smiling. 'Didn't know I was a council worker.'

'You'd be fine,' he said seriously. 'I'll just quickly show you the dining room and my office, then I suggest we make for the kitchen where we'll have a cup of tea.'

# Thirty-Four

It seemed that on Sundays Rod, or his assistant, Dougie Howat, whichever was on duty, had to manage alone for part of the day. Mrs MacArthur, the woman who cooked for the hostel, always left after Sunday dinner, and Florence, the one maid, never came in at all.

'It's no trouble,' Rod explained, making Lindy sit down at a long scrubbed table in the large, dreary kitchen after he'd put a kettle on one of the two gas stoves. 'There's a cold supper on Sunday evenings and the men take it in turns to wash up, so no problem there. We like 'em to help with the chores, anyway, and most don't mind. They've lost so many of their interests, you see, the little jobs fill the gap.'

Setting out cups, filling a milk jug and finding plates for shortbread, Rod was smiling as he proved his efficiency.

'Mind you, I'm not saying that the end result is always what you'd want. You should see some of the beds they make – like great mounds concealing heaven knows what! But they do their best.'

'Beats me how you keep so cheerful,' Lindy murmured, shaking her head. 'Didn't you say once that these fellows could drive you mad? You seem to me to be very patient.'

'I told you, you just have to keep calm, do what you can. But there's the kettle going – I'll make the tea.'

Passing Lindy her tea and the shortbread biscuits, Rod's eyes seemed to her, as she glanced up, to be rather considering, as though he had something he wanted to say. 'Yes?' she asked, sipping her tea. 'What did you want to tell me?'

'Why, Lindy, how well you read me!' Rod, stirring milk into his tea, seemed embarrassed. 'I can see I'll have to try to develop a poker face . . . Well, the fact is, I haven't been altogether straight with you.'

'What do you mean?' Her eyes widening, Lindy gazed into his face. 'You're always straight!'

'Except when I say you're from the council.' Rod ran his hand through his hair. 'Look, it's just that when I said I wanted you to come here because it's important to me, well, that was true, but it wasn't the whole truth.'

'What other reason was there, then?'

'I was thinking – if you saw the sort of work people like me do, the sort of difference it can make, to some, anyway – you might be interested in it yourself. I mean, I know you want to change your job, do something more worthwhile, and this could be it.'

Rod's eyes on her face held such appeal that Lindy's own eyes fell and she stared for some moments into the interior of her teacup. What to say to him? She couldn't think of how to put it, although she had once told him, she remembered very well, that never in a million years could she do his job. Had he not believed her? His hand suddenly on hers was warm and firm, he was making her look up at him, answer him . . .

'Oh, Rod,' she murmured at last, 'I did say your sort of work wasn't for me. Do you no' remember? When we were first walking together?'

'Of course I remember, but I know you were only saying that because you didn't understand what you could do. Lindy, you're a very caring person. I know. I know from things you've said and from the way you are, and I can promise you that you'd be perfect for my sort of job. And, helping others, you'd soon find out there's no better way of earning a living.'

'Honestly, Rod, can you see me running a hostel? I know it'd be one for women, but can you see me dealing with the sort of girls that'd end up like your fellows here? I'd never have the patience; I'd always want to be doing something else.'

'You wouldn't have to be running a hostel, Lindy. It's true, there aren't a lot of us in social work at present, but it's something that's taking off, and there are other openings you could go for. Maybe visiting folk in their homes, or working in a hospital, or with children. Won't you even think about it?'

'Rod, even if I wanted to do your sort of work, I haven't got the education. They wouldn't want anybody like me.'

'They would if you were keen enough. And you could always go to evening classes, get some more qualifications.' Rod's eyes were shining. 'Lindy, you're a very bright girl – the world's your oyster. And I'd always be here, to help, remember.'

She sighed, moving her hand in his. 'I don't know, Rod –'

'Promise me you'll at least think about it. Promise, Lindy.'

'All right, I promise.'

'Oh, Lindy, I knew you would.'

Drawing her into his arms they sat together, her face against his, and kissed long and deeply, over and over, until their breath was gone and gradually they pulled apart.

'Oh, God,' Rod murmured, 'I've got to organize the tea. The chaps will be back soon, starving, as usual.'

'Let me help!' Lindy cried eagerly. 'Come on, it'd be no trouble.'

'Thanks, you're a sweetheart, but better not.' He sighed. 'Hate to say it, but it's already dark and I think you should be going home. I'm going to get you a taxi.'

'A taxi?' She laughed. 'That's crazy, Rod! I don't need a taxi, I can take the tram.'

'Not in the dark, not on your own. If I can't take you home, a taxi it has to be.' He leaped to his feet. 'I'll phone for one now before the lads start coming home.'

It was useless to argue – his mind was made up – and all too soon she was at the door of the hostel, Rod at her side, waiting for the taxi and his half crown in her purse.

'I just wish you'd at least let me pay for it myself,' she told him. 'And you've given me too much, anyway.'

'Best be on the safe side.' He kissed her cheek and crushed her hand in his. 'I asked you to come; I'm not having you out of pocket.'

'I've enjoyed it, honestly, it's been grand.'

'And you haven't forgotten your promise?'

'I haven't forgotten, Rod.'

'Here it is, then – the taxi.'

Rod let go of her hand. 'When will I see you again? Dougie's on duty Saturday night – shall I come round for you, say, six? We can go to the pictures.'

'Oh, that'd be lovely, Rod. I'll be waiting.'

The taxi arrived at the door, the driver jumping out to let Lindy in, asking where she wanted to go.

'Nineteen, Scott Street, please.'

Am I really going home in a taxi? Lindy asked herself, seated in the back, waving to Rod as the driver closed her door and drove away. Bet he doesn't get many fares going to Scott Street. Except for Miss Rosemary, of course, when she wasn't amusing herself going on the tram.

By strange coincidence, when Lindy arrived home, having paid off the taxi as though it was the most usual thing the world, Rosemary herself was in the hall of number nineteen, seemingly about to knock on the Gillans' flat door.

'Oh, Lindy, there you are – so lovely to see you. I was wondering – that is, Jemima and I were wondering – if you'd like to come up later to my place for a little chat?' Rosemary was opening her blue eyes wide. 'Would that be convenient?'

A little chat? What was all that about?

Intrigued by the invitation, Lindy, though not filled with warm feelings for Rosemary, who had, after all, hurt Neil, even if she hadn't meant to, found herself willing to accept. 'About seven?' she asked.

'Perfect!' cried Rosemary.


# Thirty-Five

Having survived Myra's probings on her visit to Rod's hostel, Lindy, on the dot of seven, made her way to Rosemary's flat. Oh, dear, how her stepmother did go on, she reflected, climbing the stairs.

'What was it like then, Rod's place? Did you see any o' the homeless men? Did they behave well? Didn't try anything on? You never know what these folk off the street will do, eh? You have to think, if they were respectable people, they'd no' be on the street in the first place. Now is that no' true?'

Thank the Lord that Lindy had been able to

put Myra right and told her how it was – that Rod was with her all the time and that the homeless men had behaved very well indeed. No need to mention Jem's accusation of snooping! The poor fellow was depressed, anyway. Now, however, she could put the hostel out of her mind, at least for the time being, and concentrate on finding out what the little chat with Rosemary and Jemima was about.

Rosemary was looking as charming as ever in a blue woollen jacket and matching skirt, while Jemima was also dressed smartly in a dark red two-piece Lindy didn't recognize. The pair of them seemed rather excited as Rosemary poured coffee for Jemima to hand out, and it seemed to Lindy that they were cooking something up. She just wished they'd hurry up and tell her what it was.

First, however, Jemima had to ask brightly, 'How's the romance going, Lindy? With the gorgeous Rod?'

'I don't think of Rod as romantic,' Lindy answered coolly. 'Today he wanted me to see his hostel for homeless men. That's where I've been.'

'A hostel for homeless men?' Rosemary cried. 'Lindy, whatever was it like?'

'In very good order, I thought. I only saw a few of the men and they were very nice. Very polite.'

'He's a saint, doing that sort of work,' Jemima commented. 'No' for us, eh?'

'He wants me to do it,' Lindy said after a pause. 'Well, something in that line, anyway.'

'He wants you to do social work?' Jemima

174

glanced at Rosemary. 'I thought you'd told him you'd never be able to do anything like that?'

'I did. But he wants me to think about it.'

'Lindy, don't,' Rosemary said firmly. 'Don't consider it for a moment. We have – well, we have something else we think you might like to do. That's why we've asked you up this evening, to tell you about it, and we hope you're going to be interested. Isn't that right, Jemima?'

'It is.' Jemima leaned forward, her hazel eyes fixed on Lindy. 'This work would be perfect for you, Lindy. It was my idea for Rosemary – you remember I told you once that I'd suggested something? And now it's Rosemary's idea for you. You'll have to go with it – mustn't turn it down.'

'But what is it?' cried Lindy. 'You're talking in riddles. What is this job that'd be so wonderful?'

Rosemary took a breath, smiled and answered, 'Modelling.'

Lindy, astonished, for a moment could only stare from Rosemary to Jemima and back to Rosemary. 'Modelling?' she repeated at last. 'You mean, fashion modelling?'

'Yes, fashion modelling, with mannequins. You know the sort of thing?' Rosemary smiled. 'Girls like you, showing off new clothes. Making every-thing look marvellous.'

'Girls like me? Are you joking? You're no' being serious, eh? I'm a tenement girl. I can't be a mannequin, or whatever they're called. They'd never want someone like me.'

'No' true,' Jemima told her calmly. 'Since I've been working at Logie's I've seen the fashion shows and the girls who come. I do adjustments, help make things fit, so I've got to know the lassies who model and they're no' grand ladies. No' like Miss Rosemary here, for instance.'

'Oh, Jemima!' Rosemary murmured. 'You're wrong. If I could be as good at their jobs as those mannequins, I'd be very proud.'

'Aye, but you've had trouble making your mother agree to you doing that sort o' work after I'd suggested it, eh? She thinks it's no' for you, no' the sort o' thing the debs would do – I'm only glad she's given up arguing now.'

'I told her I needed the money,' Rosemary said frankly. 'And I made her see that it was fascinating work for anyone who likes clothes, and that would be you as well, Lindy, wouldn't it? Oh, I know you do, and you're so wonderfully slim and pretty you'd be a great success. You must give it a try. You must!'

'I wouldn't have the first idea how to do it,' Lindy protested. 'I mean, the models must know how to walk and show off the clothes – how could I learn all that?'

'Why, the same as I'll have to learn it,' Rosemary exclaimed. 'Oh, I've done a bit of walking around with a book on my head – for posture, you know – and I learned how to curtsy for my presentation, but otherwise I know no more than you. The thing is, there's a lady from London who's just opened a modelling agency in Edinburgh. She's very keen to be successful here and wants to find the right girls.'

'I can see you'd be one,' said Lindy.

'Well, she's agreed to take me on and I'm sure

she'd take you too, Lindy. No need to worry about what to do – she gives classes for new models.'

Lindy's frown showed she was not convinced. 'She might have taken you on, Rosemary, but who's to say she'll want me?'

'You can but try,' Jemima put in. 'I mean, it's a job tailor-made for you, I'd say, because you've always been interested in clothes, eh? Clothes and fashion? And as a mannequin you'd be working with clothes all the time.'

'Maybe, but I still say I won't be what this lady will be looking for, and even if she did want me, there'd be something to pay and I couldn't afford it.'

'No, there'll be nothing to pay until she finds us work,' Rosemary said quickly. 'Once we begin to earn she takes commission. That's the system. Do say you'll at least apply, Lindy.'

'Yes, you should,' Jemima added with some impatience. 'You did say you wanted to change jobs – this is your chance, so don't mess it up.'

'I just don't want to look a fool,' Lindy answered quietly. 'I'd feel so bad if I was turned down.'

'Nothing ventured, nothing gained. And you're lucky – you look so right, you've everything going for you. If you ask me Mrs Driver will snap you up.'

'I agree,' said Rosemary. 'Look, Lindy, I'm going to one of her classes next week. If you write a letter with all your details and add a snapshot of yourself, I could give it to her and arrange an interview. How about that?'

'It'd have to be on a Wednesday afternoon, when I'm no' at work,' Lindy said slowly. 'But that's very kind of you, Rosemary. I appreciate it. You and Jemima have both been so nice, thinking of me – I'm sorry if I've seemed ungrateful. I was just that surprised, you see. I never thought I'd even be considered for a job like modelling.'

'Confidence, Lindy, confidence!' cried Jemima. 'Don't ever let on that you thought you'd be anything but perfect for the job. And – a word of advice – don't mention the interview to Myra, or even your wonderful Rod, until it's all decided one way or the other. No point in getting them interested before they have to be, eh?'

'That's good advice,' said Lindy, rising. 'I'll take it. Will you let me know, then, Rosemary, if this lady wants to see me?'

'Of course. I'll give you all the details. But won't you stay and have another cup of coffee?'

'No, thanks all the same. I've had a busy day – got a bit of a headache. I'll just get back home.'

A bit of a headache? A lot of a headache, Lindy thought, having said goodbye to Jemima and Rosemary, and set off down the stairs. One that wasn't going to clear in a hurry; certainly not till she'd had this interview and knew what was going to happen.

And had told Rod about it, if she was successful. He'd be pleased, though, wouldn't he, if she got the chance of this modelling job that had dropped from nowhere into her lap? Because she did want it, she really did. Tailor-made for her, Jemima had said it would be, and that was true, even if she was a tenement girl. Thinking of that as she reached her door, she took a deep breath and straightened her shoulders. Confidence, Lindy! Make this Mrs Driver believe you think you're perfect for the job! And in the meantime, not a word to Aunt Myra. Or her wonderful Rod.

# Thirty-Six

On the following Wednesday afternoon, Lindy and Myra, as usual on early closing day, had a snack meal at home, after which Myra said she'd do some cleaning and Lindy said she'd go shopping.

'Shopping?' Myra frowned. 'What are you going to use for money?'

'Window shopping, I meant,' Lindy said, not meeting her stepmother's eyes. 'I can't afford to buy anything but I like to look around.'

'You meeting Rod?'

'Oh, no, he's at work. It's – well, it's Rosemary who's coming with me.'

'Miss Rosemary? That's a change of heart, eh? I thought you weren't keen on her any more after what happened with Neil.'

'She did ask me up the other evening. I think she wants to be friends.' Lindy glanced at the clock. 'Look, I'm away. She's calling for me at two o'clock, so I'd better get changed.'

'Why, you look fine as you are, Lindy. What's all the excitement?'

What indeed? Lindy, hurrying with Rosemary for the tram, felt quite eaten up with guilt over telling little lies to Myra, but what else could she do? She really didn't want to tell her she had an interview with Mrs Driver in the West End, and not just because Jemima had warned against it. Lindy herself knew how it would have been if she'd had to give all the details to her stepmother, and then maybe returned to say she hadn't got the job after all. No, no, better keep it secret till she had something definite to say, and then face the music.

'You're not nervous?' Rosemary whispered as the tram jolted along towards the West End of the city. 'You needn't be, you know. As Jemima said, you're everything Mrs Driver will be looking for, so try to be as confident as possible.'

'I am trying, but it's no' easy. Before you told me that Mrs Driver would see me, I thought I could carry an interview off, no trouble, but now it's really staring me in the face I just feel she'll think I'm no' suitable.'

'She won't, she won't! I've told her you're from a tenement and that you haven't much money, and she understands. She's had other girls like you and they've done very well. Why shouldn't you?'

Lindy sighed and shook her head. 'What's she like, then, this Mrs Driver?'

Rosemary looked down her high-bridged nose. 'She's all right. Very fair, I'd say, but rather like her name, you know. Drives people hard – drives herself hard – and expects one hundred per cent from everyone. That's what I've heard.'

Lindy groaned. 'A bit of a tyrant, eh? Well, I don't mind hard work. No' so sure I want to be driven, though. Why'd she come to Edinburgh if she's a Londoner?'

'Oh, she isn't a Londoner, she's from Edinburgh. Seems she worked in a London modelling agency even when they were quite a new idea and did very well, but then she thought, why not open one at home? There's nothing much here, you see, and she felt she could fill a gap. So far she's doing very well.'

'And how about her husband? What did he think about coming here?'

'I don't think he is here,' Rosemary said cautiously. 'From what one of the girls at the class said the other day I think she might be – divorced.'

'Divorced?' Lindy stared. 'I've never met anyone who's been divorced. Very expensive, eh?'

'Costs a fortune!'

'You're right. Mrs Driver must be doing well, then. Unless Mr Driver paid. How sad, though, that they had to split up.'

'We don't know if it's true, but I should think it is. Maybe Mrs Driver is married to her job.' Rosemary smiled as she left her seat. 'She certainly gives you that impression. But here's our stop, Lindy. The agency's just round the corner from here.'

In a rather grand part of town, thought Lindy, taking in the width of the streets in the Victorian West End and the size of the houses, but as she and Rosemary made their way towards Mrs

Driver's, Rosemary said that she only had the ground floor of one of the conversions, not a whole house.

'I know someone who has a whole house here,' Rosemary went on, 'and it's huge – big enough for a hotel, which is not what everybody wants. So some of the houses have been divided into flats, or offices, doctors' surgeries and so on. All Mrs Driver has is a couple of rooms – one for her office and one for her classes.' She touched Lindy's arm. 'For people like you and me.'

'Like you, maybe. We don't know about me yet.'

'Confidence, confidence!' cried Rosemary, halting at the handsome front door of the house they were seeking. 'Take heart, Lindy, here we are. I'll just ring the bell.'

It seemed for ever before the bell was answered and the door opened by a tall, slender young woman dressed in a black tunic and skirt, with blonde hair scraped back in a silk scarf and a paper in her hand.

'Oh, hello, Rosemary!' she cried in a high, fluting voice. She glanced at her paper. 'And is this Miss Gillan, then? Please come this way.'

'Lindy, this is Miss Forbes, Mrs Driver's assistant,' Rosemary said easily. 'She puts us through our paces.'

'My dear, you scarcely need it. Now, Miss Gillan, if you could just take a seat in the hall, Mrs Driver won't be a moment. Rosemary, would you like to go ahead into the practice room? I'll be with you shortly.'

I'm to be interviewed on my own, thought

182

Lindy, perched on a chair outside a mahogany door, one of several in the vast, polished hallway of the West End house. Well, of course, she'd expected nothing else. Still, she felt vulnerable. Exposed. For the first time in her life she was to be scrutinized, criticized, maybe found wanting, and had only herself to rely on. Confidence! she repeated to herself. Put your shoulders back. Go in there as though you mean to succeed.

'I'll just take you in,' Miss Forbes whispered, tapping on the mahogany door. 'Mrs Driver will be ready to see you now.'

'Fine,' answered Lindy hoarsely, feeling her false courage running away from her like sand through her fingers.

'Come in!' called a strong Edinburgh voice.

'Miss Gillan to see you, Mrs Driver,' said Miss Forbes, putting her head round the door.

'Show her in, please, Stella.'

Shoulders back! Confidence!

As Miss Forbes stood back, holding the door for her, Lindy, walking tall, advanced into Mrs Driver's office and heard the door close behind her. Such finality. How would she be feeling when the door was opened again?

# Thirty-Seven

The woman who rose from her desk in the large, well-appointed office was, Lindy guessed, in her forties. She was tall, not particularly thin, but held herself well, and in her dark jacket and matching dress looked elegantly at ease. Her hair was pale blonde, beautifully cut, her face rather plain, her eyes brown, but a much darker brown than Rod's and quite without their warmth. Already Lindy could feel their appraising power taking in every detail of her appearance. If only she'd had something better to wear than her twinset and tweed skirt! But Rosemary had said Mrs Driver would not be expecting Lindy to wear expensive clothes. No, she'd be looking for something quite different.

'Good afternoon, Miss Gillan,' Mrs Driver began. 'I have your letter here, saying that you wish to become a mannequin with my agency. You heard about it from Miss Dalrymple?'

'That's right, Mrs Driver,' Lindy answered, wondering if she would be asked to sit down. There was a chair facing the desk, but Mrs Driver was making no move to invite her to take it.

'You won't mind if I ask a couple of questions before we go any further? They are essential.'

'Oh, no, Mrs Driver.'

'Well, then, let me look at you.'

Moving swiftly, Mrs Driver came to Lindy and, taking her arm, turned her round, studying her, it seemed, from every angle.

'Height's what?' she murmured. 'Five feet nine? Am I right? Yes, I can tell because I'm the same. How about your measurements?'

'Thirty-four, twenty-three, thirty-four,' Lindy answered readily, thanking Rosemary's foresight in reminding her to measure herself the previous evening.

'Excellent.' Mrs Driver gave a small smile. 'That's the first hurdle over. Come and sit down, Miss Gillan.'

When Lindy had seated herself, Mrs Driver fixed her with her dark brown gaze. 'I have your letter and your photograph. I see that so far you have only worked in a grocer's shop. What makes you think that modelling is for you?'

Lindy hesitated, unsure how candid she should be. In the end she said, simply, 'I love clothes. I've always been interested in them, from a wee girl. I never thought about modelling till Miss Dalrymple suggested it, but then I thought it might be what I was looking for, because I'd be involved with clothes.' Her eyes met Mrs Driver's. 'But I knew I'd have to be suitable.'

'You thought you might not be?'

'Well –' Lindy lowered her gaze. 'I'm a tenement girl. I'm no' sure I'd fit in.'

'Miss Gillan, your background has nothing to do with your suitability to work as a mannequin. People who want their clothes to be shown are looking for the right sort of girls to wear them. Those with not only the looks and height, but the style and flair to make customers want to buy what they see being modelled. Do you think you could learn to attract people to clothes in that way?'

'I'd like to,' Lindy said earnestly. 'I'm sure I could learn what to do.'

'It's hard work, you know. Changing in and out of clothes all the time, always looking your best, never showing you're tired.' Mrs Driver shook her head. 'It's not the glamorous job people think it is, though it has its rewards, of course,

185

and there other types of modelling some think make for an easier life.'

Mrs Driver hesitated. 'Before we go any further, I think I should explain just what my agency does for those who sign up for it. I look after all their interests, finding them work, making them known, seeing they have what is needed – a portfolio, photographs and so on. What I can't do is to promise to provide full-time work.'

'I see,' Lindy said blankly, not feeling that she did. Here was a problem Rosemary hadn't mentioned.

'The thing is, Miss Gillan,' Mrs Driver went on, 'you need to know something about the situation for modelling here in Scotland. It's not the same as in London, where there are big fashion shows requiring lots of models. Here, most of the work comes from the big department stores and though there's plenty of it, there's still not enough to guarantee full-time work.'

'So the girls have to be part time?' Lindy asked, her heart sinking. There was no way she could manage on one part-time wage, and Mrs Fielding wouldn't give her extra part-time work at Murchie's.

'I hadn't realized that the modelling wouldn't be full time,' she said slowly. 'Maybe I'll have to think again.'

'That would be a pity. What a lot of models do is have a part-time job in the background. Couldn't you do that, Miss Gillan?'

'Maybe I could,' Lindy answered, her mind working overtime. Something other than the shop? 'Yes. Maybe I could.'

'As a model you'd earn about fifteen shillings a session, which is not high, but not bad for these times. And once you became known and got more work, you could do quite well. With photographic work, too.'

'Photographic work?'

'That's mainly for advertising in magazines and so on, and catalogue modelling, where you'd be photographed in various outfits or with articles for sale, for what the Americans call mail order. Or even modelling the finished products for knitting or dress patterns. All very useful for bringing in work – and payment.' Mrs Driver leaned forward a little. 'Now, are you still interested, then? You think modelling could be for you? Because I should tell you that I'm willing to take you on to my books, certain formalities being completed.'

For a moment Lindy could not reply, then she said breathlessly, 'Mrs Driver, I'm no' just interested, I'm thrilled that you want me. Thank you. Thank you very much indeed.'

'Well, let's get down to the formalities. I'll try to be brief.'

It seemed that there would be a contract to sign, and that Lindy must fully understand the financial position, what the commission would be and so on. Having carefully read all the terms at home, she would have to return to the agency to meet Mrs Driver's legal adviser, who would check that she knew what she was doing and answer any other queries. As Miss Gillan was a minor, it was important that her parents were happy about her contract too, and it would be helpful if Miss Gillan could provide a written assurance on that.

'Are they happy about you changing jobs, anyway?' Mrs Driver asked, rising.

As she also quickly stood up, Lindy bit her lip. 'I haven't told them about it yet. I thought I'd wait – see how I got on.'

'That's not satisfactory, Miss Gillan. You must tell them about it immediately and make sure you have their approval. The last thing I want is parents being upset.'

'I will tell them, Mrs Driver, and I'm sure they'll be happy for me.'

'Very well. Next, you'll need a portfolio with photographs and we'll arrange for you to have those taken, the cost to be repaid when you're earning. And perhaps I could say, about your professional name, that Lindsay would be more appropriate than Lindy – Miss Dalrymple's name for you. You don't mind about that?'

'I don't mind at all.'

'Then I think that's all for the present.' Mrs Driver escorted Lindy to the door. 'I'd like to say, my dear, that I think you'll do very well. You have a lovely face, but there are many girls with lovely faces. What impressed me about you was your love of clothes and your positive attitude. Now, see my assistant about an appointment next week for your modelling class and we'll soon have you part of Driver's.'

'Thank you,' Lindy said again. 'Thank you, Mrs Driver.'

She should have been walking on air – after all, she'd been accepted, she'd been taken on by Mrs Driver – but instead her head was aching and she felt quite numbed by the shock of her change of fortune. The contract in her hand seemed to belong to someone else – she couldn't imagine reading it, knew she must, but it would be later. Later, when she'd told her father and Myra that she was leaving the shop and embarking on something quite new. Whatever would they say? She couldn't imagine even telling them and put her hand to her brow, then heard Rosemary's voice in the hall and saw her coming running towards her, Miss Forbes with her, and with immense effort put a smile on her face.

'How did it go?' Rosemary was calling. 'Heavens, Lindy, you're so pale! Are you all right?'

'Fine.' Lindy was still smiling. 'It went well. Mrs Driver's taking me on.'

'I knew she would! Didn't I say so?' Rosemary hugged her. 'Oh, I'm so pleased for you! Stella, isn't that good news?'

'Wonderful,' Stella Forbes agreed. 'Congratulations, Miss Gillan. I'll just get my book for your appointments for the class and to see Mrs Driver again.'

'Thank you,' said Lindy, beginning to feel better until, going home in the tram, she thought of her parents again and of how it would be, telling them. And Rod – she must tell him, too. But he, she was sure, would be pleased. It was, after all, wonderful news she had to give him.

189

# Thirty-Eight

'Well, I don't know what to say!' cried Myra, her green eyes outraged. 'George, what do you think of your daughter, then? Going off behind our backs and finding herself another job. One she's no' sure will be full time, for a start, but something we'll all be ashamed to mention, that's for sure. A mannequin! As though folk don't know what goes on with those girls, showing off clothes and I don't know what else! We'll no' be able to hold up our heads again!'

'What are you talking about?' asked Lindy, pushing back her chair from the table where, after tea, she'd finally broken her news and found the reaction worse than she'd feared. 'There's no disgrace in being a mannequin, Aunt Myra! Mrs Driver, who runs the agency, is a very respectable lady and said I had to have your approval to take up modelling, so that shows she wants everything to be above board. All she does is find the girls work showing off the new clothes in the shops or doing modelling for catalogues and such. It's wrong of you to talk as though it's something shameful!'

'So, why'd you no' tell us about it before?' Myra demanded. 'Why all the secrecy?'

'Aye, that's what I don't understand,' George muttered, his eyes on his daughter, bewildered. 'We've never had secrets before.'

'Lindy just wanted to have it definite before she told you,' Struan put in, giving his sister an unusually sympathetic glance. 'What's all the fuss about? Lindy's done well to get herself a new job, even if it's no' guaranteed to be full time. You shouldn't be upsetting her, Aunt Myra.'

'Upsetting her?' cried Myra. 'She's upsetting me! And what do you know about this fashion business, anyway? I'll ask you to keep out of this, Struan!'

'Where'd you hear about it, then?' George asked Lindy. 'How'd you get the idea?'

'From Rosemary. She told me.' Lindy fixed Myra with a truculent gaze. 'Maybe you'd like to tell her what you think of my new job, Aunt Myra. She's going to be a mannequin herself.'

There was a stunned silence. Myra's mouth had dropped open, Struan was grinning and George looked mystified.

'Miss Rosemary?' Myra whispered. 'Going to do that sort o' work? I don't believe it.'

'It's true. I told you it was quite respectable. Her mother's agreed to it as well.'

'Her mother?'

'That's right.' Lindy stood with her arms folded, staring down at her stepmother, not caring to mention how long it had taken Rosemary to gain her mother's approval. The fact was she had it and was all set to do the work Lindy would be doing, which meant there was no doubt that Myra's opposition was now shaken.

'Well, I never thought it,' she murmured. 'I never thought Miss Rosemary would take on a job like that.'

191

'Shows it's different from what you thought,' Struan told her. 'Don't know where you got your ideas from, anyway.'

'Aye, it must be suitable for our Lindy if it's suitable for Miss Rosemary,' George said, his brow clearing. 'I knew Lindy wouldn't get herself mixed up in anything wrong.'

'That's right, Dad,' Lindy said quickly. 'And after I've read the contract, I'll be seeing a lawyer and he'll make sure I understand it. You'll be able to give me your approval and no' worry.'

'Well, I'm saying no more,' Myra declared, rising and beginning to clear away as noisily as possible. 'If it's what you want for your girl, George, it's no' for me to interfere. But I'd just like to point out that I'm the one who's going to suffer and nobody's given a toss about that!'

'How d'you mean, Myra?' George asked worriedly. 'Why should you suffer?'

'Why? Because I'll be left without help in the shop, won't I? And as soon as Mrs Fielding finds out Lindy's left, she'll say she's no' replacing her. She wanted to give her the sack before, if you remember, but then she changed her mind. This time she'll say I can manage and I'll have everything to do – as though I didn't have enough to do already!'

'You don't know Mrs Fielding will say that,' Struan pointed out. 'She might be happy to get you a new assistant.'

'Oh, it's all right for you to talk! Talk's cheap, eh?' Myra turned cold eyes on Lindy. 'Are you going to help me wash up, then?'

'Yes, leave it, I'll do it.'

But as she started on the dishes, Lindy's thoughts had moved from her parents to Rod. She wasn't seeing him till Saturday night. However could she wait that long, with her amazing news bubbling on her lips, ready to be told? At least she could run up and see Jemima and show her the contract, maybe see Rosemary as well. It was time for a celebration with somebody – she just wished it could have been Rod. Roll on Saturday!

# Thirty-Nine

It came at last, that Saturday, with its meeting with Rod, and Lindy was up in the clouds, thinking of giving him her news. She was sure he would be pleased, this new job being such a step up for her. Certainly she never had any misgivings. Only afterwards did it occur to her that she might have been doubtful; might have learned a lesson from the mistake she'd made with Neil, believing that he would want what she wanted. But then, Rod wasn't Neil. He was much more reasonable, much steadier in every way, and when he arrived to collect her on that Saturday evening, all she had in her heart was joy.

'Got the car at the ready,' he told her when she ran out to greet him as soon as she heard his knock on the flat door. 'It's a terrible night – throwing it down!'

'Never mind. I don't care about the weather – it's just so grand to see you again!'

'Snap,' he murmured, kissing her quickly. 'Oh, God, snap!' And they ran through the rain into the little Morris waiting at the kerb.

'Where are we going?' Lindy asked, shaking drops from her hat as they drove away. 'I've never even looked to see what's on at the pictures.'

'That's not like you. What's been keeping you busy?'

'Aha! I'll tell you in a minute. But what do you want to see, then?'

'Well, there's a Hitchcock film in Princes Street. *The Thirty-Nine Steps* with Robert Donat.'

'Robert Donat? My dreamboat!'

'Hey, none of that. Any more talk of dreamboats and you're out in the rain!' Rod was grinning as he peered through the windscreen. 'But what have you been doing this past week without me, then?'

'You'll never guess. Never in a thousand years.'

'Oh, come on, now, no teasing.'

'Well . . .' Lindy paused, smiling in the shadows. 'I've been finding myself a new job.'

'A what?' Rod risked a quick glance sideways to catch a glimpse of Lindy's face. 'Did you say a job?'

'That's right, a job. It's no' definite yet, but it soon will be. You'll never guess what it is.'

'All right, why don't you just tell me what it is?'

'Wait for it.' Lindy couldn't help pausing again for dramatic effect. 'I'm going to be a model.'

A silence fell over the little car, except for the

drumming of the rain on the roof. Lindy, taken aback by Rod's lack of speech, tried to see his face, but only his profile was visible and it told her nothing.

'A fashion model,' she said quickly, feeling a stab of unease, and gave a little laugh. 'A mannequin, you know. In case you thought I meant an artist's model.'

'An artist's model would be more honest,' he replied shortly. 'Look, I'm going to have to pull in – maybe in Thistle Street. I can get in there.'

'But aren't we going to the cinema, Rod?'

He made no reply until they'd turned into Thistle Street, where the shops were all closed and there were spaces vacant by its narrow pavements. Here he parked and sat for a moment gazing ahead until, finally, he turned and looked at Lindy. 'You want to go to the cinema?'

'Well, we said we would,' she answered, her voice trembling. 'To see the Hitchcock picture.'

'You think I could take an interest in a film when you've told me what you're planning to do?'

'Rod, I don't understand you! What are you talking about? I thought you'd be pleased for me – it's no' everyone gets accepted for the agency. Instead you start talking in riddles. I mean, how can being an artist's model be honest? Are you saying being a fashion model is dishonest?'

'When I said an artist's model was honest, I meant that she was offering her body just as it is to those who wanted to paint her. No fuss with hairdo's and cosmetics, making herself what she's not. No putting on expensive clothes to try to get

195

rich, idle women to buy them, no living a totally artificial life.'

Rod's expression in the dim light of the car was hard to see, but Lindy didn't need to. She knew from his voice and his manner that his face would show the contempt he felt for the job she'd chosen, and it was the sort of contempt she'd never thought to see in him, never thought would be directed at her. Every word he'd uttered had been like a dagger in her heart, not just because of what he thought but because what he said made him seem like a stranger – someone she thought she knew yet didn't know at all.

'It's no' like that,' she said in a low voice. 'The girls aren't trying to be something they're not; they're just wanting to seem more attractive. Is that a crime? The people who make the clothes have to sell them, and if there's money made, is that no' a good thing? Money's needed, Rod, you know that, to make the world go round.'

'Not the sort of money we're talking about here, Lindy. Where rich women who contribute nothing to society stare at beautiful young girls and think they can look like them if they buy what they're wearing. And pay out God knows what to dress themselves up, while outside there are people without jobs living in squalor, going hungry. Children as well – children most of all. And this is the kind of work you want to do, Lindy? To keep that great divide going?'

'You're too hard, too hard!' she cried, her tears beginning to flow. 'You're no' being fair, Rod, no' being fair at all. When the people come to

Logie's and such they're often just ordinary women – no' the idle rich like you say.'

Suddenly she was crying in earnest, but when Rod tried to take her hands she jerked them away and sat with her face averted, letting the tears come. 'I suppose you won't approve if I just do some photographic modelling, either,' she said thickly. 'Where are the rich folk there? It'd just be for catalogues and stuff, to send to ordinary folk, but you'll find something wrong with it, won't you?'

'Photographic modelling? Good God, what's that? You're shut up for hours with some man pointing a camera at you, Lindy? Is the idea of that expected to make me feel better? Well, it's bad enough, but it's not as bad as all that strutting around trying to make idle folk spend money.'

Rod tried again to take her hand, finally holding it for a moment before she again wrenched it away. 'Oh, Lindy, Lindy,' he whispered, 'how is this happening? We were so happy. And you promised you'd think about doing the sort of work I do, so when you said you'd found a job I thought for a minute that was what you'd found. Of course, I knew it wasn't likely, but that you wanted to be a model – that never crossed my mind!'

'I did tell you once what I liked,' she said in muffled tones. 'I said I liked dresses and make-up, and you said it was only natural – nothing wrong with it at all. But now it's terrible, is it? Terrible and shocking? Rod, I canna believe you've talked to me the way you have tonight.'

'Of course it's only natural for a young woman to think about dresses and make-up, Lindy. As long as they're just for herself – not part of a professional armoury she shouldn't want to have. You see the difference, don't you?'

'No,' she said resolutely, wiping away her tears and straightening her hat. 'The only difference I see is in you, Rod. You're like a stranger.'

'Don't you think I feel the same?' he asked quietly.

'I'm a stranger?' Her beautiful, drenched eyes were wide open, her lips parted as she tried to take in what he'd said. 'How can you say that?' she whispered. 'You're the one who's different. The Rod I knew would never have hurt me like you have.'

'Ah, I never wanted to hurt you!' he cried, trying again to take her hands that she again snatched away. 'It's just that I got such a shock, you see. I had such different ideas of what you wanted, because I really thought you cared for the same things that matter to me. But when I heard you could take a job that just revolved around money, well, I saw you'd got very different ideas.' Rod suddenly sat back, putting his hand to his face, covering his eyes. 'Can't you see what that did to me?' he asked, his voice shaking. 'What it's doing to me now? Because I still love you, Lindy. I still care.'

'There's no future, though, is there?' she asked slowly. 'No future for us now.'

'You won't think again? About this job?'

'No, because I think you're in the wrong, Rod. You want me to do what you want, but this is my life we're talking about, eh? I've a right to do what I think is best.'

'That's it, then,' he said, sitting up, facing her. 'There's nothing we can do.'

She dried her tears with her handkerchief, straightened her hat, looked out of her window and opened the car door. 'Goodbye, Rod,' she whispered. 'You needn't take me home. I'll get the tram.'

'Don't be silly, of course I'll take you home! It's raining.'

'No, it's stopped. And I don't want you to take me home, it'd be too sad.'

'Lindy –'

'Goodbye, Rod.'

Before he could put out a restraining hand she'd stepped from the car and was hurrying away down Thistle Street, not looking back. For some moments he watched, then leaped out to follow her, but at the end of the street she'd vanished into the evening crowds. There was nothing for him to do but walk back to his car and sit in desolation, until a policeman in the distance seemed to be staring, and finally he drove away.

# Forty

Telling her family of her split with Rod was something she could scarcely face, yet must get over with as soon as possible so that they would say no more and leave her to her own misery.

Of course, when she told them the reason for the break – and she'd felt she must be honest about it – Myra was able to say smugly, 'Well, that makes two of us. You might have guessed a sensible laddie would agree with me on modelling, Lindy. He knows what's right and what isn't.'

'No, he does not!' Lindy flared up. 'He's got the wrong end of the stick altogether, and so have you, Aunt Myra. I said so the other day.'

'Aye, and you seemed happy enough when you heard Miss Rosemary was going in for this work,' George told Myra in a rare moment of defiance. 'She'd never get mixed up in the wrong sort o' thing, eh?'

Leaning forward he patted Lindy's arm, his gaze mournful on her tear-stained face. 'Poor lassie, eh? This'll have upset you just when you thought everything was going well. Try to remember it'll all seem better one day.'

'No' much comfort,' said Struan, who had come in early from the pub, saying he was somewhat broke. 'Today's what counts, Dad, no' tomorrow.'

'It'll all be for the best,' Myra said decisively. 'Better to find out now if you disagree on things instead o' waiting till you've tied the knot.'

'Maybe, but meantime I get no more drives in that grand little Morris,' Struan said sadly. 'Sorry, Lindy, I know you've got other things to think about but I'm really going to miss your Rod, and that's a fact.'

At which remark Lindy burst into tears, her parents shook their heads, and Struan was all injured innocence.

'Why, what did I say?' he asked, as Lindy ran to her little room, saying she was going to bed. 'It's true, eh? We'll all miss Rod.'

'Can you no' try a wee bit o' tact?' snapped Myra. 'Lindy's got more to be upset about than a few car drives!'

'Did I no' say that very thing?' cried Struan. 'I'm as tactful as the next guy, I'd say. When are you going to put the kettle on, then?'

Grateful to be alone, Lindy lay on her bed, hearing but not listening to the noises of her family next door, only wanting to shut out the unhappy world in which she was caught and longing for sleep that she knew would never come.

Oblivion. That was what she wanted. To be away from feeling that could only be heartbreak, for with his loss had come an even clearer understanding of how much she cared for Rod. The new job, the prospect of an exciting future, doing what she wanted to do, working with fashion that had always been a bit of a dream – none of that mattered now. Why had she not abandoned hopes of a change from shop work after she'd found Rob? Why hadn't she just let their love blossom, as she knew he wanted to do, so that they came to the logical end, which was marriage? Forget all the worries over childbirth. Forget all the efforts to be something better. She would have had something better with Rod, and together they could have worked, as he already worked, for other people's welfare. Why had she not taken that path?

Because – she had to admit it – she did want

to follow the dream. She did want to see if she could succeed in doing something that seemed right for her, and the modelling job seemed so exactly suited she couldn't turn it down. It had never seemed to be an 'either/or' situation to her. She'd thought she could have both – Rob and her new work – for modelling wasn't like teaching or other professions where women had to give up their work on marriage. No, she could have kept it going, perhaps made her mark, satisfied herself, at least until she had a family. (And she might have found the nerve to get through that, mightn't she? With Rob as a father?)

But none of that was going to happen because Rob was not what she'd thought. The wonderful understanding he had for other people had not been given to her or the girls who would be her companions. He had despised what they wanted to do and could not seem to see that he was missing the point completely and that they weren't as he believed. Worst of all, he hadn't trusted Lindy herself, hadn't tried to see that the new job she really wanted to do wouldn't be anything to be ashamed about.

No, he had made himself a stranger and her a stranger, too. So be it. She would concentrate now on doing well in the work she wanted, and put Rod completely from her mind.

'Cup o' tea, pet?' she heard her father asking on the other side of her door, and told him to come in. Yes, she'd have some tea, then perhaps she would sleep.

'Thanks, Dad,' she murmured as he put the cup by her bed. 'That's nice.'

'Remember what I told you,' he said softly. 'You will get over this. Everybody goes through it, you ken, at some time or other.'

'It was worse for you, Dad.'

'Aye. Well, time passed. And I'd you, eh?' George smiled slightly. 'And Struan.'

And Myra, of course. They exchanged weak smiles, then George told Lindy to try to sleep. Things would look better in the morning.

When he'd gone she drank the tea. Was it true? Would things ever look better again? Oh, yes, tomorrow might not be better, but one day she'd be free of the heavy stone she seemed to bear in her heart. And in the coming days there was much ahead, much to learn, to take into her new life.

I will sleep, she told herself and, finally, though her face was still damp with tears, she did.

# Forty-One

Of course, she could not put Rod completely out of her mind. He was there, even though she had so much else to think about, especially as she couldn't stop herself from wondering – hoping, even – that he might suddenly appear in the shop, say he was sorry, and could they just be as they were again? She knew in her heart that he wouldn't, and he didn't, but every time the shop bell went in those last days at Murchie's there'd be a catch in her breath and she'd be looking at the door. Only another customer would come in, smiling at her, and she'd smile back. Somehow.

Myra, reporting back from Mrs Fielding, said there'd be no need for Lindy to work another week of notice. As all had gone well at the second meeting with Mrs Driver she could start at the agency the following Monday, which was just what Mrs Driver and Lindy wanted.

'So it's really going to be goodbye at the end of the week,' Lindy said a little tremulously. 'Aunt Myra, I'm going to miss Murchie's.'

'Oh, yes? Well, you can always change your mind, eh? Just stay on?'

At Lindy's expression, Myra laughed.

'Och, no need to look like that! I'm only joking. Wild horses would no' keep you from going to that agency. Just hope it works out for you.'

'Well, like I told you, everything seems to be OK. The lawyer fellow was happy about me signing the contract, and I know what sort of wages I'll be getting.' Lindy heaved a sigh. 'But first I've to go to Mrs Driver's class to learn how to walk. I'm worried about that.'

'Why, what's to learn about walking around wearing smart dresses? I should've thought you could do that without any training at all.'

'Oh, no, Aunt Myra, seemingly there's a lot to learn. And how I get on will be very important, eh? At least I've got the contract, so I won't get the sack straight away!'

'That's good,' said Myra coolly. 'Because it'll be no good trying to come back here. Mrs Fielding says I've to manage without an assistant. Just as I said she would.'

204

'Oh, Aunt Myra, I'm sorry!'
'Too late for that, Lindy, too late for that.'

After fond farewells from all the customers, who even clubbed together to give Lindy a box of chocolates, it seemed strange on the following Monday not to be going to the shop but to be taking the tram to the agency instead.

Lindy had spent all of Sunday deciding what to wear for her first day, getting into long discussions with Jemima and Rosemary, who viewed her wardrobe with her, making suggestions and encouraging noises, until she finally settled on a mid-calf black skirt lent by Rosemary and a white blouse of her own.

'Will these be all right for the class?' she asked Rosemary anxiously. 'You'll know – you've been through it.'

'They'll be perfect. Unless you'd like a jacket as well?'

'My dark one, if you want it,' put in Jemima, her voice sympathetic as she looked at Lindy. 'Ah, you're doing so well, eh? It's such a shame that – well, that you've had such an upset at the wrong time. I won't say any more.'

'We do feel for you,' Rosemary added softly. 'But you're being so brave; it shows you're strong. You'll do well. We admire you.'

'No need to admire me,' Lindy answered quietly. 'I'm no' brave, I'm just getting by.'

'Well, that's what's brave!' cried Rosemary. 'But try not to worry about the class. It's all just about how to use your hips and how to make turns and so on. It will soon become second nature, and you'll' – she waved her hands – 'flow, if you understand me.'

'Is that what they call it?' Jemima asked, laughing. 'No wonder mannequins seem different from ordinary mortals!'

'You make it sound so easy,' Lindy sighed. 'And now you've finished and are going for a job?'

'Yes. I'm so worried – my first assignment is on Tuesday,' Rosemary told her, not looking worried at all. 'A spring show at Forsyth's – in December! But that's the way things go. Now, Lindy, are you all right for shoes? Remember, you'll be wearing heels most of the time. If you can wear mine you're welcome to take what you like. I've got heaps. And be sure to take your make-up with you, and your brush and comb, and anything else you think you'll need. Models always have their little bags with them, you know. They're like Girl Guides – have to be prepared!'

Well, she was prepared, all right, thought Lindy as the tram delivered her to her stop for Mrs Driver's agency. She felt she had so much packed into her bag she might have been going on an expedition to some far-off country. Maybe the agency was just that? Something removed from all that she knew?

Now that she was so close she couldn't wait to get started, complete the training and be given her first job. And keep Rod Connor to the back of her mind? That she still couldn't do.

# Forty-Two

Learning to walk the models' way was, as Lindy had guessed, not as easy as Rosemary had said. 'It will soon become second nature,' she had airily declared, but when Lindy and the other new models watched Stella's demonstration in Mrs Driver's practice room, they had serious doubts that they would ever manage to achieve her smoothness, her flow, her almost ballet-like movement.

Apart from Lindy there were five other young women attending their first class in the long, narrow room that had probably been used for dining in the original house. With its long windows, parquet flooring and handsome plaster work, it still bore signs of its old grandeur, but now an upright piano stood in one corner with a wind-up gramophone nearby, and in the middle of the room a low, curved platform – a models' catwalk, no less – drew the newcomers' eyes like a magnet.

Although a small fire burned in the chimney piece, the room was cold enough that December morning to have the girls shivering as Mrs Driver outlined what they would have to do, while Stella, in a mid-calf-length black dress and high-heeled black shoes, stood by, waiting to demonstrate.

There seemed to be so much to remember! And it wasn't as though they couldn't all walk anyway, was it? But models' style of walking was something quite different to theirs, and not something you'd normally use to get from A to B.

'First, girls, you have to think about your feet but not look at them,' Mrs Driver began. 'What you do is walk in a straight line, one foot in front of the other, placing all the weight on the ball of the foot, never the heel. At the same time, your head must be held high, your shoulders brought forward, the arms naturally loose and the hips swung in an emphasized movement. Turns at the end of the catwalk can be tricky, but must be completed in the same flowing movement as the walk, the head tilted to one side, a smile perhaps given to the audience, and then you're ready to return.'

'I know this sounds a lot to remember, but when you see Stella it will all seem clear,' Mrs Driver finished, smiling. 'In no time, if you practise hard, it will all become second nature to you, I promise!'

So that's where Rosemary heard that, Lindy thought, wondering like the other novices if it could possibly be true. Certainly it was lovely to watch someone so accomplished as Stella, as Mrs Driver put on a scratchy record of sweet music and her assistant drifted gracefully down the catwalk.

The trouble was she was almost too good. It was hard for the watching girls to imagine themselves in her place, yet that morning they would be attempting to achieve that very thing in front of Mrs Driver's critical eye. Tall, slim and strikingly attractive as they all were, they could feel nothing but their nerves.

As Stella finished her routine and stepped aside, Mrs Driver joined in the little clap the girls gave her, then took a list from a pocket in her black cardigan.

'Right, now comes your turn, girls.' She gave another of her brief smiles. 'In alphabetical order, I think, which means that Jennifer, you will be first.'

'With a name like Abbot I always am,' sighed Jennifer, an elegant blonde with forget-me-not blue eyes.

'Better than being me,' put in a dark-haired, dark-eyed young woman next to her. 'If you're called Kitty Yarman as I am, you're always last.'

And I'll be in the middle, thought Lindy. Oh, my, how did I get into this?

Yet it was what she wanted, eh? Better do her absolute best, then. As though she was already preparing to do her walk she held her head high, moved her shoulders forward and, without looking at her feet, placed them one after the other in a straight line. Easy! Except that she was, of course, standing still. Moving was never going to be the same.

Meanwhile, Jennifer, at the outset of her walk, was being given more advice on the dreaded turn, with Mrs Driver instructing her to stop on one foot, face the side where an audience would be, smile and move round to make the return journey.

'To make it easier to begin with, I'll call out "Turn", to remind you of what to do. All right?'

'Yes, Mrs Driver,' Jennifer replied, her blue eyes terrified. 'Do I have to keep in time with the music?'

'No, we'll leave the music for the moment, until everyone is more practised. Off you go, then.'

Away went Jennifer, not doing too badly, her blonde head up, her hips swinging, even managing a smile. Though no one could say her turn was elegant, she completed it without trouble and arrived back at her starting point with a gasp of relief.

'Well done!' cried Mrs Driver. 'Not bad at all for a first attempt. Now, let me see – Christine Crawford, I think you're next, my dear. Remember what I told Jennifer about the turn. Try not to be too stiff, let your hands be free and look straight ahead without staring.'

'Yes, Mrs Driver,' said Christine, swallowing hard but, like Jennifer, doing reasonably well when she performed her walk, even turning quite neatly, though she forgot to smile.

Oh, will I do as well? Lindy was wondering. If only it was her turn! Suddenly she heard her name called.

'Lindsay Gillan!'

She had never felt so nervous as she did standing at the head of the catwalk with so many pairs of eyes watching her. Though the only pair that counted belonged to Mrs Driver, it didn't help that Stella and all the beautiful girls were watching, too. Head up, shoulders forward, hips ready to swing, she reminded herself again, arms and hands hanging naturally, feet in a straight line, one before the other . . .

'Off you go, Lindsay!' said Mrs Driver. 'Be ready for the turn when I call and don't look down!'

Oh, no, she wasn't looking down, only staring unseeingly ahead, feeling quite glassy-eyed, like some sort of puppet, yet aware as she progressed that her movements were quite smooth, as she'd never imagined they might be.

'Turn!' cried Mrs Driver and Lindy paused, her head turned to one side, her weight on her left foot, and smiled, taking her time, before bringing herself round on her right foot and moving lightly back to the starting point. There, it was over. However she'd got on, her first walk was over.

'Very good!' cried Mrs Driver. 'You managed that very well, Lindsay, except for looking at the beginning as if you were afraid for your life! Next time, I guarantee, you'll be looking quite different. Now, Rhona Reynolds – I think we're ready for you, my dear, with Belinda Sinclair to follow, and then you, Kitty – at last!'

Oh, the relief! With their walks completed and Mrs Driver temporarily out of the room, the girls relaxed around the fire with coffee served by a young maid who gazed at them all with something like awe, causing a few smiles.

'She needn't look like that,' Jennifer whispered when the maid had left. 'We're not dazzling mannequins yet!'

'Will we ever be?' asked Christine.

'To tell the truth, I hope we're not too far off,' said Rhona Reynolds, a redhead. 'I'm pretty broke; I need to earn some money soon.'

'So you will,' said Mrs Driver, returning. 'You've all made such excellent beginnings it won't be long before I can start finding you work. Of course, there's more practice to be done – you

211

still have a lot to learn – but I'm pleased to say well done!'

'Thank you, Mrs Driver, but do you mind if I ask you something?' said Rhona.

'Go ahead. I'm here to answer questions.'

'Well, I was wondering – if I only want to do photographic modelling, say, why do I have to learn all the catwalk techniques?'

'It may seem strange, but to learn fashion modelling techniques is really very valuable in whatever you do, Rhona. Learning to walk and stand correctly and to use your body to its best advantage to give you poise and confidence. Think how useful they can be at interviews!' Mrs Driver laughed. 'I hope I've convinced you?'

'I think you have,' Rhona agreed. 'I'm walking tall already.'

'Perfect. Well, now, if you've finished your coffee I'd like to give you all some tips about what you need in your model bag and what should be in your portfolio. And Lindsay – after you've had lunch I'll take you to the photographer I've selected for you. Now don't look so alarmed – you can't be a model without photographs to be shown to clients. The others have them already. And Hamish MacMaster is very good and very patient. Be ready at two o'clock.'

'Yes, Mrs Driver,' said Lindy.

# Forty-Three

It was already teatime when Lindy arrived home to kick off her shoes and slump by the range. Although George and Struan had not yet returned from work, Myra was back from the shop and curious to know how Lindy's day had gone.

'Don't mind if I say so, but you look worn out,' she cheerfully told her. 'More tiring than you thought, eh?'

'Yes, it was tiring – nerve-racking, in fact – but it went well all the same. We had our first try at walking like the models and it wasn't easy. We've a lot to learn, but I think we felt we'd get there in the end.' Lindy yawned and stretched. 'Think I'll make some tea – is the kettle on?'

'I'll fill it.' As Myra busied herself putting the kettle on and setting out cups, she still seemed to be keeping watch on Lindy. 'You spent the whole day doing this walking?' she asked at last.

'No, this afternoon Mrs Driver took me to have photographs taken. I think that was most tiring of all. I mean, he took so many.'

Thinking back to her afternoon at Hamish MacMaster's studio, Lindy reflected that it had been less worrying than she'd feared. After Rod's remarks about photographers she hadn't known what to expect, but Hamish turned out to be a pleasant, easy-going young man, intent only on getting the best results for his clients, not at all interested in making up to them.

Finding him so nice after Mrs Driver had departed greatly relieved Lindy's mind, and she quite got used to his casual appearance. Dark, spiky hair on end, a shirt without tie or collar, a half-grown beard – she supposed it was what was called the artistic look – Bohemian, was it? Anyway, he was easy to talk to and told her from the start that she would be no problem to photograph. She had the sort of face that looked the same from any angle, whereas most people had a good side and a bad side.

'So, if you're interested in photographic modelling, I can recommend it to you, Miss Gillan. And I think what I produce for you should get you on your way. Two full face shots, I think Mrs Driver suggested for you, plus two profiles and one full length.'

'That's quite a lot,' Lindy commented. 'I've only ever had snaps taken before. My dad's got a Brownie.'

'Nothing wrong with Brownies,' Hamish replied. 'But I think you'll agree that my photographs will not look like snapshots. I'll send them over to the agency in a couple of days.'

It was surprising how much trouble he took over his work, how many shots he seemed to need before he was satisfied and how wearying it was for her, trying to please. Yet she had enjoyed the experience. Maybe, if there was more work to be had on the photographic side, she might do well to consider it. At the end of the session, however, she was glad to thank Hamish and say goodbye. Excited though she was by all that had happened that first day, home, high heels off and a cup of tea had never seemed so attractive.

'Photographs, eh?' commented Myra, pouring out the tea. 'And how much are they going to cost?'

'The agency's paying, then I'll pay Mrs Driver back from my first earnings.'

'But you're paying her a percentage anyway. Seems to me you'll have very little left.'

'Till I've cleared off what I owe, maybe.'

'And then you've to think of what you owe elsewhere, don't forget.'

Lindy's eyes widened. She was opening her mouth to ask what her stepmother meant when the flat door banged, signalling the arrival of her father and brother, and Myra began hurriedly to clear away the teacups.

'There they are, then – I'll have to get the table laid and see to that stew. Lindy, can you give me a hand?'

Over the meal there were questions, of course, from George and Struan about Lindy's day, and it was only when they'd finished eating that Myra spoke again of Lindy's debt. This time she brought in George.

'I was saying to Lindy, George, that till she gets proper work she has to think about what she owes, eh?'

'Owes this agency?' asked George, as Lindy stiffened.

'No, no, me, of course! I mean, you and me.' Myra's eyes rested on Lindy. 'We canna keep

215

her for nothing, and she's no' got the shop work now.'

As George and Struan turned to look at Lindy, the colour flamed in her cheeks and she put her hand to her lips.

'Oh, Aunt Myra, Dad, I forgot – I forgot all about my board! Oh, this is terrible – what'll you think? I was all the time worrying about the agency – I'm ever so sorry. Honestly.'

'Aye, I dare say,' Myra returned, 'but what are you going to do about it? I mean, when you've nothing coming in?'

'I will have, and probably quite soon. Now I've got the photographs I can put together what they call a portfolio and Mrs Driver will send that around, you see. To the people who want models. Then I should get work.' Lindy gave a nervous laugh. 'I mean, somebody should want me, eh?'

There was a short silence, then, as the kettle shrieked, Myra stood up. 'Maybe, but how long will all this take? You say it'll be soon, but in the meantime I'm missing out, eh? I'm one short, and that's a fact.'

'I'll pay for Lindy,' George said swiftly. 'Till she gets on her feet. It's all right. I've a bit put by, I can do it.'

'No, Dad!' Lindy cried. 'I don't want you to do that!'

'No, because what he's got put by is for a rainy day,' snapped Myra. 'Who knows how long your job'll last, George? And if you get the sack we'll need what you've got.'

'Too right,' put in Struan. 'And there's rumours

216

going around that none of us are safe at the brewery.'

'It's all right,' Lindy said clearly. 'I've got something in the post office. I can use that, Aunt Myra. I'll see you're no' short.'

'Ah, pet,' her father murmured sadly. 'This job – it's no' looking like the bed o' roses you thought, is it?'

'I said that from the start,' said Myra. 'And the thing is, it's pretty clear to me that it's only ever going to be part time, anyway. Until you get known you'll be waiting around for the next bit o' work, and in the meantime, what? Canna work at the shop – no part-time work there.'

'I know that, Aunt Myra,' Lindy said shortly. 'I intend to find another part-time job. It's what a lot of models do, Mrs Driver said.'

'Easier said than done these days. Where'd you start looking?'

'How about temporary Christmas work?' Struan suggested. 'There's the Post Office for a start. Off you go, Lindy, delivering the cards, eh?'

'Good idea,' Myra commented. 'At least it'll tide you over for a bit.'

'I suppose so.' Lindy gave a despondent sigh. 'Oh, I'm away to fetch my mending. I've stockings to darn.'

As she moved into her little room, Struan, however, followed her. 'Hey, I forgot to tell you –'

'Tell me what? I think I've heard enough from you, Struan.'

'No, listen. Guess who I saw in my dinner hour?'

'Who?' she asked, slowly turning her head.

'Rod Connor!'

'Rod? Where? Where did you see him?'

'In town. I'd gone for some cigarettes. He was in the shop.'

'Did you speak to him?'

'He spoke to me. Asked me how I was, asked how you were.'

'And what did you tell him?' she asked fearfully.

Struan shrugged. 'Just said you'd started your modelling classes today.'

'You told him that?'

'What else? You did start today, eh?'

Lindy looked away. 'Did he say any more?'

'Just, "So she's going ahead with it, then?" That was all. Then he said goodbye and walked out. Never bothered about his ciggies.'

'I wish you hadn't told me you'd seen him.'

'Why? At least he asked after you.'

'And wouldn't have liked what you said. He's just against what I want to do, for no good reason at all.'

'OK, forget him. Come and have a cup of tea.'

'No, thanks. I want to darn my stockings.'

When he'd left her she did begin her mending, making a poor job of it, her concentration elsewhere. Dad was right: there was no bed of roses in modelling. Or anywhere else, for that matter.

# Forty-Four

Everything seemed brighter the following day, mainly because Lindy met Jemima leaving for work as she was herself leaving for her class, and Jemima, as usual, was helpful.

'A Christmas job?' she cried. 'Why, I'd no idea you wanted one! Logie's are taking on people at the end of the week. I can put in a word for you.'

'Oh, Jemima, could you? Thing is I can't earn anything just yet and I need money for my board. I can't go full time, though – would Logie's take me on?'

'I could ask. They're looking for staff to work on the Christmas catalogue stuff, packing hampers and such, and also in the Christmas shop. I'm sure there'll be a few part-time vacancies.' Jemima gave a confident smile. 'Leave it with me, anyway.'

'You're an angel!' Lindy squeezed Jemima's arm. 'I'd better run for my tram. Shall I see you tonight?'

'Fine, but wait a minute – have you heard about Miss Rosemary?'

'No, what? I haven't seen her lately.'

'She's leaving.' Jemima's smile had faded, leaving her looking as bleak as the wind rattling down Scott Street. 'Aye, she's found a flat in the West End. Put her notice in here already.'

'Oh, heavens, she'll be missed, eh? In spite of all that trouble over Neil.'

'I'll certainly miss her, that's for sure. Never thought she'd stay, of course.' Jemima smiled wryly. 'She was never going to want to keep on having baths in an old tin hip bath, was she?'

'That's my problem, too,' sighed Lindy, 'but I won't be leaving. Do we know who's coming in, then?'

'The landlord told Rosemary a middle-aged couple had taken it. Both work at the biscuit factory.'

'They'll have a nice wee flat, eh?'

'They won't be much like Rosemary,' said Jemima.

'Who would?' asked Lindy.

The brightness of the day continued at the class, where the girls worked really hard at perfecting their walks under Stella's supervision while Mrs Driver interviewed new clients. Later, though, they felt rather ridiculous when they were all made to progress around the room wearing books on their heads while Stella told them sternly, 'No laughing!'

'Honestly, we can't help it,' Kitty protested. 'What must we look like?'

'Like models of good posture!' Stella retorted. 'Posture, posture, posture – that's what's so important in a model. Makes her stand out in the crowd, gets her noticed. Can't you tell, all these years later, that Mrs Driver was once a model, just from the way she holds herself?'

'Can certainly tell with you, Stella,' Christine said honestly. 'Maybe we should just try to forget what we look like.'

'Forget what we look like!' cried Jennifer. 'Never! It's all that matters, yes?'

'I only meant what we looked like with books on our heads,' Christine answered. 'Of course I know our looks matter.'

'They're all we have to sell,' Kitty remarked. 'That's why we have so many photographs.'

'And interviews,' reminded Stella. 'Don't forget nobody looks past your face and figure at an interview. It's usually instant approval – or not.'

At the girls' expressions, she smiled. 'Don't worry. We're going to continue classes tomorrow with lessons on make-up and hair. Every model has to know how to do her own hair, and add hairpieces if necessary, but always have it looking just how the client wants.'

'Hope all that'll be easier than model-walking,' red-headed Rhona put in. 'Oh, my, nobody knows how hard that is, eh?'

'Make-up is certainly easier,' Stella told her, 'and I think you'll all enjoy yourselves learning how many different looks you can achieve just by adjusting your make-up and your hair. But, now, back to work, girls, and don't let me see any books falling to the floor!'

Hurrying up to see Jemima that evening, Lindy, after her 'good' day, felt happier and more confi-dent, even though, as so often, the thought of Rod Connor still hurt at the back of her mind. She had to work so hard to overcome that niggling pain, she wondered still if she would ever be free of it; certainly, Struan's account of meeting him had not helped. Maybe if there was good news from Jemima she'd forget that for a while.

There was good news – Jemima had managed

to arrange an interview for Lindy at Logie's on Friday afternoon, one that would probably be a walkover, she said. Before they could discuss it, however, Rosemary arrived and Lindy had to hear all about her new flat and how sorry she was to leave number nineteen, except that there were advantages to her new place and she hoped everyone would understand.

'Of course they'll understand!' Lindy exclaimed. 'Nobody expected you to stay so long.'

'It's been a terrific experience, being here, meeting everyone,' Rosemary said seriously. 'I'll never forget it.'

'For whatever reason,' Jemima commented dryly.

'Oh, don't think I didn't enjoy it, Jemima! Everyone's been so kind!'

'Of course you enjoyed it,' Jemima's mother put in. 'We know that, don't we, Jemima?'

'I'm just sorry you're going,' Jemima murmured, and Lindy agreed.

'You've been a breath of fresh air, Rosemary. It's been grand to know you.'

'So kind of you to say so.' Rosemary cast down her eyes. 'Especially when – well, I needn't say what happened. I still feel guilty.' She looked up. 'Do you ever see him, Lindy?'

'Neil? I haven't seen him for ages, but he still comes to visit his mother, I know that.'

'If you do see him –' Rosemary stopped. 'No, better not. Better not mention me, I think?'

There was a short silence, broken by Rosemary herself.

'Look, I'm sorry, I think I interrupted

something, didn't I? Weren't you telling Lindy about a job at Logie's, Jemima?'

'That's right, a temporary Christmas job – they're interviewing on Friday.'

'But I don't understand.' Rosemary's blue eyes on Lindy were perplexed. 'Why would you want another job, Lindy, when you'll soon be getting modelling work?'

'No' soon enough. I'm afraid I need some money now.'

'Oh.' Rosemary flushed. 'Stupid of me. I know you're not quite ready to work yet. But it won't be long. I mean, I've already had some work and it went so well – I really enjoyed it – and Mrs Driver has other clients in mind for me. It will be the same for you, Lindy.'

'Even if I do get some work, it will still be part time. And even with photographic work added in I'll need something more.' Lindy tried to smile. 'I'm no' complaining. I'm sure I'll enjoy whatever comes along.'

'Just a wee bit disappointed?' Jemima suggested.

'Because it's part time, no' full time? I suppose I am, but I'm just hoping I'll get plenty of work one day.'

'You will!' cried Rosemary. 'Anyone with your looks will have no trouble at all!'

Lindy smiled and shrugged. 'All the models I've met have my looks, Rosemary. You, too. That's the problem. How to be singled out for work when everyone's the same.'

'All beautiful?' Jemima glanced at her mother, who had got up to put on the kettle. 'Never had to worry about being beautiful myself.'

To cries from Rosemary, Lindy and her mother, all assuring her that she was very attractive, Jemima laughed and rose. 'OK, OK, I'm very attractive, but sit down, Ma, I'll put the kettle on.'

'I don't know why she's always running herself down,' Mrs Kerry whispered. 'Thinks she should have a young man, I suppose.'

'They were talking at the agency today about looks,' Lindy remarked. 'How important they are to models. Maybe too important, d'you think?'

'I'm afraid looks are important to everyone,' Rosemary replied. 'I've seen that all my life. From dancing school to debutantes' balls, if you weren't pretty you were a wallflower. There's not much anyone can do about it.'

'I never thought about it before,' Lindy said thoughtfully. 'But maybe it is wrong to think too much about looks.'

'Heavens!' laughed Rosemary. 'If you're going to think on those lines, Lindy, you're in the wrong profession!'

'What's so funny?' asked Jemima, returning with a tray of tea and biscuits, but Lindy only asked for more information about her interview.

'Well, as soon as they heard you were a trainee model they knew you'd be a good candidate,' Jemima told her. 'So all you've got to do is look wonderful, which you always do, and turn up at three o'clock on Friday – all right?'

'Look wonderful for packing hampers?' asked Lindy, laughing. 'Well, I'll do my best. Wish me luck, everybody, on Friday!'

Their thoughts would be with her, they promised, but honestly, Jemima stressed, Lindy had no need to worry.

'You can never be sure of anything, Jemima,' was all Lindy replied.

'That's very true,' sighed Mrs Kerry, and the others fell silent.

# Forty-Five

Whether she'd expected it or not, luck was with Lindy at her interview for Christmas work at Logie's when the assistant manager offered her three days a week with wages of a pound. Wonderful! From that she could pay Myra for her board and have a bit for her own expenses, the only problem being that if she did manage to be selected for modelling work before she left Logie's the dates might clash.

'We must just hope for the best,' Mrs Driver told her. 'It's a problem all models face because they are, as you know, mainly part time, but we'll have to see how it goes. Certainly it's good to have another source of income. You've done the right thing, especially getting into Logie's – such a superior store.'

This was true, for, like Jenner's and Forsyth's, also in Princes Street, Logie's was famous for its excellent merchandise, selling the best in clothes, linens, china and glass, carpets, soft furnishings, even provisions in its high-class food hall. Of course, for Lindy, its added attraction was its fashion shows, which had first given Jemima the idea of model work for her and for Rosemary. She couldn't help hoping that if a show were arranged again soon she might get the chance to take part. All in all, things were looking up!

Although fully expecting that she would be spending her time packing hampers, she was pleased to be given work instead in the Christmas shop, where she would be selling cards, decorations, crackers, artificial trees and everything needed for a festive season for the privileged few. Just the place to upset Rod, was Lindy's thought when she arrived for her first day, but she put it to the back of her mind, along with all her other thoughts of Rod, preferring to hope that one day all children would be able to enjoy Christmas, rich or poor.

Not that Christmas was always celebrated in Scotland, anyway, with many families preferring to keep their festivities to Hogmanay when they saw in the New Year. Certainly Myra and most of the tenants at number nineteen did not provide Christmas cheer, there being no money to spare for it, but Lindy had always admired the lovely baubles she'd seen on shop Christmas trees, the tinsel and stars, as well as the balloons and paper lanterns that opened out in such a fascinating way. Finding herself surrounded by such things at Logie's she was in her element, and soon impressed the senior assistant running the shop with her keenness and interest.

'Your shop experience has been worthwhile, Miss Gillan,' Miss Burnett told her one morning. 'You've no trouble with the cash register and your way of dealing with customers is just what we like to see. Maybe you'd like to consider permanent retail work?'

'Well, I'm really hoping to succeed as a model,' Lindy answered, flushing with pleasure. 'But maybe if it doesn't work out, retail would be something for me.'

'Well, see how you go, my dear. It's a good rule always to keep your options open.'

Although she agreed, Lindy knew that she'd really meant what she'd said about modelling and, as her time at Mrs Driver's class drew to an end, found herself longing to make a start, to see how she managed when faced with the real catwalk and real audiences watching her, with work in front of the camera providing another test she was anxious to complete.

Everything, of course, depended on Mrs Driver – on when she would pronounce them ready for professional work and find them clients who might engage them. Girls from her other classes were already fulfilling engagements – Rosemary, for instance, now had a second job in Glasgow – and those who'd come after Lindy's group were still practising their walking. They were all at different stages – but when would it be their turn to work? asked Lindy, Jennifer, Kitty and the others. No one liked to question Mrs Driver.

The day came, however, halfway through December, when Mrs Driver announced that they were all now ready for professional work and she would be submitting their portfolios to various clients, including photographers.

'It's not the best of times for you,' she told

them, 'because all the Christmas shows and so on are organized already, but be prepared for work in the New Year. There are various things in the pipeline, I can tell you that.'

More time would have to pass, then, and though they were dying to begin work, what could they do? Having reconciled themselves to waiting to see what came up in the pipeline, three of them were thrown into instant excitement when, out of the blue, Mrs Driver told them to report to John Johnson's, a large department store on Edinburgh's North Bridge, for interview the following day. Not much notice, but Miss Revie, the head of Ladies' Fashion, was desperate to replace three models for the store's spring collection show in only two days' time. Apparently they'd all gone down with flu – could Mrs Driver, who'd already sent a couple of her girls to the show, send three more?

Of course she could! And the three she had selected were Jennifer, Kitty and Lindy. Though hard luck on those left, it was lucky for Lindy that she was not due to work at Logie's on the following day. Lucky, indeed, that she could try for her first real job. But that night, she hardly slept.

# Forty-Six

'My, you're in a state,' Myra remarked, observing Lindy hurrying to get herself ready to go to Johnson's early on the day of the show. 'Running around like a headless chicken, I'd say.'

'I'm just checking to make sure I have everything I need,' Lindy told her, putting aside Gingerboy who was, as usual when she was going out, trying to get under her feet. 'There's my bag with my hair stuff, my make-up, my flat shoes – I'm wearing my heels – no, I'll take my heels and wear the flats till I get there – now, what else?'

'Umbrella!' cried Myra. 'I'm just getting mine, seeing as I'm away now to open the shop.'

In her raincoat, her umbrella in her hand, she stood looking at Lindy, now in her own raincoat and pulling on a brimmed hat. 'Come a long way, haven't you?' she murmured. 'Since you used to work in the shop?'

'I don't know yet how far I've come,' Lindy answered, checking her appearance in the mirror by the door. 'I'll have to see if I pass this interview.'

'Seems to me you'd be just as well off at Logie's,' Myra remarked with a sniff. 'A nice place to work and no worry about being wanted by all these other folk, eh? A regular job is best, Lindy, take my word for it.'

'Maybe, but I've got to rush. See you tonight, eh?'

'Good luck, then. Hope all goes well.'

'Oh, thanks, Aunt Myra!' Lindy cried, giving her stepmother a hug before finally flying out of number nineteen to catch her tram. As she climbed aboard, clutching her bag, her model bag, her shoe bag with her heels and her umbrella, it gave her a nice feeling to think that Aunt Myra had wished her luck. How much was she going to need it?

* * *

229

Johnson's, though not as grand as the Princes Street department stores, was still extremely popular, offering a wide range of quality goods, including fashion. Every year it gave two shows – one for autumn clothes directly after its summer sales, and one in December for spring styles, when an entrance fee was charged, proceeds going to a Christmas charity. Both of these were very important to Mrs Driver, who always managed to get some of her models included, and had already told Lindy's group that she would be suggesting them for the autumn show. The three, who now had the chance to appear earlier than that, might have been congratulating themselves when they met together at the entrance to the store – if they hadn't been so nervous.

'Oh, I'm so worried,' sighed Jennifer. 'This is the big test, eh? I mean, our first one?'

'I wouldn't feel so bad if I didn't have a spot coming out on my chin,' groaned Kitty. 'It feels like a football. I can't think of anything else.'

'I can only think of my butterflies,' said Lindy, feeling loaded down with her different bags, her raincoat and her umbrella. 'And I know I look like a drowned rat, but come on, we'd better find this Miss Revie.'

'You go first, then,' said Jennifer. 'You're the strong one, Lindsay.'

'Me?' Lindy pushed open the store's revolving door. 'What a laugh!'

Miss Revie, they were informed, was waiting for them in the dress department, the scene of the fashion show to come, but the first thing they saw on entering was a catwalk set to one side, out of the way of the few customers looking round.

'Yes, it's all ready for you!' cried a tall, thin woman approaching them, with suspiciously bright red hair. She wore a black dress and an emerald jacket, both beautifully cut, black patent shoes with straps and buttons, and dangling earrings that caught the light. 'You're from Mrs Driver's? Thank God for that. I'm Beatrice Revie, head of department for Ladies' Fashions. Now who is who here?'

As they introduced themselves, her eyes, dark as Mrs Driver's, took in their looks, from faces trying to show confidence to shoes that were damp, and even the bags, umbrella and coats they were clutching in their damp arms.

Then she smiled. 'So far so good, ladies. I can tell you're the right height for me and have the right looks. But you're all new to modelling, Mrs Driver tells me, and if you don't mind, I'm going to ask you all to walk for me on my temporary catwalk. Like to come this way, so that you can leave your things?'

Leading them into a narrow room off the dress department, she informed them that this was where the models would be changing on the day of the show. As they could see, it was lined with rails of the clothes they would be wearing – suits, coats, day dresses, evening dresses, tea gowns, nightwear, as well as the fashionable pyjamas for leisurewear, together with hats and accessories.

'Of course, it won't be like this on the day,' she said, laughing. 'More like a football match. But everyone will know what they're wearing and when they should be appearing – that I can promise you. Now, hang up your coats, comb your hair and I'll take the first one to the catwalk. Miss Yarman, I think that will be you. Miss Gillan, Miss Abbot – would you wait here?'

'I'm going first?' asked Kitty, opening her eyes wide. 'That's a change. I'm usually last.'

'I always like to do things differently,' said Miss Revie.

I'll be in the middle again, thought Lindy. Just as long as I get through it.

'You know there are customers out there, watching,' Jennifer whispered. 'I shan't like that.'

'If you get selected for the show there'll be more people watching you than the folk out there,' Lindy answered, her eyes straying to the racks of waiting clothes she would have loved to examine.

'Somehow that's different,' said Jennifer.

Only a short time later Kitty was back, smiling, and Miss Revie was calling, 'Miss Gillan!'

So Miss Revie doesn't do things that differently, thought Lindy, in the middle again, as she had thought. Not that she minded, though she couldn't help wanting to get this key test over with as soon as possible.

Yet, when she was out there, poised on the temporary catwalk in the dress department, watched by only a couple of interested customers and Miss Revie at the side, her nerves suddenly left her. It was as though all that she had learned had come together for this moment, giving her the confidence she'd always sought to present herself in the best possible way as she began gliding down the walkway, her head held high, her shoulders forward, her hips swinging. And she was remembering to smile – maybe at the two anonymous watchers – as she approached her corner and paused, turned, paused again and, with a final smile, made her return to where Miss Revie was waiting.

'Very good!' cried Miss Revie. 'Why, if I didn't know how nervous you were I'd say you enjoyed that, Miss Gillan!'

'Think I did,' said Lindy, wondering – had she really been that girl out there? Wearing her ordinary blue dress, her hair still damp, her make-up not repaired? She longed to ask if she'd passed the test, but Miss Revie was already bringing on the lovely Jennifer, who was finding the courage to smile, and all Lindy could do was return to the models' room.

'Think we've done all right?' Kitty whispered as Lindy went across to the clothes rail and began studying the selections, examining flared skirts, wide collars, cuff buttons, little jackets, silk pyjamas – everything that was in vogue for 1936.

She shook her head. 'Who knows? I just want to have a crack at wearing these outfits.'

And it seemed she was to get her wish, for when Miss Revie returned with Jennifer, it was to tell all three of them that she was pleased with their performance and that she would be happy to see them at the show two days later.

'I want everyone here from nine a.m. onwards,' she announced, 'for the show starts at eleven, as soon as coffee is served, and you'll need to be

233

trying things on, getting ready and so on. Any questions?'

'Yes,' answered Kitty. 'How do we know what we're wearing?'

'All taken care of. I have my own methods.' Miss Revie walked them across to the rails. 'Each model has her own selection, beginning with coats through to leisurewear, and they are hung here in order of appearance. There'll be a list up when you come. That clear?'

'Very clear. Thanks, Miss Revie.'

'Thank you for coming then, and filling the gaps for me. Good luck, ladies, and I'll see you at the show.'

In a flash of time it was all over and they were back outside in the rain again, coats on, hats over their hair, umbrellas up, but in such a state of euphoria none of it mattered.

'Let's have lunch,' suggested Kitty. 'There are plenty of cafés round here.'

'Yes, let's celebrate!' cried Jennifer. 'Girls, do you realize, we've landed our first jobs!'

'I feel so happy I shouldn't mention that we still have the show to do,' said Lindy, laughing.

'Except that you already have mentioned it,' Jennifer told her. 'But compared with Miss Revie's interview I think it'll be a doddle.'

'A walkover,' said Kitty. 'On the catwalk.'

'Oh,' they groaned, but then ran through the rain to find a café for their celebration meal – egg salads, pots of tea and sinful sticky buns. Perfect!

# Forty-Seven

Surprisingly, perhaps, the girls were right about the fashion show itself, for if they didn't dare to call it a 'doddle' on the actual day, all went so well for them they counted themselves lucky, especially as Mrs Driver had been spotted in the audience.

To begin with, of course, they'd had to face the expected chaos in the dressing room, where there were models everywhere: some dressed, some not, some fully made-up, others not, all milling around, talking and laughing, paying no attention to the newcomers. When they'd finally found a corner to do their hair and make-up, they were intrigued to hear on all sides that there was going to be trouble as the bride had not turned up.

'What bride?' asked Lindy.

'Why, the girl who models the wedding dress,' someone close by explained. 'They always show a bridal group here, to finish the show.'

'And the model's no' come?'

'Not yet, and Mrs Revie's furious. Look at her – like a thundercloud! Of course we all want to know who'll have to take her place. Someone blonde like you, dear.' The girl – a statuesque blonde herself – looked at Jennifer. 'You'd be just right.'

But another voice was calling from the door, 'She's here! She's here!'

And in strolled Rosemary, in a coat with a fur collar and matching fur hat, seeming quite at ease as she smiled all round and moved towards Miss Revie.

'Am I late? So sorry. I took a taxi but the traffic was terrible, we were stuck so long in a jam I thought I'd never get here!'

'So did I,' Miss Revie said grimly. 'Won't do, Miss Dalrymple. Kindly remember, for future reference, that trams don't get stuck in traffic jams. I was just about to ask someone else to be the bride.'

'Oh, dear, I really am sorry, Miss Revie, I didn't think about the traffic.' Rosemary's expression was suitably contrite. 'But I'm here now!'

'Yes, well, you'd better check on your earlier outfits; we're nearly ready to start.'

'Why did you no' tell me you were coming here today?' Lindy asked Rosemary quickly. 'I thought there were only three of us coming from Mrs Driver's.'

'Just from your group. Two of her other models were already booked for this – I'm one.' Rosemary was drifting away to find her outfits. 'I'm sorry I haven't seen you, Lindy, but I've been packing. I'm leaving tomorrow.'

The well-dressed audience assembled, the coffee cups cleared away, it was time for the show to begin. Everybody was in position: the head fashion buyer, who was to give the commentary, the manageress and senior staff of the store, Mrs Driver in the front row. Out of sight, waiting to go on, Miss Revie's watchful eye upon them,

236

were the models, each one wearing a long, straight coat of the season, with a small hat worn to one side and their own high-heeled shoes.

'Oh, Lord, I wish I was on first,' Kitty whispered, but it was the statuesque blonde who sashayed down the runway after the head buyer had welcomed everyone and somebody had put some music on a record player.

'I'm more nervous about Mrs Driver being out there than anything else,' whispered Jennifer, 'though I don't feel too bad, really.'

'Not after being watched by Miss Revie,' Lindy agreed, and was grateful that she'd had that experience, so that when it came to her turn to walk down the catwalk, wearing a grey coat with square shoulders and wide lapels, she was ready almost to enjoy herself and knew that she was acquitting herself well.

As the show continued it became clear that Miss Revie's organization was immensely efficient and of the greatest help to everyone. Though the backroom might appear chaotic, no one had trouble knowing what to wear and when, just as Miss Revie had promised, and to Lindy and the other beginners this was especially helpful to their confidence. As they worked their way through their lists of outfits – the smart little suits with short jackets and long skirts, the floating tea gowns, the pleated day dresses with pretty necklines, the silk pyjamas for leisure, the two-pieces for golf – things seemed only to get better, and at the end of the show they could relax and enjoy the bridal finale along with everyone else.

And how lovely Rosemary looked as the bride,

moving so slowly down the catwalk in her slim-fitting ivory satin gown, her blonde hair veiled, her eyes cast down! Surely, thought Lindy, she should be playing the part in real life very soon, for tomorrow she would no doubt be returning to her old life, surrounded by admirers all willing, probably, to pop a diamond ring on her finger. Oh, poor Neil, how could he ever have competed? Suddenly Lindy felt a longing to see him again, her old friend, and tears pricked her eyes as she joined in applause at the end of the show, thinking of how he'd suffered.

The little rush of sadness quickly faded as she found herself caught up in end-of-show euphoria, with the models gladly getting back into their own clothes, all chattering again as Miss Revie went about crying, 'Well done, well done, girls,' and Mrs Driver congratulated her models, especially Lindy, Kitty and Jennifer.

'A very successful debut,' she told them. 'But don't expect all shows to be as well organized as this. Miss Revie here is a byword in the Scottish fashion world for efficiency – very few are like her. But write this up in your portfolios, girls: your first success.'

'Well deserved,' Miss Revie added warmly. 'I won't forget you. Or you, Miss Dalrymple,' she added warningly as Rosemary came to say goodbye and had the grace to blush. But Lindy knew that she would always get work, not just for the way she looked but for her manner and style, both so expensive to acquire there were few who could offer the same.

'What time are you leaving tomorrow?' she

asked as she stood with Rosemary outside the store, Jennifer and Kitty having already set off on their separate ways home. 'I'd like to say goodbye.'

'Oh, probably not till late afternoon. But don't think of saying goodbye, Lindy! You must come and see me in my new flat.' Rosemary was already waving for a taxi. 'Look, I'll take this – I'm doing some last-minute shopping in Morningside – may I give you a lift?'

'No, thanks, it's out of your way. If I can, I'll see you tomorrow. I'm away now for my tram.'

A routine journey home, but her mind was still so full of her first show that when she finally caught the tram she scarcely noticed the other passengers around her. Until someone spoke her name. 'Lindy?' she heard. 'Lindy, don't you know me?'

'Of course I know you!' she whispered. 'Hello, Neil.'

# Forty-Eight

He didn't look too bad. Better than when she'd last seen him, anyway, though his face was more gaunt than she remembered and very slightly older. Was that possible? He was her contemporary – they weren't ready yet to change. Still, she was relieved to see that his eyes had lost the dead look that had upset her before, and now were bright on her face as he slid along the slatted seat in the tram to make room for her.

'I can't believe it's you,' he murmured. 'What are you doing over at this end of town, then?'

'Why, I might ask you the same thing!'

'I live round here,' he answered calmly. 'Today's my half day. I'm going to see Ma.'

'You have a flat round here? I never knew where you lived.'

'I have a room,' he corrected. 'With use of a bath. But you still haven't told me why you're in these parts? Have you got a new job?'

'Two new jobs. I'm working part time at Logie's, just for Christmas. But today . . .' She hesitated a moment. 'I've been to a fashion show at Johnson's. I'm – well, I'm a mannequin. Or a model, we like to say.'

'A model?' Neil whistled. 'So that's why you look different.'

'I look different?'

'I suppose it's the make-up. You never used to use quite so much.'

'Oh.' She put her hand to her cheek. 'I haven't taken it off yet, that's all. We need to wear it for the show, you know. I hope I don't look too different.'

'Don't worry – you're as beautiful as ever.' He shook his head. 'And it's good that you've got what you wanted, eh? You've spread you wings.'

She smiled. 'I'm no' sure yet. It was my first show today. I've had to do some training and I think I did well, but it's early days.'

'And what's happened to your shop work with your stepmother? Why've you gone to Logie's?'

'The owner wouldn't let me do part time so I

got this temporary job, selling in their Christmas shop. Cards and decorations.'

'I might come in and see you there. Buy a card for Ma.'

They were silent for a moment as the tram travelled noisily on its way, each gazing earnestly at the other's face until Lindy finally spoke. 'Neil, mind if I ask – are you – you know – all right now?'

'You mean, over her?'

As though a shutter had been rolled down, his expression became quite blank. 'Hard to say,' he said quietly. 'Partly, I suppose.'

'You don't want to talk about it?'

He shrugged. 'Why not? I'm better than I was, and I'm hoping to be better still. I can already say her name, for instance.'

'That's good, Neil.'

'So, what's *Miss* Rosemary doing now, then? She still at number nineteen?'

'She's moving out tomorrow.'

He was silent again and Lindy guessed he was remembering the day when Rosemary had first arrived and he had carried in her luggage. A disastrous day for him, had he only known; one that had brought him a happiness that was false and a pain that was real.

I wish I hadn't said anything, thought Lindy. I should never have asked how he was. Yet she had been so glad to see him again she knew she could have done little else. He had been her friend; she had to know how things were for him.

Suddenly he seemed to be making an effort to

move away from whatever dark thoughts still occupied his mind, and half smiled.

'How about you?' he asked. 'You still got that young man of yours?'

It was her turn to remember pain. 'No,' she said shortly. 'That's all over.'

'Oh? Why? He seemed a good chap.'

'He is – he's perfect. Just doesn't approve of me doing what I want to do. Thinks modelling is all wrong, selling your looks to make rich women buy clothes. I told him that was nonsense.'

'Is it?'

'Of course! Models are just ordinary girls, they're doing nothing wrong, and the women aren't all rich who like new clothes. I tried to make him see that, but he wouldn't listen, so we parted.'

'I think that's a shame. You should have tried to meet in the middle somehow.'

'Easy to say.' Lindy rose and clung to a hanging strap while trying to clutch her bags and umbrella. 'But here's our stop, Neil.'

'All too soon, Lindy. Let me carry the bags for you, eh?'

When they left the tram he looked down at her with a softness in his eyes that reminded her of the old days. This was the way they had been, she and Neil – good friends comfortable together, and it made her relieved to see him so much like his old self.

'How about your writing?' she asked as they walked slowly together. 'That going well?'

'It's saved my life,' he said simply. 'I'm writing something that's really good, something I think will succeed. Better no' say any more.'

'Is it about poor folk, Neil? Struggle and that sort of thing?'

'No, it's no' about that at all. Look, I'd rather I didn't go into detail. Maybe you'll read it one day, then you'll understand.'

And because she was still so close to him, she understood already just what his book was about, but would never tell him. She would never say she'd guessed it was about what had happened to him over Rosemary but, as he'd said, maybe he'd let her read it one day.

'Here we are,' she said brightly. 'Home again.'

He stopped and let her take back her possessions. 'Lindy, now we've met again, could we – could we have a meal together, or something? Just for old time's sake?'

'That'd be grand. I'd like that, Neil.'

His face relaxed into smiles. 'How about tomorrow night? Shall we meet in town?'

'Better make it the day after tomorrow,' Lindy told him, not explaining that she wanted to say goodbye to Rosemary the next day. 'You could come up to the Christmas shop to meet me if you like, say, before we close – half past five?'

'Lindy, I'll be there!'

Back at home there was no one to welcome her, except Gingerboy, who graciously left his sleep to see if she would put something into his bowl, for everyone was of course at work, which was just as well. Setting down her burdens, stretching and yawning, she didn't really want to talk to the family yet – there was too much to say.

'What a day, Gingerboy,' she murmured,

pouring him some milk. 'I don't know if I'm on my head or my heels. Fancy meeting Neil again, eh?'

As Gingerboy, of course, made no reply, she filled the kettle and set out a few things for a late lunch, thinking how pleased she'd been to be with Neil again. It would be lovely to have a meal and talk with him, even if he wasn't Rod and didn't aim to be.

But why was she bringing Rod into it? she asked herself. 'Meet in the middle' Neil had said she and Rod should have done. How could they have done that? There was no middle way for them. And as she made tea and ate a little bread and cheese, some, not quite all, of her new satisfaction faded.

# Forty-Nine

At teatime no one took much interest in Lindy's first fashion show; Miss Rosemary's departure, though – that was something different.

'So she leaves tomorrow?' Myra murmured. 'Well, I'll have to say, I'm sorry. She's always been one to look out for – see what she's wearing and that. And so nice if she meets you, eh? Never minds stopping to ask how you are, no' like some.'

'Aye, a very pleasant young lady,' George agreed. 'There'll be no one like her in this house again.'

'Just as well,' Struan snorted, helping himself to more apple tart. 'She's caused enough trouble while she's been here. Haven't forgotten Neil, have you?'

'Och, I've no time for Neil,' Myra snapped. 'I used to have, but no' any more. He's no use to anyone, him and his writing, eh? How he's kept his job as a printer I'll never know.'

'I think you're being a bit hard on him, Aunt Myra,' Lindy fired up. 'He's very talented and he's going to do well. It wasn't his fault he fell for Rosemary, and he's trying to get over her.'

'Oh? And how do you know what he's going to do?' Myra demanded.

'I met him on the tram. In fact, we're going out for something to eat the day after tomorrow. Just as friends, the way we used to be.'

'Well, now you tell us! Were you going to tell us at all, I wonder?'

'I think it's grand,' said George. 'I always liked Neil. I'm sorry he left us.'

'You're no' the only one going out the day after tomorrow,' Struan said, finishing his apple tart. 'I've got a date, too.'

'With the lads as usual?' asked Myra. 'I don't call that a date.'

'No' with the lads,' Struan said, smiling broadly. 'With Jemima.'

There was a stunned silence. Myra exchanged looks with George, while Lindy stared at her brother.

'Are you joking?' she asked. 'Why would Jemima want to go out with you?'

'Why shouldn't she? I met her in the hall and

we got chatting, and I thought, Jemima's an attractive lassie, why've I never noticed before?'

'Lassie!' Myra exclaimed, finding her voice. 'She's no lassie! Why, she's years older than you, Struan.'

'Two years older than me. What's that? I tell you, she's very attractive, dresses well, and is clever and all. Anyway, I asked her if she'd like to go to the pictures and she said she would. That's the end o' that.'

'Beginning, more like,' said Myra. 'Once you ask someone out they know it means something, eh? I thought you'd have more sense!'

'I think he's showing sense,' George declared, leaving the table to take out his pipe and sit by the range. 'Jemima's a grand girl and you'd be complaining if he was taking out some little miss that'd never fit in, Myra. Good luck to Struan, I say.'

'Look, we're only going to the pictures,' Struan protested. 'Hardly getting engaged.' He leaped to his feet. 'Think I might as well see the lads tonight, anyway. 'Bye all.'

'And I might as well wash up,' said Lindy into the silence, and as she cleared away was thinking full marks to Struan for taking the limelight away from her own concerns. While Myra was fussing over his going out with Jemima, she'd have no time to think about Lindy and Neil. But what, oh what, was Jemima thinking of?

'Oh, I knew you'd be coming round,' Jemima said, flushing, as Lindy arrived at her door later that evening. 'I suppose Struan's told you, has he?'

'Aye, at tea time.' Lindy's eyes were seeking Jemima's without success. 'Honestly, I didn't believe it.'

'Better come in.' Jemima showed her in to the flat and offered her a seat. 'We can talk. Ma's out at a whist drive.'

'She doesn't know?'

'Oh, yes, but she's – well, she doesn't believe it either.' Jemima's colour was fading; she seemed willing now to let her hazel eyes meet Lindy's, their expression truculent. 'Why does everyone think it's so impossible that I should go out with Struan? Ma says he's just a boy, but he's only two years younger than I am!'

'I know, but some men seem to take a long time to grow up.'

'Well, maybe if he wants to go out with me it's a sign he wants to grow up now,' snapped Jemima.

'Maybe,' Lindy agreed, privately thinking that he might just have thought Jemima would be the ideal person to spoil him. 'But listen, Jemima, you're very attractive—'

'Oh, don't start that again, Lindy! I know how attractive I am.'

'Well, then, you'll know you can meet someone who's right for you, someone who can take care of you, no' the other way round.'

'I can take care of myself. I don't need a man to make decisions, and that sort of thing.'

'I know, I know, but—'

'All I'm doing is going out with Struan to see a Marx Brothers film and have a good laugh. That's all there is to it.'

'OK, if you're happy about it—'

'I am!' Jemima's tone was fierce, but then she put her hand on Lindy's arm. 'Sorry to be so snappy. I'm just a wee bit depressed, you ken, with Miss Rosemary leaving and everything. I need something to cheer me up.'

''Course you do. She's going to be hugely missed. Made a lovely bride at the show today.'

'Oh, and I never asked you how it went! Oh, Lindy, I'm sorry – how could I have forgotten?'

'It went well. I wasn't nervous at all.'

'Well done, well done! Listen, let's have a cup of tea, eh? Miss Rosemary gave me some Earl Grey – she's clearing out her cupboards, of course. I'll put the kettle on.'

'My favourite words.'

When they were trying the Earl Grey tea – 'smoky' was their verdict – Lindy told Jemima of her meeting with Neil, and that he was doing fairly well.

'In fact,' she finished, 'we're going out together for a meal, the night after tomorrow. When you'll be watching the Marx Brothers.'

Jemima laughed, then said seriously, 'I'm glad you're seeing Neil again, even if he isn't Rod. It will do you both good, in my opinion.'

'Why mention Rod, Jemima?'

'Well, I'm just so sorry that it all went wrong for you. There must be some way you could get back together again.'

'I don't think so. Anyway, I'm going out with Neil again. That's good enough for me.'

'Is it?' Jemima asked sadly.

248

# Fifty

Two days later Lindy, at her counter in the Christmas shop at Logie's, was thinking of Rosemary's farewell the previous evening. Strange, the way it seemed to have had such an effect on the tenants who'd come down to the hall to say goodbye. It was as though this young woman, elegant in her fur-trimmed coat and matching hat, had taken away something special from those left at number nineteen. Some spark, some touch of magic that they would not see again. Left them facing their own hard lives without the interest they'd been able to take in hers – maybe that was the point?

Of course she'd had her critics, especially over Neil's personal misery, but she was so different, she gave such an insight into a world they could never know, it was certain they were going to miss her, even if they wouldn't admit it.

'Och, she should never have been here in the first place,' one of Neil's brothers still muttered to Lindy as Rosemary posed at the front door to give her last smiles and waves. 'Lassie like her – she never belonged, eh?'

'That was what we liked, I suppose,' said Lindy. 'We liked her to be different, eh?'

'All I know is that number nineteen won't be the same without her,' Jemima said glumly.

Mrs Kerry agreed, adding: 'She's a lovely lady,

right enough, but we always knew she'd never stay.'

And that had been poor Neil's mistake, thought Lindy. He'd believed she would.

'You've all been so kind,' Rosemary was calling. 'I'm going to miss you all so much. But Jemima has my address and if you're ever in the West End – do look me up! I mean it – do!'

As though they would! When would they ever be going calling in the West End! Still, it was nice of her to say.

'Ready, miss?' asked the taxi driver, who'd been waiting patiently for some time.

'Just coming,' said Rosemary and, turning to Jemima and Lindy, hugged them both hard. 'Oh, dear, I feel rather weepy! Better go, I think.'

And with a last wave she climbed into the taxi.

'Goodbye, goodbye!' the watchers called as the taxi driver closed the passenger door, took his own seat and drove away, soon to be swallowed up in the traffic of Scott Street.

That was that, then – she'd gone. The tenants turned to climb the stairs, not saying much, while Jemima lingered for a moment to speak to Lindy. 'I offered to go with Miss Rosemary, you know, to help her settle in, but she said there was no need. So I just helped her tidy up here.'

'All ready for the new folk, then.'

'Oh, don't remind me. But here comes your stepmother, Lindy.'

'Have I missed the grand farewell?' asked Myra, bustling in. 'I couldn't get away any earlier.'

'Aye, Miss Rosemary's gone,' Jemima told her, at which Myra smiled coldly.

'You'll be missing her, eh? But then you'll have Struan to think about instead.'

'We are only going to the pictures,' Jemima said shortly. 'Nothing important.'

'You never know.' Myra laughed, tossing her head. 'Well, I must get on. Lindy, you'll give me a hand?'

'Don't I always?' asked Lindy.

Now in Logie's, quieter as closing time drew near, Lindy's thoughts turned to Neil. Of course, it hadn't been true what she'd said to Jemima – that going out with him was enough for her, but she was looking forward to being with him again, to see him approach his old self, maybe, and to help him with that. Rosemary had gone and would not come back, leaving him to build his own life again, which he was doing with his writing. It would be strange, wouldn't it, if he really did have success with his novel?

She had turned aside for a moment, deciding she should stop thinking about Neil and begin tidying the counter before closing time, when someone behind her asked, 'Where are the Christmas cards, please?'

And her heart leaped.

Slowly she looked around and met the eyes of the man who had spoken. She knew his voice. She knew his eyes. Yet still couldn't take it in. This was Rod standing in front of her, not Neil. Rod, asking for Christmas cards and staring as though he'd seen a ghost. She knew her look on him must seem the same.

'Lindy?' he was stammering. 'Lindy – what are you doing here?'

Only after a long pause could she gather herself together enough to say, 'Rod, I work here.'

'I don't understand –'

Coming round the counter, she could no longer meet his eyes. 'You wanted to see the cards? They're just over here. I'll show you.'

'Thank you.'

And he followed her to the Christmas cards.


# Fifty-One

There were still cards left, though the racks in the corner where a few people were browsing were no longer full.

'You've left it a bit late,' Lindy said, making an immense effort to sound normal, as though she was talking to any other customer. Snatching a quick glance, she saw that Rod's eyes were fixed on her.

'Always do. Just want one or two.'

'There's still plenty of choice.'

'That's lucky.'

'I'll leave you to it, then.'

As she turned away he put out his hand as though he would touch her arm, then let it go. But she made no move. At last, their eyes met in a long, troubled gaze.

'How come?' he asked. 'How come you've left the grocery shop?'

'I needed some part-time work and I couldn't do it there.' As she knew what he would ask next, she answered the question. 'I found out that modelling isn't a full-time job.'

He lowered his eyes. 'You've begun, then? Last I heard you were taking classes.'

'I did my first show a few days ago.'

'I expect you did well.'

She made no reply, her heart beginning to beat heavily in her chest. It seemed to her that there was no point in talking any more, no point at all.

'I must go, people are waiting,' she said, still trying to speak normally, though to herself sounding a little wild, and hurried back to the counter where two customers were standing. At least, one was a customer. The other was Neil.

'No need to rush,' the customer, an elderly man, said kindly. 'Just want this artificial holly. No hurry.'

'That's all right, sir, I'll just find a bag.' Lindy's lips were dry, her eyes desperate as she looked at Neil.

'Am I too early?' he whispered, smiling.

She shook her head and finished serving the customer. 'We'll be closing soon.'

In fact, she could see Miss Burnett, who had been finding balloons for a customer, looking at her watch.

When would Rod come to the till with his Christmas cards? Did he know Neil? What would he think? What did it matter what he thought? Neil would be of no interest to him, as she herself

253

could be of no interest. She had told him about her first show – that meant she was serious, doing what she'd said she would. And why not? It was Rod who was in the wrong . . . Oh, but it didn't help to think that! Not at all.

'Please excuse me a minute,' she said to Neil. 'I just want to see –'

See what? That Rod was still choosing his cards, but that she didn't say.

'Back in a tick.'

Over in the corner, by the racks, two people were debating between pictures of robins on snow and holly with berries. No one else. No Rod. Surely he hadn't just gone? Hadn't bothered in the end with cards? Hadn't wanted to come to the counter? She'd said herself, there was no point in talking . . . But to go without even saying goodbye? A dull pain was consuming her as she returned slowly to the counter and Neil.

'All right?' he asked.

'He's gone.'

'Who? Who's gone?'

'Rod.'

Neil stared. 'Your fellow? I thought you said you'd finished with him?'

'He came in to buy cards. He didn't know I was here.' Her eyes fastened on Neil. 'He must have seen you.'

'What do you mean? I frightened him off? He doesn't know me – how could I have done that?'

'I don't know – but I think he must have guessed who you were. We were talking –'

'You want me to go?' Neil asked in a low voice. 'I've upset your fellow, so you want me to go?'

'No!' She put her hand on his arm, looking round to see if Miss Burnett was near, but she was still with her customer. 'No, I don't want you to go, Neil, it's nothing to do with you what Rod thinks, and he's no' my fellow anyway. It's true what I told you. He didn't even know I was here.'

'You're sure you want to go out with me tonight?'

'I'm sure. But will you wait for me at the main entrance? We'll be closing here any minute.'

'At the main entrance. You'll come?'

'Neil, I've said so.'

'OK, then.'

His shoulders drooping, he left her, looking back once before he reached the escalator and vanished from sight.

'Ladies and gentlemen, we're closing now,' she heard Miss Burnett call. 'Please come to the till if you have anything to purchase.'

Thank God, Lindy was thinking, soon she would be out of the shop and not having to put on a pretend face before customers. And she needn't worry about Neil. He would understand, anyway.

# Fifty-Two

In spite of avoiding any mention of Rosemary or Rod, they had a pleasant meal in a West End café, Neil chatting fairly easily about things in

255

general, Lindy telling him about her model training and how she'd had to walk about with a book on her head, which brought a smile to his face. Then there was the news about Struan and Jemima – had he heard about them?

'No, what about them?'

'Well, it's just that they're going to the pictures tonight – together. We're all so amazed.'

'Struan and Jemima?' Neil drank coffee. 'I reckon that is amazing. Isn't he a bit young for Jemima?'

'Everyone says that, but there's only two years between them. Thing is, he seems a lot younger because he's so immature. Well, I think so, anyway. Look how he used to tease you!'

'I remember.' Neil shrugged. 'Well, Jemima must've wanted to go out with him or she wouldn't have said she would. I agree, it's surprising, but you can never be sure what folk will do.' His face had darkened, his eyes losing their brightness. 'That's a lesson everybody needs to learn.'

After a pause, when Lindy could think of no reply, he said he'd ask for the bill. It was a rotten night out, cold and sleeting, and they'd better be on the move.

'You don't have to take me back, Neil,' Lindy told him. 'It's right out of your way. I'll just get the tram.'

'No, it's all right – I'm staying at Ma's tonight. We can go back together.'

'Do you think you might come back to number nineteen permanently?' she asked when they were shivering at the tram stop. 'It'd be nice if you would.'

'Aye, but I'm best off where I can write in peace. You'd never believe what a difference it makes to be on your own.'

'On your own . . . sounds sad, somehow.'

'No' for a writer. I can see folk when I want to, and that's different to having your brothers knocking about whenever you're trying to get on.'

'I suppose number nineteen isn't the quietest place anyhow.'

Neil laughed as their tram drew up and they climbed aboard. 'You can say that again, Lindy.'

They were almost home when she turned to him. 'That was lovely, Neil, thank you. But next time, no arguments – the meal's on me. No need for you to always pay. We often went Dutch in the old days.'

'Next time?' Neil took her hand. 'Maybe there won't be a next time.'

'What do you mean?' Her eyes searched his face in the gloomy light of the tram. 'You don't want us to meet again?'

'I do. You know I like to be with you. Though why you'd want to see me after the way I treated you, I've no idea.'

'Oh, come on, that's in the past. We can still meet as friends.'

He let go of her hand. 'It wouldn't be right for you. Things aren't the same as they used to be.'

She hesitated. 'I thought you'd come back.'

'I have. Or, I might have. But I could tell this evening, when you were looking for Rod, that nothing was over for you where he's concerned. I know you've got your new career and you want it, but you want him, too, eh? There's no place for me in your life, Lindy. Better get that straight.'

'No, Neil, no, you've forgotten something – oh, God, here's our stop – why do we try to talk on trams?'

'Forgotten what?' he asked, taking her arm on the slippery pavement as their tram rumbled unconcernedly away.

'I may still want Rod, but he doesn't want me. I'm different from what he thought – I have the wrong ideas, so he'll want to do without me. I think he's the one with the wrong ideas and won't be changing mine, but I'd have liked to find what you said – you know – a middle way.'

'There you are, then. Proves what I said.'

'We'll never find it, though. We're too far apart.' Lindy, her face spattered with drifting sleet, looked up at Neil. 'So, I can still see you, Neil. There's still a place for you in my life.'

They had reached the door of number nineteen and were stumbling in together, shaking off their wet coats.

'Are you listening, Neil?' she asked.

'Yes, but I think we should see how things go, eh? I'll be here at Christmas. Why don't you come on up to Ma's sometime, eh?'

'All right, if that's what you want.'

He kissed her on the cheek. 'It's what I want.'

'Wonder how Jemima enjoyed her evening out with Struan,' she murmured, trying to sound light-hearted as Neil began to move towards the stairs.

'I'm sure you'll find out,' he said with a grin. 'Goodnight, Lindy.'

'Goodnight, Neil. Thanks again.'

She watched him go, her old friend who thought it would no longer be right to see her because of Rod, something she couldn't believe. She and Rod – well, as she'd told Neil – could never be together. All she could do now was learn to do without him and look to her new life, her new career, to give her what she needed. If Neil understood that, maybe they could meet from time to time? Best to do what he said, though, and see how things go. Yes, that would be best. Quietly, she let herself into the flat.

# Fifty-Three

The following day was not one of Lindy's Logie's days, and she planned to use it putting up Christmas decorations Miss Burnett had let her have at a reduced price.

'Why not?' she asked Myra, showing her the collection of paper chains and lanterns, balloons and artificial holly. 'Why shouldn't we decorate at Christmas? Other folk do.'

'Some, you mean,' said Myra, preparing to leave for Murchie's. 'Most here haven't the money to spare. Lot o' fuss about nothing is my view.'

'You don't mind if I do?'

'Suit yourself, if it cheers you up. Look a bit like a wet weekend, if you don't mind me saying so.'

'Oh, thanks,' said Lindy. 'That makes me feel grand.'

When Myra had gone she worked steadily, dusting down and cleaning before putting the decorations in place, and by the time she'd finished it was time to see if any post had come.

Nothing. Oh, well, she hadn't expected anything, except maybe a card or two. There wouldn't be anything from Mrs Driver until after New Year, she'd said, and then it would probably be photographic work. Anything would be acceptable, thought Lindy, for all she'd had was one payment, of which quite a high percentage had had to go to Mrs Driver anyway, and the part-time money from Logie's didn't go very far. Furthermore, that would be coming to an end once the festive season was over, and then what?

Even the sight of the newly decorated flat and comforting cup of tea did nothing to lift Lindy's spirits as she looked into a doubtful future, so that when there came a knock on the flat door, she answered it in no great hopes. Perhaps that was the way to answer a door, to expect nothing, and then to be so wonderfully, amazingly surprised . . .

For it was Rod who had knocked; Rod who was standing waiting, Rod who was saying, 'Lindy, I had to see you. Oh, God, you don't know what it's been like!'

'You think?' she whispered, as he put out his arms and as in a dream, she went into them. For blissful moments they clung together in the hall, their eyes half closed, their mouths meeting, never parting – until Lindy released herself and drew Rod into the flat.

'You think I don't know what it was like?' she

asked as she closed the door and turned to him. 'I knew, all right. Oh, Rod, I knew!'

'But I was the one who was a fool. I was the one who started laying down the law, telling you what to do.' He shook his head as she made him walk with her into the living room, where they sank on to the old couch and sat entwined together, looking into each other's faces.

'What could you have thought of me?' he murmured, his hand smoothing her face. 'I've hated myself for weeks but I couldn't manage to tell you, and when I heard you'd started your modelling classes, I thought, well, that's the end, Lindy's going ahead with her career. She doesn't want me. I didn't know how I was going to face it.'

'And then you came into Logie's and saw me,' she said softly. 'Couldn't you tell then how I felt?'

'I thought I could, and then I saw this fellow at your counter and something told me – I don't know how – that he was Neil. You were both talking and I thought, so he's come back, he's over Rosemary and he wants Lindy, and I just – well, I saw the door at the other end of the department and I went through it. Couldn't face seeing you with him, you see.'

'Oh, Rod, you didn't give me a chance! That was Neil you saw, but I'd only just met him again and we said we'd meet, but he isn't truly over Rosemary and he's still only my friend. If only you'd said something yesterday!'

'How could I, when he was standing there with you? I just went back to the hostel and began doing some jobs, trying to keep my mind blank, but it was no good. I'd seen you again and all I wanted was to put back the clock, make you come back to me. Make us as we used to be.'

'And you came to find me. But how did you know I'd be here?'

'I didn't. I left Dougie in charge and I went to Logie's and asked for you. They wouldn't say where you were, but they said it was a day you didn't work there, so I took a chance and came to number nineteen.' He held her away from him, looking at her. 'And, thank God, here you were!'

'I was putting up some decorations. We've no' had any before. What do you think?'

'Snap, I've been decorating the hostel.' He looked around at her streamers and balloons, the holly placed over the pictures, and smiled. 'Very nice. So, can we enjoy Christmas now?'

'But tell me first – have you really changed your mind about modelling? Do you think it's no' so bad?'

He hesitated. 'I'll be honest, Lindy, I still think in principle it's – well – what I said before. But I was wrong to think the girls themselves are only interested in making money the wrong way. I know you're not like that – you don't see it that way, and I should have respected that from the beginning. Will you forgive me, because I didn't?'

'If you'll forgive me. Because I was so sure I was right, I never thought you might have a point. I was upset because you seemed to be disappointed in me, and I couldn't see why.' She shrugged. 'So I dug my heels in and wouldn't think of meeting halfway. That was what Neil said we should do.'

'Neil said?'

'Yes, he told me there must be some way we could stay together.' Lindy lowered her eyes. 'But I said – I said we were too far apart. I'm sorry, Rod.'

'Lindy, it was my fault you felt that.' He held her close then let her go. 'Listen, shall we really be as we were before? The only difference being that you have a different job?'

'You want me to keep it?'

'I do. You'll be good at it and you should have your chance with it.'

'Rod, it's grand you should say that.'

'The whole point of the new us is that I should say it.'

'The new us?'

'The tolerant, understanding us,' he said with a grin. 'And we'll agree never again to put ourselves through what we've just been through. Promise?'

'I promise.'

Their kisses then were long and serious, until Rod tore himself away and said he had to get back to the hostel. 'I've played truant long enough. But there's something else I want to say before I go – I'm on duty on Christmas Day, but I've got Boxing Day free. Would you come and have tea with my dad and me?'

'Tea with your dad?' she echoed. 'Oh, of course I will, Rod. I'd love to meet him.'

'I'll come for you then, about three o'clock? There'll be Christmas cake, because Dad's got an admirer who's baked him one, and some mince pies and scones – bought, I'm afraid . . .'

'As though I care what we eat,' she said fondly, walking with him from the flat to the outer front door. 'Rod, I couldn't be happier.'

'Me too,' he said quietly. 'See you on Boxing Day, then.'

'On Boxing Day.'

They embraced once more, then Rod went out to his car and Lindy watched and waved until he had driven away.

Alone in the flat, she felt strange, still feeling as though she'd been dreaming and the dream was still with her. Had Rod really come? Really put his views aside and asked her to forgive him? Yes, it had happened, but was it any wonder she was thinking it was too good to be true?

'Sometimes good things do happen, though,' she told Gingerboy, who'd come stalking in from her room. 'So you should never give up – that's the thing to remember.'

His yellow eyes only stared.

Later, when the family was back, she basked in their surprise and pleasure when she told them her news. Rod was back? And wanted to take Lindy to meet his father?

'That says it all,' declared Myra. 'I always knew he'd come back, anyway. He was that keen from the start.'

'And such a grand lad,' said George. 'I've always liked him.'

'Me, too,' added Struan. He looked around at the decorations. 'Don't blame you for putting the flags out, Lindy!'

'Never mind the streamers,' said Myra. 'How'd you get on with Jemima, then? You were late back; we'd all gone to bed.'

'We got on very well. She's a nice lassie, Jemima, and the Marx Brothers had us in stitches. Groucho – Harpo – och, the things they got up to! I never thought Jemima could laugh so much. Always seemed a bit serious, eh?'

'Seeing her again?' asked Lindy.

'Ah, that'd be telling.'

'Well, tell, then.'

'OK, yes, we're going out after Christmas. Might have a fish supper.'

Myra and George exchanged glances.

'Well, well,' Myra murmured. 'Both of 'em, eh?'

'What do you mean?' asked Lindy quickly.

'Just thinking o' you and Struan – both your dad's children – no' children any more.'

'You just found that out?' asked Struan. 'But Lindy, now you're back with Rod, do you think he'd let me drive his car again? I really missed that, you ken.'

# Fifty-Four

With her thoughts fixed firmly on Boxing Day, Christmas passed like another dream for Lindy, except when she saw Jemima and Neil, for they, of course, were important to her and had to share in her good news about Rod.

'I knew it would happen,' Neil told her, under the cover of the noise in his mother's flat on Christmas night when all the tenants of number nineteen, including the Websters – the new couple from Rosemary's flat – had squashed in for a sing song and leftover mince pies.

'I could tell from the way you were,' Neil went on. 'I mean, when you'd seen him and thought he hadn't stayed. He was the one, I thought, and you see I was right.'

'But I didn't know he'd come back then,' Lindy pointed out. 'You couldn't have known what would happen.'

'I'd a pretty good idea that you two would get back together somehow. One of you would have to give in.'

'I feel bad it was Rod, Neil. It should have been me.'

'No, it's good it was Rod. He was the one who caused the rift; he was the right one to mend it.'

'It will never happen again, we've promised,' she said quietly, and then felt a pang to be talking about her happiness and Rod's, while poor Neil . . . Och, he'd find happiness himself one day, sure he would! In the meantime, he had his book.

As for Jemima, Lindy thought she'd never seen her looking quite so much at ease. Why, even coming up to the MacLaurens' for a get-together would never have been her sort of thing, but here she was, enjoying herself, helping to hand round the mince pies and joining in the singing.

'Hear you had a good time with the Marx Brothers?' Lindy ventured during a lull. 'So Struan said.'

'Oh, I did, Lindy! I've never laughed so much and that's the truth.'

'And you're going out again?'

'Just for a bit of supper,' Jemima agreed cautiously. 'But don't go getting carried away for me, eh?'

Am I the one who's carried away? thought Lindy. But of course it was too soon to tell whether these outings meant anything or nothing. To change the subject she asked about Rosemary. How was she?

'Oh, I looked in to see her – she's got a lovely wee flat. She was just getting ready to spend Christmas with her mother.' Jemima gave a little smile. 'But I think she won't be going on her own.'

'Are you talking about a young man?'

'Definitely a young man. He's always been in the background – now he's stepped forward.'

'How about her modelling, though?'

'Ah, she'll keep on with that, I'm sure.'

Like me, thought Lindy. What would the New Year bring? Just for a little while she wondered what might be in the pipeline, but soon returned to thinking about Boxing Day and what she might wear to meet Rod's father over the Christmas cake made by 'his admirer'. It would have to be her same old blue woollen dress, she decided, but at least Mr Connor wouldn't have seen it before. Not that he'd care if he had, if he was like most men, but she did want to look her best for him. This meeting was important.

Boxing Day came at last, and Rod with it, collecting Lindy at three o'clock for the drive to

267

Leith. Aware of eyes at windows looking down, they didn't kiss, only let their eyes send the messages each wanted to see, and then were on their way.

'Had a nice day yesterday?' asked Rod.

'Oh, yes, though Dad and Struan were at work as usual. But we all went to a neighbour's in the evening and that was very nice. The new tenants were there.'

'Not like the famous Rosemary, I suppose?'

'More like the rest of us,' agreed Lindy, smiling. 'How about you? The hostel folk had a good time?'

'Certainly did. Dad came over for Christmas dinner, which I helped to cook, and all went well. No dust-ups. But I'm looking forward to today.'

'And I want to meet your dad.'

'You soon will. Here's the grand Port of Leith coming up now, busy as ever, Christmas or no Christmas. Work never stops at the docks, you know – that's where Dad's ship is now, being checked over.'

'Always seems strange to me that Leith's a part of Edinburgh now. I mean, it's so different, eh?'

'A lot of Leithers would agree. They like to think of themselves as independent still, but it's too late to think of that now. There are compensations, anyway, being part of a great city.'

'You don't live near the docks?' Lindy asked, looking around her as they turned from Leith Walk to enter streets new to her.

'No, by the Links. Know the Links? It's a huge open space, full of history – battles with the

268

English and all that sort of thing. Now it's more like a park – very popular. Our house is one of a terrace quite close by.'

'You have the whole house?'

'Why, yes. Dad bought it on a mortgage when he first got married.'

'Oh,' said Lindy, wondering how you got a mortgage. 'So he's no' a tenant? He owns the house?'

'He does now. Did well, in fact, because there was no money in the family. I think I told you, my grandfather was a fisherman, never had much, but Dad had a good technical brain; he earned enough to get a property.'

'And it sounds nice – near the park.'

'Spent half my childhood there,' Rod told her. 'Would still play cricket if I had the chance. Golf as well, maybe. Did you know that golf was said to be invented on the Links? There's fame for you.'

Seemingly, thanks to his dad, Rod's life had been different from that of anyone else Lindy knew. Except for Rosemary, of course, but then Rosemary was just a ship who'd passed in the night. Hadn't Lindy once thought that of Rod? Clasping her hands together with sudden nerves, Lindy thanked her lucky stars that that had turned out not to be true.

'Well, this it!' cried Rod, turning into a terrace of solid, stone-built houses and drawing up at one of them. 'Here's my home, Lindy.'

Stepping from the car, Lindy's eyes went over the three-storey house, taking in the oak front door with polished letter box, the sash windows, all with net curtains, the small strip of front garden with evergreen shrubs. She turned to Rod.

'The whole house?' she repeated.

He nodded. 'It's just a terraced house – see 'em all over Edinburgh.'

'But half the time there's no one here.'

'It's the way things have worked out. Dad's away and my job's partly live-in. I get home when I can. But come on in, he'll be waiting for us and it's getting dark already. Hello, Dad!' he called as they entered the house. 'We're here!'

And into the neat, polished hallway, came another, older Rod, smiling as he put out his hand. 'Hello, Miss Gillan!' he cried, in a deep, pleasant voice, more of a Leither's voice than Rod's. 'Or can it be Lindy?'

'Oh, please, call me Lindy,' she answered quickly, and once they'd shaken hands he took her arm. 'Come away in, then, by the fire.'

# Fifty-Five

The sitting room, or parlour, into which Rod's father showed Lindy, was instantly charming. Long, dark red curtains at the bay window had already shut out the darkening afternoon, while table lamps and a bright open fire gave mellow light. There were watercolours of ships around the walls, the frames decorated with berried holly; photographs on a small desk, one of a sweet-faced woman Lindy guessed to be Rod's mother; two easy chairs and a sofa before the fireplace, and a round table already laid for tea with a white cloth and pretty china.

Admiring all of this, it was only when Mr Connor had taken one of the armchairs and waved her to the sofa that she saw he wasn't quite as much like Rod as she'd thought. True, he was the same height and still had chestnut-brown hair only slightly touched with grey, but his eyes were blue, not brown, and his features were heavier – not quite so handsome. Still, he had Rod's friendly smile and easy manner, which were what counted.

'You must call me Lindy,' she said as Rod took away her coat and hat. 'Only people at work call me Miss Gillan.'

His brilliant blue eyes – sailor's eyes, she supposed – were fixed on her face that was a little flushed by the heat of the room and her own excitement.

'And at present you're working at Logie's?' he asked.

'Just for Christmas, but I might get something else after Hogmanay.'

'I've told Dad about your modelling,' Rod said quietly. 'Was quite impressed, weren't you, Dad?'

'Sure I was! I know nothing about it, but I'm sure to get into that line of work is quite a feat. The main thing is to enjoy it. If it's what you want to do, you'll do well.'

Rod opened his mouth as though to speak, but in the end said nothing, while his father, after studying him for a moment, turned back to Lindy. 'I expect you've heard that I'd have liked Rod to follow in my footsteps, but it's his decision what he does and I'm glad he's found his niche. No, I mean it, Rod. We can't all be the same.'

'He does wonderful work, Mr Connor,' Lindy put in earnestly, at which Rod rose and said he'd put the kettle on.

'Spare my undeserved blushes, I think. And no, Lindy, I don't want you to help me. This is your time off.'

'Rod does do good work,' she insisted when he'd gone. 'I really admire him.'

'Oh, so do I.' Mr Connor rose to make up the fire, then sat down, looking at Lindy again. 'Am I right in thinking your father's with Bayne's Brewery, Lindy? Tell him their bitter's my favourite tipple. Not that I drink much, but I like Bayne's when I do.'

'I'll tell him, Mr Connor. My brother, Struan, works there too.' She paused. 'At least, they do for now. Never know for how long.'

'People will always want their beer. I think Bayne's will weather the storm. But are there just the two of you, yourself and your brother?'

'Yes, just the two of us. Our mother died when I was born.'

'I'm sorry.' Mr Connor's eyes went to the photograph of the sweet-faced woman and he gave a heavy sigh. 'Rod lost his mother too, as you probably know, but he was twelve. That's her picture there – my Mildred. We still miss her, Rod and me.'

'I'm sure,' whispered Lindy. 'I have a step-mother. She's very kind, but it's no' the same.'

'No, couldn't be. I'll never marry again.'

'Here we are!' cried Rod into the silence that had fallen between his father and Lindy. 'Here's the trolley, all loaded by my own fair hands. Want to move to the tea table, folks?'

# Fifty-Six

Lindy, taking her seat and accepting a toasted teacake, couldn't resist thinking, as she looked at the iced Christmas cake made, Rod had said, by his father's admirer, that the lady in question would not have much hope of being anything more. Perhaps she didn't want that, anyway, and such appeared to be the case, for when Rod passed her a slice of the cake he explained about the donor.

'Mrs Landers is a widow who lives next door. She's always very kind to us, and I tease Dad about her, but really she's wrapped up in her family – got three daughters and five grandchildren, so we're lucky she gives us some of her baking when she can. This is an excellent cake, eh?'

'It's lovely. We don't really celebrate Christmas much, but I think I'd like to have a go making one of these one day.'

'Secret's in the baking,' Mr Connor declared. 'That's as much as I know, but I've been told that if you bake a cake too long it's dry as dust, and if you bake it too little it collapses.'

'Best of luck, Lindy!' cried Rod and they left

the table laughing, Lindy having insisted that she wanted to do the washing up. In the kitchen, of course, they closed the door and kissed long and happily before getting down to work.

'Don't know how long I've been wanting to do that,' Rod murmured as he washed and Lindy dried, standing together at the sink in the large, warm kitchen. 'How'd you find my dad, then?'

'He's grand, I like him so much, Rod. I think he's a lot like you.'

'Much cleverer. But I could tell he likes you, Lindy. Oh, yes, like son, like father.' Rod, drying his hands, surveyed their pile of plates and teacups and said they could leave them on the table – he'd put them away after he'd taken Lindy back home. First, though, he had something to give her.

'Give me?'

'It's nothing special.' He was taking a package wrapped in Christmas paper from one of the kitchen cupboards. 'It's just a scarf. I didn't know what to get you.'

'A scarf?' Lindy smiled. 'Rod, I'll just get my bag.'

'You haven't got me something?'

'Guess what – it's a scarf, too.'

'Let's compare, then.'

Rod's was a lightweight woollen scarf, one of Logie's special lines in Royal Stuart tartan, as he had no tartan of his own, and which he said was just what he wanted and that he'd wear it that very evening. Lindy's, however, was a shawl, rather than a scarf, made of white Shetland wool in a cobweb pattern so delicate, so beautiful, it brought tears to her eyes.

'Oh, you shouldn't!' she whispered, when they'd spent time kissing again.

'Nor should you,' he told her. 'What were you doing, spending your hard-earned money on me? But I'll wear my scarf for ever!'

'We must go back to your dad, Rod. We've been in here for ages – what will he think?'

'We've been working, haven't we? But we'll go back now.'

'First, there's something else in my bag,' she told him. 'It's for your father.'

'Oh, God, Lindy, this is crazy! Giving Dad a present as well!'

'No, it didn't cost much. You'll see.'

It was a miniature bottle of Drambuie, which took Mr Connor completely by surprise. His favourite, he exclaimed! Well, favourite whisky, of course, not Bayne's bitter, but Lindy should never have—'

'No, she shouldn't,' Rod said firmly, 'but she wanted to, so drink up, Dad. Meanwhile, I'll take Lindy home.'

There was a farewell kiss on the cheek from Mr Connor and his murmured hope to meet again before he returned to his ship, and then she and Rod were wrapped up well and in the car on the way home. In Lindy's bag were her present from Rod and a large piece of the Christmas cake for her family, while Rod's scarf was round his neck and he was saying he'd never been so warm.

'Never been so warm?' Lindy repeated. 'And

I've never been so happy. Did I tell you that before?'

'If you did I can hear it again, any time. And, of course, I'm telling you the same thing.'

Parked outside number nineteen their eyes met, but as Rod made to take her in his arms, Lindy shook her head.

'Wait, there's something I want to say, Rod. It's . . . important.'

'Help.' He made a face. 'I'm not sure I like the sound of this. Am I going to be upset?'

'No!' She took his hand and held it. 'It's just that I feel you've been so good, giving in to me, I should – well, I should do the same for you.'

'Lindy –'

'What I'm saying is if you really don't want me to do the modelling, I won't. I can do something else. I've thought about it and that's what I'm offering.' She stroked his hand. 'What do you think, then?'

'What do I think? I think I'm a lucky man.' For some moments Rod held her tight, pressing his face against hers, then releasing her. 'That you'd do that for me – I can't believe it.'

'You did as much for me.'

'But I honestly want you to keep on with the modelling now. You've done your training, you've proved yourself, and I feel that if you give it up you'll always regret it.'

'I don't know –'

'You do. It could always be in your mind when we're married, that you didn't have your chance to do what you wanted to do. I don't want to take that chance away from you.'

276

She was sitting very still, her breath coming fast, her head reeling.

'Married?' she said at last. 'You've never mentioned being married, Rod.'

'Why, I thought it went without saying. Of course we're going to be married. Aren't we?'

'But you've never asked me, Rod! A man has to ask and you never did. I never knew what was in your mind.'

He was silent for a moment. 'I suppose I just didn't have the nerve to put it into words.'

'The nerve?'

'Yes. I knew you were keen to have a life of your own. I thought you'd turn me down and I couldn't face it. Better to keep on, see what happened – and then, well, you know what did. Seemed like the end of everything and I was to blame.'

'We were both to blame. But we needn't think about that now.'

'Let's never think about it again.' Rod paused, smiled a little. 'Lindy, shall I ask, then? I can't exactly go down on one knee in the car but, will you marry me?'

'Yes!' she cried. 'Oh, yes, Rod!'

Eternity went by as they celebrated their betrothal with kisses and caresses, until at last Lindy said she'd better go as folk would be wondering at the car being parked for so long.

'No, they won't,' said Rod. 'They won't be wondering at all. But before you go in, let's decide – do you want to be officially engaged now? Or when you've worked a while?'

She thought for a moment. 'I'd like to be

engaged, but I think maybe I needn't tell Mrs Driver, in case she thinks I'm no' serious about work.'

'All right, this is our plan. Get engaged at Easter, say? And marry – when?'

'Christmas?' Lindy suggested. 'I want to do some saving up.'

'You won't mind a winter wedding?'

'Winter weddings can be lovely.'

'Christmas it is, then. And you could still work afterwards, if you want.'

'Oh, Rod, I don't know if I'm on my head or my heels! I can tell my folks, though? And Jemima?'

'And Neil,' he said quietly.

'And Neil,' she agreed.

And finally, slowly, they left the car and walked, entwined, to the door of number nineteen.

'Meet me soon – I'll be in touch?' Rod whispered.

'Meet you soon,' she whispered. 'As soon as we can.'

'As soon as I can sort out my next time off. Happy Boxing Day, my darling.'

'The happiest ever, dearest Rod!'

However was she going to tell her folks? she wondered, but it turned out to be the easiest thing in the world. As soon as they saw her they seemed to know, and when she got the words out and told them her plans there were cries and smiles, and George said he'd get out his bottle of port he'd been saving for Hogmanay.

'And let's have some o' that Christmas cake with it,' suggested Struan, who'd just come in from seeing Jemima again. 'Best news ever, eh? A brother-in-law for me with a car!'

'I always knew he was the one for you,' said Myra. 'Why ever didn't you bring him in, Lindy?'

'I don't know – I'm all at sea. But he will be coming in, Aunt Myra, and you'll be meeting his father, too. Oh, I'm so happy; it's like a fairy tale, eh?'

'You'll be giving up your modelling, then?' asked Myra, but Lindy, about to drink her port, only smiled.

'Oh, I don't think so, Aunt Myra. Rod doesn't want me to, you see.'

# Fifty-Seven

On January 20, 1936, King George the Fifth died at Sandringham. He had been suffering for some time from chest problems and after his Christmas broadcast seemed to go quickly downhill, finally retiring to his room on January 15 and never leaving it again.

There was widespread grief, of course, and a period of mourning, during which Mrs Driver warned that there would be no work available for her models, which was a setback for Lindy, who to date had only had one photographic assignment and was anxious to be offered more. One good thing was that she'd been offered part-time work in the stationery department at Logie's so at least had some wages coming in, but it was a huge relief when the mourning for the late King was over and suddenly modelling work was again to be found.

Maybe it was to do with the different atmosphere that was about, caused by the new King's love of parties and social life filtering down to all his kingdom, that there was renewed interest in fashion. Certainly there was a feeling that those who could afford it wanted a brighter social life too, and the clothes to go with it.

Whatever the reason, the winter days brought more fashion shows and Lindy finally began to get interviews. Sometimes she didn't pass, sometimes she did, but when she was successful she knew it was because her face fitted. That was the thing about her new life – you had to look right, and sometimes you couldn't tell what was wanted and what was not. All you could do was concentrate on your looks and be ready for anything that came your way. Being beautiful was essential, but you had to accept that you could never rely on it to get you a job. Not, as Lindy had said, when everyone else was beautiful, too.

Still, when she did get work, she was with the clothes she loved and the experience of modelling was important. If only there was more of it.

'Early days,' Mrs Driver told her girls when they complained about their lack of success. 'Always remember, however good you are, however lovely, you must be known, you must become a name. Yes, I know it's difficult – you need the name to get the work, you need the work to get the name – but it will come, it will.' As they sighed and still looked dubious, she added: 'But one thing I don't advise is to run off to London and think you'll do better there. Believe me, you won't. Better to stay here and swim than to go to London and sink.'

London? As though she would ever leave Scotland! thought Lindy. Ever leave Rod! Never.

'I'm relieved to hear it,' Rod said, his face serious when she told him what she thought of the idea of going to London and Mrs Driver's advice against it. 'You're sure you wouldn't try it, though? Bright lights are tempting.'

'We have bright lights here – I don't need London.'

'So, it's going well, then?'

'Well, slowly. Most people have gaps. I'm glad I have Logie's in reserve and sometimes photographic work. I'm doing a knitting pattern job next week.'

'Knitting pattern job . . . Why does that not sound glamorous?' Rod laughed and hugged Lindy to him. 'Main thing is, you haven't forgotten our plan, Lindy?'

'To get engaged at Easter? I think about it all the time.'

'Even when you're modelling jumpers?'

'All the time,' she repeated firmly. 'Rod, you come first.'

Which made him smile again.


Jemima, of course, was delighted to hear of the engagement, and so was Rosemary. Such a relief to know Lindy was back with Rod – he was so right for her! As for Neil, he seemed pleased,

281

even though he said he'd lost his dearest friend, however much Lindy denied it.

'You'll always be special to me,' she told him earnestly. 'And one of these days you'll be in love again yourself.'

'I'm in no hurry,' he said quietly. 'I have my book to finish.'

No one knew for sure if Jemima and Struan were in love or not, but they certainly met so regularly some of 'the lads' were feeling aggrieved, saying they never saw Struan and what was so good about Jemima that he couldn't find time for them? But Jemima never admitted that there was anything serious between her and Struan.

'It's because she's waiting to see what happens,' Myra said sagely. 'Wants to know what Struan's got in mind before she says anything. But my guess is that he's suddenly keen to get married – maybe because of you and Rod looking so happy, eh?'

'That wouldn't matter to Struan. He always knows what he wants.'

'Well, then, there's Jemima's mother. She's probably not too thrilled about things. Unlike your dad and me, and Rod's dad, eh? Oh, what a lovely man, eh? So kind of him to take us out that time!'

Yes, that had been a grand idea of Mr Connor's, to take Lindy's parents and her brother out for supper at a nice little place in Leith. They'd all enjoyed it so much, except that Myra had spent a lot of time worrying about entertaining him back, and was only saved when he had to rejoin his ship.

'Aye, you've been lucky, finding Rod,' Myra said thoughtfully. 'Long may it last.'

But why shouldn't it last? thought Lindy. What could go wrong?

And when Rod slipped his mother's engagement ring on Lindy's finger at Easter time, she could think of nothing but the joy that had come to her and that it must last, anyway, for she couldn't live without it.

# Fifty-Eight

When Mrs Driver was eventually told of Lindy's engagement she was not pleased, though not at all surprised.

'When you're working with attractive young women, it's an occupational hazard, as they say, to lose some to marriage,' she told Lindy, fixing her with a stern eye. 'What are your plans, then?'

'Well, I won't be giving up work, Mrs Driver.'

'H'm. You'll have to see how things go, then. Once married, it's never wise to plan too far ahead.'

'We're no' thinking of starting a family,' Lindy said, blushing. 'I mean, these days—'

'These days mistakes can happen just as always,' Mrs Driver told her crisply. 'But for the time being, I'll just keep on trying for bookings for you. I hope you're not too disappointed that you haven't had so many?'

'I suppose I am, a bit.'

'Takes time, Lindsay, to get known. And competition is fierce – always will be.'

'Oh, I know,' said Lindy.

Her disappointment wasn't, however, due entirely to the shortage of work. Sometimes, when she did have a job and went into the dressing room to prepare, it was to see every single girl studying her face or, if not her face, her body, trying to decide if she'd put on an ounce or two, or maybe her hands needed a manicure, or her hair wouldn't do what she wanted it to. And this to Lindy, though she knew it was maybe foolish to think so, seemed depressing. Of course, looks were what the girls had to offer – they could hardly be blamed for being obsessed with them. It was only to Lindy that such obsession had become worrying.

'I know it's unreasonable,' she said once to Kitty Yarman, someone who rather shared her views, 'but I sometimes wonder if we couldn't sell clothes without always having to be so perfect.'

'It is unreasonable,' Kitty agreed cheerfully as she worked away, plucking her dark eyebrows. 'Folk expect to look perfect themselves when they buy new clothes, so they're not going to be impressed by models who don't look any better than they do.'

'And the buyers and dress-shop owners know all that too.' Lindy sighed. 'No hope of change, then.'

'Unless you change your job.'

'But I've done all the training!'

'Well, there's always catalogue work.'

'Even there your face hasn't to have one single flaw. No spots allowed!'

They laughed and Lindy, putting aside her misgivings, began on the serious work of making up her face.

It was some days later, on a day when she was not working at Logie's, that she was at home studying some new eye shadow she'd been given to try out. One of the perks of the job was that models were frequently given such handouts, and Lindy didn't mind experimenting with something new.

'Do get tired of looking at my same old face,' she told Gingerboy, who was on his way to her bed for a nap. 'I see it so often, eh?'

She had just applied a little of the new shadow to one of her eyes and was checking the effect in her mirror when she heard a noise outside the flat door. Sounded like someone crying. A child? She ran to the door.

It was a child. Matty Andrews, Aggie's wee daughter, wearing a grubby little dress, was standing crying in the hall, her small fists to her eyes.

'What is it, Matty?' cried Lindy, stooping down to put her arms round her. 'What's the matter?'

'Mammie's no' well,' wailed Matty. 'And there's porridge all aroond.'

'Porridge?' Lindy, mystified, suddenly turned pale. There was blood on Matty's dress. Probably not hers . . .

'Come on!' she cried, snatching up the child. 'Let's go and see Mammie, eh?'

285

The door of Aggie's flat stood open and, terrified of what she might see, Lindy hurried in, Matty still in her arms, to stop and stare. Porridge all around? It was a good description, for lumps of porridge were lining the floor, stuck on the backs of chairs and on the cluttered table, while a large pan was upside down beside the stove. There was also a terrible smell of something burnt hanging in the air – but no sign of Aggie.

'Where's Mammie?' Lindy asked, setting Matty down. 'Aggie, Aggie, where are you?'

'Here,' came a faint voice, and Aggie herself appeared at a door. 'Oh, Lindy, is that you?'

'My God, what's happened?' Lindy asked, taking in Aggie's bloodstained face and half-closed eye, rapidly turning black. 'Aggie, Aggie, come and sit down. Tell me what happened. Was it Tam?'

'Aye, he lost his temper,' sighed Aggie, speaking painfully through swollen lips. 'It was because I'd . . . burnt the porridge, you ken . . . and there was no more oats . . . so he threw the pan around and the stuff . . . went everywhere . . . and then he . . . but it's no' as bad as it looks.'

'Isn't it?' said Lindy, almost trembling with rage. 'It's bad enough. Come and sit down – this chair's OK – while I look at you.'

'Mammie, Mammie,' wailed Matty. 'I want Mammie!'

'In a minute, pet,' said Lindy. 'I'll just see to her. Where's Alex, then?'

'Gone to school, and the baby's still asleep next door.' Aggie seemed as though she might try to laugh, but decided against it. 'Imagine – sleeping though it, eh?'

'Aggie, are there any cloths I can use? Just to mop you up? There's a cut over your eye –'

'On the pulley.' Aggie pointed. 'A couple o' wee towels. They're clean. I did the washing yesterday.'

Working fast, Lindy soaked the towels from the kitchen pulley in cold water and sponged Aggie's poor face until it looked better, but when she asked for a sticking plaster for the cut, Lindy found she'd have to go and get her own.

'Just hold that cloth over your eye while I nip down the stair for my bag – I always carry plasters. Now just sit tight, Aggie.'

'I'm no' going anywhere,' said Aggie.

As soon as she'd put on the plaster, Lindy made Aggie a cup of tea, then made her lie down on her bed, with Matty close and the still-sleeping baby in his cot. Next she filled a bucket with water and scrubbed away the porridge, put the burnt pan in to soak, washed up the breakfast dishes and told Aggie she was going to get her a few things from the shop and wouldn't be a minute.

'Oh, Lindy – I've no tick—'

'Don't worry. These are on me.'

'Och, that Tam!' cried Myra, helping Lindy to put together a box of groceries. 'Wait till I see him! But what's wrong with your eye, Lindy?'

'Help, my eye shadow! Och, I must look a clown, but I'd no time to take it off. If you could've seen poor Aggie!'

'Oh, I don't need to. I know what Tam's like, but what can you do?'

'I'd like to report him to the police!'

'You'd get nowhere. They don't like interfering with married folk.'

All the same, when Lindy ran back in to number nineteen with her groceries and saw Tam Andrews about to climb the stairs, she didn't hesitate to tackle him.

'What are you doing here?' she cried fiercely. 'Come back to see what else you can throw around? Frighten Aggie and your bairns?'

He gave her a hangdog look and shook his head. 'You've no idea how bad I feel,' he muttered. 'It just comes over me, you ken, and I canna help lashing oot!'

'Maybe a visit from the police might help you, then? I've a good mind to report you!'

'No' the polis? Lindy, you wouldn't do that! I've just got this job at the tyre factory – if you set the polis on me, I'll be finished.'

'Well, will you promise to try to control yourself? In the meantime, let's go up and see how Aggie is now, eh? Then you can make the dinner.'

'Did she come and tell you about me?' he asked as they slowly climbed the stairs. 'That's no' like her.'

'No, she didn't tell me. I found wee Matty crying in the hall.'

'Oh, God, Matty!' Tam put his hand to his eyes. 'Lindy, I promise I'll never let this happen again.'

'Keep to it, then.'

Later, when she'd left the penitent Tam preparing a meal for the family while Aggie rested, Lindy sat down again with her eye shadow and her mirror. For some time she stared at her face in the mirror, before suddenly pushing the mirror aside and shaking her head. All she could seem to see was Aggie's face, battered and swollen. All she could seem to think was that there should be something she should do about it, and that gazing at her own beauty was not enough.

I always liked the clothes, she thought. That was what I wanted. But the clothes came with modelling and modelling was not what she'd imagined it would be. True, Mrs Driver had always stressed the importance of looks for a model and she'd gone along with that. It was only after she'd come up against the obsession with looks day after day and realized she must have it too that she'd begun to think – oh, dare she whisper it? That there was something hollow at the centre of her new career and that modelling was not for her?

There was nothing wrong, in her view, in modelling clothes for people to buy, as Rod appeared to think, and for most models the life might seem satisfying. But, she had to admit it was no longer true for her. For her, it was no longer enough.

When to announce her decision to her family, though? Only after she'd told Rod, of course. As she and Myra finished preparing the evening meal she found herself trying to find the right words to explain her views. She knew that Rod, at least, would be delighted, though Myra would have a grand time saying 'I told you so', no doubt about that.

But then her dad and Struan came in from work and everything changed.

'What's wrong?' cried Myra, instantly alert to the looks on their faces. 'What's happened?'

'Can you no' tell?' asked George, sinking into his chair, feeling for his pipe. 'I've been let go.'

'Oh, no, Dad!' Lindy cried, as Myra for once seemed unable to speak. 'No, they wouldn't – they wouldn't do that to you!'

'Done it to plenty,' said Struan flatly. 'To me and all. They've put me on half time.'

'I'm on no' time at all.' George was lighting his pipe with trembling fingers. 'Worked for Bayne's all my life, and then they let me go with nothing at all. Just till things improve, they say. Come back when the depression's over. Well, I know who's depressed!'

'George, mebbe they mean it?' Myra said at last. 'They'll no' want to lose you – soon as things get better, you'll be back –'

He shook his head. 'It's me for the dole, Myra. Don't ask me how we'll manage, with Struan only on half time and all.'

'I can help,' Lindy said clearly. 'I'm earning, and I might earn more. I'll see you're all right, Dad, Aunt Myra – you needn't worry.'

Modelling, she was thinking, I still have it. Maybe it's true what I said: more work might come my way. Thank the Lord I didn't tell 'em I was giving it up!

'We'd never take your money—' George was beginning, when Myra cut in.

'Lindy, that'd be grand if you could – help us, I mean. Just till your dad finds something else, eh?'

'Like what?' asked George, and Struan sighed as he lit a cigarette.

'I'm going to have to tell Jemima. What's she going to say?'

'Why, what everybody says when money gets tight!' cried Myra. 'She's going to have to pay for you for a change, and why not, eh? We're all going to be feeling the pinch.' She glanced at Lindy. 'Don't know what'll happen about your wedding, Lindy. There'll be nothing to spare for that.'

'Don't worry, Aunt Myra. I never expected you to pay, anyway, and it'll only be very quiet. Leave it to Rod and me.'

'What a relief you've got someone like Rod, eh? Thank goodness one of us had a bit o' luck! Now, you two men can stop your smoking and come to the table. I'm going to start dishing up.'

# Fifty-Nine

Rod, of course, was deeply concerned to hear of George's losing his job, his good-natured face darkening, his brown eyes losing their gentle look so beloved by Lindy.

'It's disgraceful!' he cried as he and Lindy took a Sunday walk in Cramond, a village at the mouth of the River Almond, part of Edinburgh but with a beauty and history of its own.

'And so typical!' Rod went on. 'A firm makes a fortune out of a product made by loyal workers, and when the going gets tough, who's first to go?

291

Those who've given the best years of their lives!'

'I know, I know,' sighed Lindy. 'And with Bayne's there's no cushion, no money when folk get the push. Myra used to say Dad should try for work elsewhere with better conditions, but he said it was too late and he never did.'

'Struan could. He's young.'

'Yes, but the other breweries are no' recruiting anybody now. He'll have to stay where he is till things improve. Poor Jemima – she's really upset for him.'

'We're all upset,' said Rod. 'But tell your parents not to worry – we'll see they're all right.'

'Oh, I've said I'll help all I can.'

'Things looking up for you, then?'

'Sort of.' Lindy lowered her eyes, feeling guilty that she hadn't told Rod of her change of heart over modelling, her view being that he'd want her to give it up straight away, which she couldn't afford to do. If the situation changed maybe she'd tell him then. But she couldn't see the situation changing.

'Dad's so depressed,' she continued. 'He's like someone who's lost his prop and can't manage without it. He doesn't know what to do with himself.'

'I can imagine.'

'Sometimes he goes to the library and reads all the job adverts, but he hasn't seen anything so far. Trouble is, even if he does find something, there'll be half of Edinburgh in for it too.'

'We'll have to help him, that's all.'

But how? After walking on a while they paused, then quickly checked that no one was looking and exchanged kisses.

'About our wedding,' said Lindy after a pause.

'Not got second thoughts?'

'Of course I haven't! No, I was just thinking that I feel bad because I can't save up much towards it now, the way things are.'

'Don't worry about that. I can pay.'

'Rod, I don't want you to. And my folks wouldn't want that either.'

'Look, they can't pay for anything at present, and neither can you. So leave it to me. Nearer the time we'll decide what we want. Something quiet, I guess?'

'Oh, yes. And it needn't be in the kirk. A registry office will be all right for us, eh?'

'Fine for me. I'm not much of a kirkgoer.'

'Nor me.' Lindy put her hand in his. 'Are we really talking about our wedding, Rod? Seems like a dream.'

'If you wake up it'll still be there, on the horizon.' They clung together lovingly, then made their way to the little café facing the estuary where the gulls were gathering.

'I'm going to do all I can to find your dad another job,' Rod promised when they'd found a table and were waiting for tea. 'That's what he needs more than money. He has to have something to do – something he wants to do as well. That's important.'

Don't we all want that? Lindy sighed to herself. And I thought I'd found it. Now, though, she must make the best of what she had and be grateful she had anything at all.

* * *

293

It was one evening a day or so later that Rod called at number nineteen and told Lindy, who'd answered his knock, that he'd like to speak to her father.

'Why, Rod, I wasn't expecting to see you!' Lindy's face was suddenly hopeful. 'Have you got some news for Dad?'

'No, I'm afraid not – just an idea I want to discuss with him. Is he in?'

'Oh, yes, he's always in. He'll be so pleased to see you.'

Both George and Myra managed smiles when Rod walked in, though the marks of strain on their faces were plain to see. George, who had been sitting near the window, for the room in the warmth of the summer evening seemed airless, shook Rod's hand and Myra said he must have tea, which he declined.

'Grand to see you, Rod,' George remarked. 'Don't see many folk at the moment.'

'You could go out more,' Lindy told him. 'Struan's going out, aren't you, Struan?'

'Just with the lads tonight.'

'And what you're using for money I don't know,' snapped Myra. 'Still, I'm glad you're no' moping.'

'Like me, you mean?' asked George. 'Struan's still got work, remember, even if it's short time.' He rested weary eyes on Rod. 'Did you want to speak to me, Rod?'

'Well, this is just an idea, Mr Gillan.' Rod took a chair near him. 'I've been thinking that as your skills lie in brewing, your best bet is to try to get back to it.'

'And how do I do that? Bayne's have laid me off.'

'Doesn't mean you won't be wanted elsewhere.'

'Och, there's no point in trying – the other breweries would advertise if they wanted men.'

'Maybe they're planning to – you won't know unless you ask. Consider how many breweries there are in the city – twenty-three! Think of all the famous names! Bayne's might be facing reduced sales, but you don't know about the others.'

'What are you saying George should do?' Myra asked. 'Just ask for a job?'

'I'm suggesting he should write to some of them and ask if there are any vacancies, or likely to be. Include a reference if possible. I suppose you got a good one from Bayne's – Mr Dillon?'

'Aye, it was good, all right.' George laughed shortly. ' "To whom it may concern" it said, and talked about me as if I was a marvel. If I was that good why the hell did they let me go?'

'Still, it's good you have something to show.' Rod gave a persuasive smile. 'What do you think, then, of what I've suggested?'

'I think it's a damn good idea,' put in Struan, at which Myra frowned.

'He's asking your dad, no' you, Struan!'

'Aye, well I'm no' one for writing letters,' George said slowly. 'Haven't had to write a letter since I don't know when.'

'I'll help you,' Rod told him. 'And type your letters up for you, too. I've got a typewriter back at the hostel. Why don't we get on with writing something out now?'

'Rod, thank you,' Lindy said quietly. 'We're very grateful. I'm no' sure if we've any writing paper, though.'

'I brought some.' Rod opened a small briefcase he'd brought with him which no one had noticed. 'Be prepared is the motto, eh? Mr Gillan, I'll rough something out for you and see if you approve. Will that be all right?'

As he nodded, seemingly amazed, Myra leaped to her feet. 'I'm sure we can do with a cup o' tea now. Struan, did you say you were going out?'

'Aye, but first I want to say I'm going back to the idea I had before, and Dad needn't put me down this time.'

'What are you talking about?' asked George. 'When did I put you down?'

'When I said I'd join the Territorials. You said Bayne's wouldn't be pleased but I'm going for it anyway. I reckon I can make quite a bit at weekends and I need it.'

'Of course you do!' cried Myra. 'Things are different now. You try for it, Struan – it'll be just the thing.'

After tea and seed cake had been passed around, Rod wrote out the sample letter to the breweries and George, having studied it, gave his opinion that it was grand. 'Will you really type it for me, Rod?'

'Certainly will, as well as a copy of your reference if you'll let me have it. Then I'll get everything back to you so you can sign the letters and post them off to whichever breweries you think best.'

'Rod, I couldn't be more grateful. To take all this trouble for me – it's unbelievable.'

'You've been unfairly treated; I want to do what I can for you. Now, I'd better be going.'

Seeing Rod to the door, Lindy threw her arms round him and almost burst into tears. 'Oh, Rod – you've been so kind.'

'May not do any good, my idea, but it's worth a try is all I'm saying,' he told her. 'Now, I'll get back. Don't forget I love you.'

'As though I could!'

Moving back to her family after Rod had driven away, Lindy decided that her cup of happiness must be full. All that was needed now was to find her dad a job, and the cup would be running over.

# Sixty

The first replies that arrived for George were from the largest breweries and all said the same: no workers required. Though they'd keep Mr Gillan's letter on file, any vacancies would be advertised and in future he should check the newspapers.

'Did I no' say?' George cried as the disappointing replies arrived. 'Did I no' say it was all a waste of time?'

'There are still some to come in,' Lindy told him. 'We can't say it's been a waste of time till you've heard from 'em all.'

But her father would not allow himself to hope and sank once more into his depression.

'I'm very sorry,' Rod groaned when given the

news, 'but it's right what you say, Lindy – we don't know for sure we've failed until all replies are in.'

All the same, as he and Lindy sat over a late coffee after a visit to the cinema, Rod himself seemed despondent. 'Everywhere you look there's trouble,' he murmured. 'Suffering, inhumanity, poverty – what's wrong with the world?'

'Whatever it is there's no' much we can do,' sighed Lindy. 'I mean, this Hitler fellow in Germany, he's doing terrible things, they say, and so is Mussolini, but we can't stop them.'

'Well, we should be able to.' Rod stirred his coffee gloomily. 'It should be possible to take action to help victims, even if they are in other countries.'

'How, though? How can folk interfere?'

'Well, through some sort of international action. We missed the boat with the League of Nations after the war. Should have organized something then.'

'Too late now.'

'I wish that wasn't true. I mean, it's not just Germany and Italy we have to worry about. There's unrest all over the world. Take Spain, for instance. According to the papers, it's like a powder keg ready to explode, with a load of generals all set to oust the government. We'll have to watch what happens there.'

'You talk of other countries,' sighed Lindy. 'How about here? How many people are like Dad, thrown on the scrap heap? I sometimes think we're so happy, you and me, but we shouldn't be. I mean, with so much misery around.'

'Ah, don't say that!' Rod caught at her hand. 'Look, I'm sorry, it's my fault, acting like an old

298

misery guts. Let's think of something to cheer us up.'

'Well, I've had some more catalogue work – that's money coming in, and I forgot to tell you that Struan's been accepted for the Territorials. Part time sort of thing. He's over the moon.'

'That's great news, Lindy.' Rod's brow had cleared, his eyes were brightening. 'The silver lining, eh? Suppose that's what we should look for?'

'Every time,' said Lindy, as they rose to go.

Walking instead of driving back to number nineteen, the July evening was warm around them and they felt a little better in themselves. After all, they had each other – they couldn't be blamed for feeling happy, could they?

'No more depressing talk,' Lindy said at her door. 'Let's look on the bright side. Dad might get good news soon. And I've thought of something else that's cheered me up.'

'Me?' Rod asked fondly.

'Apart from you! You remember I told you about the wife who'd been beaten up by the husband who threw the porridge around?'

'I do remember. Shocking thing.'

'Yes, well, Aggie – that's the wife – saw me the other day and said Tam has been amazing. Still lost his temper a couple of times, but he'd just gone out and stood on the stair, shaking all over, till he'd calmed down, and then he'd been OK. Oh, she was so happy, Rod! I just hope he'll no' go back to his old ways.'

'No guarantee, but it's a start.'

'Yes, and I think I helped, Rod. I did threaten to report him and he might have listened.'

299

Rod's eyes on her were considering. 'Did you enjoy being able to help, Lindy?'

'I'd no' say "enjoyed", I was just glad I could.'

'It's what people find rewarding in my sort of job. Makes up for the times when it's anything but.'

'You know much how I admire you,' Lindy told him, and was beginning to move into his arms when the flat door opened and Struan looked out.

'Lindy – Rod – thought I heard you – come on in. Dad's got some good news!'

'Came by the evening post,' George told them, smiling widely and waving a sheet of paper. 'From Wellmore's – that's one o' the smaller breweries out Northfield way. I never thought they'd come up with anything.'

'They want him to go for interview!' cried Myra. 'They said they've a key job that's just come up and they were impressed with George's reference. What d'you think, Rod?'

'I couldn't be more pleased. It all sounds very hopeful – promising, in fact. When's the interview?'

'Thursday,' said George. 'Think my brown jacket'll do, Myra?'

'Dad, I'll get you a new shirt,' Lindy told him, hugging him tightly. 'The sales have started – I've seen a real bargain. Oh, I'm so happy for you!'

'No counting chickens before they're hatched, but I'm just glad I've got as far as an interview. Rod, it's all thanks to you. I'd never have done it alone.'

'Don't thank me, Mr Gillan – it was your reference they liked and your good work got you that.'

'Aye, well, I'll see how I get on. But I wish

you'd call me George, Rod. After all, you'll be one o' the family one o' these days, eh?'

'Not too far away, we hope.'

'Christmas,' said Lindy happily. 'That'll give us time to prepare and save up.'

'And if I get this job I'll be saving up and all,' said George. 'We'll want to put on a nice show, eh, Myra?'

'I'm planning it already,' said Myra.

# Sixty-One

Thursday came and George set off for his interview with Wellmore's Brewery looking, Myra said, 'as smart as paint' in his brown jacket, newly pressed trousers, crisp new white shirt and brown striped tie. Smart – yes, he knew he looked smart, except for his face that was as apprehensive as a condemned man's, while as for his earlier euphoria – that had vanished as soon as Thursday dawned.

'Aye, it's one thing to get an interview,' he'd muttered to Myra, 'it's another to get the job.'

'Just do your best,' she told him. 'We're all thinking of you.'

Of course they were: Lindy, Struan and Rod, but there was nothing they could do. It was all up to George to prove he was better than the others being seen, for there would be others. Younger, perhaps; more articulate; better at selling themselves.

As she smiled for the camera at work on a

toothpaste advert, Lindy was secretly praying her father would be successful, for if he weren't she couldn't imagine what he would do. While Struan, doing one of his days at Bayne's, was feeling as tense as a too tight string, partly for his father's sake and partly because that evening would be his first at the Territorial drill hall, where he would be given his uniform and meet the sergeant to begin training. Suppose it didn't work out? Suppose the sergeant was one of these sadistic guys who liked making new recruits feel bad?

Maybe if George got into Wellmore's he might put in a word for Struan in the future? With a full-time job he might manage without the TA money. On the other hand he liked the idea of being a part-time soldier. Hell, he'd just make it work and that was that. And he'd be able to take Jemima out as often as before and cut the arguments about her paying. 'When I take a lassie out,' he'd told her, 'I pay, all right? I don't want any woman paying for me.'

'Oh, what a piece of nonsense!' Jemima had cried, but she'd taken his point. She was very sensible, Jemima.

Over at the hostel, Rod's thoughts were certainly with George, for it would not be easy to pull him back from depression if he failed his interview, but something else had sent his heart sinking: an item in his newspaper. Several times over his coffee break he read it through, and when he folded the paper and put it in his desk drawer his face had assumed a grim thoughtfulness Lindy would not have recognized. Trouble was, he didn't know how things would go, whether he could do anything

302

or not. Could he face the difficulties, anyway? Or ask so much of the girl he loved? When his phone rang later that day it was a lifeline – it gave him something else to think about. For it was George on the phone, ringing from a call box.

'Rod, it's me!' His husky voice echoed in Rod's ear, for George always thought you needed to speak up on the telephone. 'I've got the job! I start next week and I want to thank you, Rod. You've saved ma life!'

Thank God, thought Rod as he gave George his heartiest congratulations. Now he could put that other matter out of his mind, at least for the time being.

Of course there had to be a celebration. Eating out was not something the Gillans went in for – except for that lovely time when Rod's father had treated them in Leith, but just for once Myra said they should all go out to a fish restaurant in the High Street and make sure Rod didn't pay. It would be their thank you to him, for as George said, he'd given him his life back, and that was enough to change all their lives.

The following evening they gathered at the restaurant, the four Gillans plus Rod and Jemima, the women in summer dresses, for the July evening was steamy, the men in jackets they took off at the table. All were intoxicated – not with alcohol, only George's good luck and their own shared relief.

'Tell Jemima about the interview,' Myra commanded as jugs of lemonade were brought and large menus. 'She's no' heard it yet.'

'Och, I just did what you told me,' George protested. 'I did ma best.'

'But tell her how many fellows were there. Six, eh? Shows how well you did, to be picked, eh?'

'Aye, well, it's true there were six others, but I don't like to think of 'em because I know how I'd have been feeling if I'd been them.' George shook his head. 'I think, to be honest, they weren't as experienced as me, and what the board told me was that they'd been impressed by me writing in the first place.'

'Rod's idea!' cried Lindy, pressing his hand.

'Showed' – George hesitated – 'initiative. Is that the word? And yes, that was your idea, Rod. Typing the letter and all – I bet they never expected a fellow like me to be able to type!'

'Please don't say any more,' Rod murmured. 'I told you, George, whatever I did would have got you nowhere if you hadn't had the experience and knowledge to back it up. So no more thanks – unless it's to yourself.'

'Think there might be an opening at Wellmore's for me, Dad?' asked Struan. 'I wouldn't mind a full-time job again, though I had a grand time at the drill hall the other night, so I'll be sticking with the TA. The sergeant was an old chap who really knew his stuff but didn't make us feel like idiots because we didn't.' Struan drank some lemonade. 'I was worried to death, I can tell you, but it turned out fine.'

'Sure, I'll keep my ears open for you at Wellmore's,' George told him. 'I'd like you out of Bayne's – they've no treated you well, either.

But now, who wants what to eat? And no arguments about paying, eh?'

'This is on us,' Myra declared. 'And I'll start
the ball rolling. I'll have the haddock.'

After the happy meal was over, they strolled
back to number nineteen in the sort of warm
evening stillness rarely met in Edinburgh. Where
was the usual wind? Didn't dare to spoil things,
eh? Oh, couldn't you wish it was always summer,
then? A good summer, of course.

When the others had gone into the flat, after
George and Myra had insisted on thanking Rod
yet again, Lindy and Rod stood by his car in a
last sweet embrace.

'I said once, if Dad got his job, my cup would
be overflowing,' Lindy whispered against Rod's
face. 'And he did get his job and my cup is
overflowing. With happiness, I mean, in case you
think I mean anything else!'

Rod, caressing her, nodded. 'It's been a wonderful
thing for him, to know he's wanted again.'

'Wonderful. You'll let me thank you again,
Rod?'

But he only put his fingers over her lips until
she drew away, laughing, and he said he must
get back to lock up at the hostel.

'See you Saturday?' he asked. 'My evening off
next week.'

'Grand.' They kissed in farewell, then Lindy, as
usual, waved him away as he drove off and turned
to go into the flat to continue the celebrations.

'For Gingerboy this time,' said Myra. 'Look
what they gave me at the restaurant. A bag o'
fish pieces!'

'Is that what you were hiding in your bag?' asked George. 'Come on, then, Gingerboy! Talk about lucky, eh?'

'You mean the cat or you?' asked Struan, laughing.

But George only grinned.

# Sixty-Two

It was a grey evening in August, warm and sticky, when Lindy left Logie's to queue for her tram. She was feeling pleasantly tired after dealing with the crowds of tourists who were looking round everywhere, even the Stationery Department. And then she and Jemima had spent quite a busy lunch hour studying materials to see if there was anything suitable for their wedding outfits.

Having decided on a registry office for the ceremony, Lindy had regretfully ruled out the traditional bride's and bridesmaid's dresses, sad though that made Jemima feel – not for herself, she hastened to say, but because Lindy would have made such a beautiful bride dressed in white satin or lace.

'I've already been a bride,' Lindy told her, smiling. 'At two fashion shows and I don't know how many catalogue shoots. Rosemary's the same – she makes a very popular bride.'

'Nice you see her from time to time.' Jemima's face was alive with interest, as it always was when she was discussing Miss Rosemary. 'Did you see the announcement of her engagement in the papers?'

'Oh, yes, she showed me cuttings. Also her ring, which was lovely.'

'But no prettier than yours, Lindy. And yours is special, being Rod's mother's, eh?'

'It means a lot,' Lindy said softly. 'I can honestly say I don't envy Rosemary at all.'

'Nor me,' Jemima returned, but though Lindy looked at her with a question on her lips, she only said they'd better get on with their choosing. In the end they couldn't quite decide, and thought it best to wait for the arrival of the winter stock, due any moment.

'Still plenty of time,' said Jemima. 'You haven't set a date yet, have you?'

'Think we should. I'll speak to Rod when I see him.'

As she waited for her tram, Lindy was wondering when that would be. Probably at the weekend again, but he hadn't fixed a time when they'd last parted. In fact, he'd seemed rather preoccupied, which wasn't like him. She'd almost asked him if he had something on her mind, but had been sidetracked, debating with herself when she should tell him she might just possibly be giving up modelling. Since her folks no longer needed the extra money she'd been giving them, she would be free to do something she wanted to do, even if it didn't pay so much. But what did she want to do?

She'd been disappointed with modelling and didn't want to burn her fingers twice, yet was finding herself increasingly drawn to the sort of work she'd thought she'd never even consider.

Would she have the courage to eat humble pie and tell Rod she wanted to do what he was doing? She'd reached no conclusion when she heard a car's horn and was taken aback to see Rod in his car, waving to her.

'Quick, jump in!' he was shouting. 'There's a tram behind me!'

'But Rod, what are you doing here?' she gasped, scrambling in and banging the car door behind her so that he could drive rapidly away.

'I was planning to go to number nineteen, but then I remembered this was one of your Logie's days and thought I'd try the tram stop.'

'But we weren't planning to go out, were we?'

'No, but something's come up. I need to talk to you. Dougie's holding the fort.'

'Thing is, they'll be expecting me at home.'

'Oh, I know, we can stop off and let them know.'

She felt she should have been excited at the prospect of unexpected time with Rod, but there was something about his manner that was rather different from usual. She couldn't quite decide how it was different, only that it was enough to make her hold back any enthusiasm.

'And where are we going?' she asked as they drove towards Scott Street.

'To Dad's house. We can be private there, and I've brought some ham and salad stuff so we needn't worry about going for a meal.'

'You seem to have thought this all out, Rod. Is it important?'

He drove without speaking for some moments.

'Very important,' he answered at last. 'You'll see.'

Very important. When they arrived at the house in Leith, after she'd told Myra what was happening, Lindy found she was hardly daring to look at Rod as they set out their cold supper in the kitchen. He seemed so unlike himself, so much on edge in a way she'd never seen in him before, she was beginning to feel the same herself. Or worse, maybe, because he at least knew what he was going to say while she didn't, except that she guessed it was something she was not going to like. Something he didn't actually want to tell her, but felt he must.

Having washed the lettuce and cut up the tomatoes and cucumbers to go with the ham, she raised her great eyes to his and was not surprised when his slid away.

'Do you really want to eat this now?' she asked quietly. 'Couldn't we talk first?'

He ran a hand over his face, then met her gaze. 'Yes, you're right. We can't eat now. Let's go in the sitting room.'

On the sofa near the fireplace she looked around, remembering the lovely Boxing Day she had spent here when Rod's father had been home. She'd seen him once since then when he'd come back briefly in the spring, but now he was on his way to Australia, far, far away. Was he to be told whatever it was Rod was planning to tell her? If so, he would have to wait a long time for it. At least she was going to know now.

Rod had come to sit next to her, was taking her hand in his and was again meeting her gaze. 'You remember I said something about Spain some time ago? Have you been reading anything about it in the papers?'

309

'I saw there'd been some sort of revolt against the government.'

'Yes, that's correct. Right-wing generals and people who sided with them organized what's called a coup against the Republican government. That had been democratically elected, it was what the people wanted, but the Nationalists, as they call themselves, are Fascists – you know, like Mussolini's Italians – and they planned revolts all over the country. The coup wasn't completely successful, so what's happening now, Lindy, is out and out civil war.'

'I see. That sounds terrible. What's going to happen, then?'

'The worst, I should think, unless something is done.' Rod leaped to his feet and began pacing the room. 'The thing is, you see, the Republican government is too weak to stand alone and if no one helps the generals will win and there'll be a regime like Mussolini's or Hitler's in Spain. We can't let that happen.'

'We? You mean this country?'

'No!' Rod angrily shook his head. 'This country's going to do nothing. They won't take sides, in spite of the injustice of it all! But people from this country can do something, just like men and women from France and elsewhere – they can fight to support the rightful government. Lindy, I saw in the paper a short time ago that an International Brigade had been formed and some British men are planning to join it.'

Suddenly Rod drew her to her feet and held her close as a great fear began to build in her heart and, even in the warmth of his arms, she was shivering.

'Lindy, darling –' He kissed her face. 'I'm asking you to let me join it too. I know it's a terrible thing to ask –'

'No!' she cried. 'No, you can't ask me, Rod, you can't! If you love me you can't ask me to let you go and get killed! I'll never agree – never!'

'Listen, listen – I'm not going to be killed. I'm only giving my support to a cause that's gripping all the thinking people of Europe. Workers, artists, nurses – all sorts of people are going to Spain. I've always been against injustice, you know that, and I couldn't live with myself if I didn't join folk who feel the same. Please, Lindy, say you understand.'

She drew herself from his arms and sank down on to the sofa, putting her hand to her head as he knelt before her. 'We were going to be married,' she said desolately. 'I've been looking at materials for my dress.'

'We are still going to be married, as soon as I come back. I love you, Lindy. I want to be married to you more than anything in the world, but I have to do this first.'

'We could be married before you went.'

He hesitated. 'No, there wouldn't be time.'

'When would you go, then?'

'September. I'll have to put my notice in with the council and make arrangements.'

She sat staring into space, thinking that this was how an earthquake must feel. A cracking open of your whole world, where nothing you'd taken for granted was safe, and where all that was before you was a great dark void.

311

'You don't want to be married now, do you?' she asked. 'Is that because you don't want me to be a widow?' He made no reply but rose to sit with bowed head on the sofa until suddenly she reached across to him and put her arms around him.

'Rod, if I did ask you for my sake no' to join this brigade, would you do it?'

He rested sad eyes on her face and touched her cheek. 'I wouldn't join,' he said softly.

'But you'd never be happy, would you? You'd always be thinking, like you said, that you couldn't live with yourself? But you could always blame me.'

'I'd never blame you, Lindy.'

With a deep sigh, she loosened her arms from him. 'It's all right, Rod. I won't ask you.'

# Sixty-Three

They couldn't eat Rod's salad and Lindy packed it in a bag to give to Aggie, but they did make some tea and sat at the kitchen table to drink it.

'There was something I was going to tell you,' Lindy said after a time. 'Before my world fell apart.'

'Oh, God, Lindy—'

'Look, it doesn't matter anyhow, the way things have changed.'

'My love for you has not changed.'

She looked away. 'Well, all I was going to say was that I don't feel the same about modelling.'

His tired eyes widened. 'How do you mean?'

'I still don't see it like you did, but I – I suppose I think now it's no' for me. I like clothes, I like to look nice, but I feel now that there's too much emphasis on looks, as though they were all that mattered.' She shrugged. 'Truth is, they are, eh? Because your job depends on 'em. But maybe I don't want that sort of job. That's all I was going to say.'

'What sort of job would you like?' Rod asked with sudden eagerness. 'One with women, maybe? Or children?'

'Something I probably can't do.'

'Something like mine?'

She sighed. 'Oh, what's the point in talking, Rod? Nothing matters now.'

'It does, it does. Your world hasn't come to an end. I'll be coming back, we'll be together, and I want you to do something worthwhile. You feel that, too, don't you? I always said, didn't I, that you were one who could care for other people? You wouldn't agree, but you just needed time to see it. And now you have!'

'It's like I say,' she said bleakly. 'What I want to do doesn't matter now. I can't think of anything else except that you're leaving me.'

They clung together, Lindy softly crying, Rod's face dark with emotion.

'I'll be coming back, I will, Lindy. It's just – like you said – something I have to do. But the time will come when we'll be together again, I promise you. Tell me you'll remember that. Tell me, Lindy!'

'And let you go? I've said I will.' She rose,

picking up their cups. 'But I don't want to talk any more. Will you take me home?'

On the drive back they didn't speak. Only when they arrived at number nineteen did Rod break their silence. 'I'll come in with you,' he told Lindy. 'I'll tell your folks myself what I'm going to do.'

'You needn't come in. I can tell them.'

'No, they've a right to hear it from me.'

'If you say so.'

Together they went into the flat, where at the entrance George, Myra, and Struan looked up with smiles.

'Rod, it's grand to see you!' cried George. 'Come and sit down.'

'I'll put the kettle on,' said Myra happily, but Rod thanked her and said no, they didn't want tea.

'Rod has something he wants to tell you,' said Lindy, sitting down and taking Gingerboy on her knee.

'No' bad news, is it?' asked Struan, drawing on a cigarette. 'You're both looking like the man who lost a shilling and found sixpence.'

'Be quiet, Struan,' said George, his smile dying. He too could see the looks on the faces of Lindy and Rod. 'Let Rod say what he wants to say.'

'I hope you'll understand,' Rod began, taking a chair. 'I'm feeling terrible, asking Lindy to understand, too, but she does and she's agreed to let me go.'

'Go where?' asked Myra, her eyes narrowing.

'To Spain with the International Brigade. There's a British contingent going to help restore the government and fight the Fascists who are trying to take over.' Rod was speaking too

314

quickly, trying to hide his nervousness, knowing that as far as Lindy's family was concerned he might have been speaking a foreign language.

'It will seem strange to you, maybe, that I want to go, but I feel I must do what I can to help,' he struggled on. 'I'm not alone, others feel the same – we have to join in, to fight for what's right.'

There was a stunned silence, during which Myra and George exchanged looks and Struan smoked furiously.

'You're going to postpone the wedding?' Myra asked at last. 'You're asking Lindy to do that?'

'I am, yes.' Rod passed his hand over his brow. 'I told you, I feel bad.'

'I'm no' surprised. How could you do it to her, Rod?'

'Aye, how?' asked George, his face bewildered. 'What's Spain to do with us?'

'As I said, it's a question of supporting the right cause. If the generals win there will be a Fascist regime in Spain. The people will be ground down; there'll be totalitarian rule. We can't let it happen.'

'And what good are you going to be?' demanded Struan. 'You're no soldier.'

'I can shoot,' Rod retorted. 'At one time I used to do a lot of target practice; I got into it at school. I admit I haven't done it for some time, but there'll be intensive training.'

There was another silence as eyes turned to Lindy, who was still stroking Gingerboy with quickly moving fingers. She was looking at no one.

'Lindy, how can you let this happen?' Myra demanded. 'Stop this foolish laddie from risking everything for a country he doesn't even know!'

For some moments Lindy made no answer. Then she let Gingerboy go and looked across at her stepmother. 'It's the way he is,' she said quietly. 'There's no way I can change him.'

'Oh, Lindy,' Rod muttered and, reaching towards her, clasped her hand.

'So you'll just wait and hope for the best?' asked Myra. 'I don't know what you're thinking of.'

'She's right,' George said slowly. 'It's the way Rod is. He's one for justice, like he was for me.'

'One for himself,' Myra said curtly. 'What about the ones he's hurting, eh? Our Lindy. His dad? What's your dad going to say, Rod?'

'I'm hoping he'll understand why I'm going,' Rod said in a low voice. 'I think he will.'

'Oh, yes, everybody has to understand, eh? Rod, I'll never think the same of you, never!'

'It's between him and Lindy what they do, Aunt Myra,' Struan told her. 'We shouldn't interfere.'

'Believe me, Mrs Gillan, I wish with all my heart that things were different,' Rod said desperately. 'Believe me, I do.'

When she said nothing, only sat staring at her hands on her lap, he rose and moved towards the door. 'I think I'd better go. Goodnight to you all. And . . . I'm sorry.'

As no one spoke he glanced at Lindy, who joined him at the door, and after a moment or two they went together from the flat into the street.

'I don't blame them for hating me,' Rod muttered. 'I wonder you don't do the same.'

'I don't hate you, Rod.'

'You know I love you? However it seems, I love you?'

'I know, Rod.'

'And you'll wait for me?'

'I'll wait.'

Their arms wound around each other, their lips met.

'This isn't the last goodbye, Lindy,' Rod whispered. 'Not yet.'

'When will it be?' she faltered.

'I'll tell you as soon as I know.'

'Goodnight, then.'

He shook his head, unable to speak, and opened his car door to take his seat. When, after a long moment, he drove away, he did not look at her and she did not wave, but stood for a while without moving.

'Don't say anything,' she murmured when she returned to the flat. 'I don't want to talk.'

'Poor lassie,' murmured George, but no one else spoke.

# Sixty-Four

The last goodbye to Rod was something Lindy never wanted to live through again. It took place at Waverley, Edinburgh's central station, from where he was due to travel to London for the boat train and Channel crossing to France. From there he'd be making for Spain to join other volunteers for training before active service.

Active service. She knew what that meant. Fighting. Danger. But all she could do was hope. In the Great War millions had been killed but some came back. Please God, let Rod come back this time, she prayed, though what right she had to ask that she couldn't say. The wives and sweethearts of all the volunteers willing to fight in Spain would be feeling the same as she did; all knew some would not be coming back.

Rod, of course, was trying to keep his once usual calm, but as they stood on the platform by the side of the long London train she could detect a tension in him which had only appeared since his decision to go to Spain. She knew that he was worrying about her and, at the same time, wondering if he would be able to face whatever he had to face. Now that the time had arrived to depart, the tests ahead had come closer, the call on his courage nearer, and the last goodbye to his beloved was upon him. Sorry as she was for herself, Lindy could feel her sympathy flowing over him and, as the hands of the station clock moved on, she flung her arms round him and clung to him, her tears not far away.

'Oh, God, Lindy will you be all right?' he groaned. 'I feel so bad – so guilty –'

'Look, you're doing what you have to do. I'll be fine. I've got my life all mapped out for when you're away.'

'All mapped out?' Rod tried to smile. 'You mean your evening classes?'

'That's right – my English and maths I've

signed up for. And then there's my Logie's job and any modelling – for the time being, anyway – and checking on your house and writing to your dad. You needn't worry about me, Rod. I won't have time to think.'

'It's good of you to write to Dad, though when he'll get the letters I don't know. He probably hasn't had mine yet.' Rod sighed. 'I wish I hadn't had to tell him what I'm doing, but I had to, hadn't I?'

'He'll understand,' Lindy said, her eyes misting as she looked across to the clock. 'Rod, dearest – it's time.'

'I'll write to you,' he said fiercely, 'even though I've been told we'll be lucky if any post gets through, in or out. But I'll get news to you somehow, Lindy, I promise.'

'The guard's got his flag ready,' she whispered. 'Better get on the train, Rod.'

'One last kiss, Lindy.'

They kissed long and passionately, both shedding tears, then Rod, moving stiffly, climbed aboard the train, staying by the door that a porter slammed behind him so that he could take a last look at Lindy. But the train was moving, slowly, slowly, then gathering speed, and though Lindy ran down the platform, waving as she went, her steps soon slowed and she was left alone, her hand dropping to her side. There was nothing to do but to turn away and go back to Logie's, from where she'd been given permission to take the time off for this last, terrible, wrenching goodbye.

But as she passed the refreshment room she felt so suddenly faint she knew she must have something to get her through – tea or coffee, a scone, maybe – and went inside.

Gratefully drinking coffee at a small table, she began to feel stronger, able to go on to work, anyway, but not better. Oh, God, no. When could she ever hope to feel better? She was crumbling the scone, keeping her tears at bay, when someone came to sit beside her and a man's quiet voice said, 'Lindy?'

She looked up and saw that it was Neil. Neil as he used to be, not anxious, not eaten up with feeling, not even a little strained, but looking well, really well – even – could it be – happy?

'Neil,' she said faintly. 'You've found me again. What are you doing here?'

'Waiting for the next London train. What about you?'

She hesitated. 'I've just been seeing Rod away.'

'Rod? Your young man? Look, mind if I bring my coffee across?'

When he'd brought his coffee over he gazed at her, taking in, she guessed, the tear stains on her face, her look of desolation.

'He was going to London, too?' he asked.

'Further than that. He's joined the Republican International Brigade. He's gone to fight in Spain.'

'Oh my God!' Neil's eyes were horrified. 'And left you? How could he do that, Lindy? Why, you're engaged. How could he leave you like that?'

She almost told him that he had once left her, too, but she only shook her head. 'He feels he has to help. It's the way he is. But I don't want to talk about it.' She drank her coffee. 'What's taking you to London, then?'

He relaxed, smiling again. 'You'll never believe it, Lindy, but I'm going to see a publisher. He likes what I've sent him of my novel. He wants to take it.'

For a moment the mists of her grief cleared and she stared in amazement. 'You're going to be published, Neil? That's wonderful! Tell me about it.'

'Well, this was the third publisher I'd tried. The others turned it down, but he thinks it's terrific. It's called *Rejection* – and if you think it's about me, it is, partly. The hero is rejected in love, but he goes on a journey of discovery, of the world and of himself.' Neil sat back. 'And he triumphs, Lindy. He comes through. So what do you think of that?'

'I think it's terrific, too,' she said quietly. 'I couldn't be more pleased for you. Will you let me read it when it's published?'

'You bet. Look, can I get you another coffee?'

'No, thanks. I have to go back to work. This is my day at Logie's.' Lindy touched Neil's hand. 'It was grand to see you, Neil. Good luck in London.'

'I wish I could walk with you but I've got to catch my train.' Neil, standing, suddenly stooped and kissed her cheek. 'Keep in touch, Lindy, and I hope . . . I hope all goes well for you and for Rod. May he come safely home.'

'Thank you.'

Slowly she made her way from the refreshment room, Neil following, then they smiled and parted, and she continued alone to travel the short distance from Waverley into Princes Street and Logie's. Now the dark clouds had descended over her again and she knew she must endure them. For how long there was no way of knowing. How could there be, when no one knew how long a war would last? Or if a soldier would return?

# Sixty-Five

Time passed but, in spite of all her attempts to keep busy, it was too slow for Lindy. She had her jobs and her studies, even the hope that she might soon be able to think of switching to work for the welfare of women and children, but nothing dulled her anxiety for Rod, whose few letters told her so little.

Even great events in the United Kingdom – the abdication of Edward the Eighth and the coronation of his brother, George the Sixth, scarcely drew her attention, most of which she concentrated on daily reports in the newspapers on the changing situation in Spain. She followed all the battles and sieges, including the vital siege of Madrid, which seemed to have ended with a win for government forces and might have been cause for celebration, except that it wasn't long before the pendulum swung the other way and the rebel nationalist forces, led by the powerful General Franco, were in control of much of Spain.

Yet the fighting went on and there were rumours

of cruelty and atrocities on both sides, and still so little news of Rod. All he would say was that he was all right, managing well, and as for her letters to him, he hardly ever received them.

Everyone she knew was sorry for her, wondering how on earth she was bearing up, to which she could only reply that people in her situation had no choice. They kept going because they had to. All the same she knew that, secretly, her family, Jemima, Neil and all at number nineteen were preparing one day to treat her as someone who, though never married, had become a kind of widow. She, though, would not accept that. Not until she had no choice.

Of course, there were pieces of good news she could enjoy. Jemima's engagement to Struan, for instance, as soon as he had managed to land a full-time job with Wellmore's, where George was doing so well. And then there was Rosemary's wedding, which Lindy and Jemima attended, stepping for a while into Never-Never Land, where everyone seemed rich and beautiful and drank champagne, but which they kept secret from Neil. His recently published book had been a huge success, and even though folk at number nineteen couldn't afford to buy it, they'd queued up to read it from the public library, amazed that their 'Mr Shakespeare' had done well after all. Lindy, of course, had her own signed copy, and did take real pleasure in that.

There were some good things in life, then, but as time moved on and news of Rod dried up, Lindy's courage slowly began to seep away and she sometimes felt she could not go on. Only when she saw Rod's father on his return from

Australia did she manage to put on a brave face, as the two of them exchanged hopes that all might still be well. In the melting pot that was Spain it was not surprising that there should be no news of individuals – they must just be patient. But when Rod's father had sailed away again, down sank Lindy's heart, never, she thought, to rise.

And then it happened. Out of the blue, for the civil war had not come to an end, it was announced in the League of Nations in September, 1938, that all Republican international brigades were to be disbanded. No more foreign nationals would be required. Why, it was not clear, though the papers seemed to think that such a move would win support from the West for the government. All Lindy knew was that there was the light of hope streaming into her life at last. If Rod were alive, surely, surely, he would be coming home?

Every day she waited for news and every day was disappointed, until one morning a postcard arrived with an indecipherable postmark. It was from Rod. Myra had brought it in before everyone left for work, and when Lindy saw it she turned so pale, Struan cried, 'Watch out, she's going over!'

'I'm not, I'm not!' she cried, but as her legs collapsed under her she sank into the nearest chair, the postcard still in her hand. 'Oh, listen, listen – he says he'll be arriving at Victoria Station, London, on December the seventh! Can you believe it? I must go. I must be there!'

'Lindy, it's only September,' said Myra.

'I know, I know.' Lindy put her hand to her

brow. 'You know, I feel so strange – everything seems to be going round . . .'

'Struan, fetch some water,' Myra ordered, but it was George who squeezed the teapot.

'A cup o' tea is what Lindy needs,' he declared. 'Seeing as we have no brandy.'

'You no' got any o' that port left?' asked Struan.

'Tea will be fine,' said Lindy, and burst into tears.

# Sixty-Six

Where was he, where was he? On the platform at Victoria, that chill December day, Lindy was bobbing up and down in the waiting crowd, searching for Rod. There were so many men alighting from the train, shaking the hands of Clement Attlee and other well-known people come to welcome them home that she couldn't single him out, yet he must be there. But where?

Most of the men, she noticed, were still in rough uniforms; others had found a variety of things to wear, and though some looked well, others were bandaged or leaning on sticks. Was Rod one of these? Her eyes were everywhere, searching, searching . . .

And then she saw him. He had just spoken a word or two to one of the official party and was now moving on; his eyes, too, were searching, searching. For her, of course, but at first she couldn't speak his name. The sight of him, so gaunt, so weary, in a jacket she couldn't remember, had seemed to close her throat and she could only wave and wave, until – thank God – he saw her.

'Lindy!'

'Oh, Rod!' she managed to speak at last as they went into a locked embrace, oblivious of everyone around them. 'Rod, you're here. It doesn't seem true.' She was running her fingers down his face. 'I hadn't heard, I thought you might be –'

'Dead? No, I'm not dead. Oh, God, Lindy, is it really you? Or am I dreaming?'

'It's me,' she said softly. 'And you're no' dreaming. But Rod, can you come with me? Can you come straight home? I've got tickets for the Edinburgh train.'

'The Edinburgh train? Lindy, how wonderful that sounds! There is some sort of welcoming party laid on, but I needn't go –' His eyes went over the faces of the waiting crowd and he smiled a little. 'I can see these people anyway – they're welcoming enough, I think. They know why we went, what we tried to do.' He grasped Lindy's hand. 'But I want to come home, Lindy, to be with you – if you've any money?'

'Money?'

'I've a confession to make. I've none till I can get back to Edinburgh. We only got paid three pesos a day, and I spent what I'd taken with me in the first couple of weeks.'

'No need to worry, I've got money,' she told him gladly. 'I've no' been doing too badly lately. So, let's take a taxi, eh? To King's Cross.'

'To King's Cross,' he said, taking a deep breath as he picked up his bag. 'And home.'

\* \* \*

326

It was late evening when they arrived back at Waverley after the long journey north, during which Lindy gave Rod all the news he'd never received in her letters. How his dad was well – everyone was well, Struan and Jemima were engaged, Neil had written a very successful novel and Lindy herself had passed her exams at evening class and was planning to try for new work soon. Though he listened with the greatest interest and was delighted to hear of Lindy's plans, he said nothing of his own experiences in Spain and she did not question him. Best to leave it till he was ready, she decided, as they arrived in Edinburgh to take another taxi, this time to Rod's house.

'I've got it all ready for you,' she told him. 'There's a steak pie waiting, the boiler's on and Struan's left your car at the gate.'

'He's let me have it back?' Rod laughed, and it seemed to her that he was looking better, even since he first arrived. And walking round his house again he was like a boy, exclaiming over Christmas presents.

'All still here,' he whispered. 'Just as I remember it. And I used to think about it so often – when I wasn't thinking about you, Lindy.'

He gazed at her before turning away suddenly, putting his hand to his eyes.

'Sorry, I'm just being a fool. Look, I can't wait to get out of these clothes and take a bath. God knows what you must think of me!'

'You know what I think of you! But I'll go down, eh, and get our supper ready.'

* * *

'This is good,' he commented later, beginning to eat the steak pie Lindy had served. 'Can't tell you what it means to me to get some British food again.'

Fresh from his bath, wearing clean clothes, with his damp hair combed, he looked so much his old self that Lindy's heart beat with joy. Whatever had happened in Spain, however long he took to return to his old life, he was back, her Rod, and she couldn't be more grateful.

'I'm glad it's OK. I thought you might be too tired to eat.'

'No. After that bath I feel fine.'

He hesitated. 'You won't mind, though, if I don't talk yet – about Spain.'

'Oh, no, I wasn't expecting you to.'

'There was the fighting – obviously, I came through, but . . . Look, all I'll just say is I don't regret what I did. None of us do. We did our best and if we lost to the Fascists it wasn't due to any lack of spirit on our part.' His eyes on her were shadowed in grief. 'You know five hundred of us died?'

She turned pale and leaned over to kiss his cheek. 'I don't like to think about it. And are you saying that the Fascists are going to win?'

'Sure, they are. General Franco's pretty well in control. He's going to run Spain like a dictator, and there's going to be nothing anyone can do.' Rod put his knife and fork together. 'But, as I say, we did our best, those of us there.'

'You did, Rod, you did! You had to go; you had to try to help the government, the one the people wanted.'

'Yes, I can think of that.' Rod, rising, drew

Lindy to her feet. 'That was lovely, Lindy, but I think I'd better get you home. Has Struan left me the car keys?'

'Oh, yes, and he's filled up with petrol. It was so good of you to lend him the car, Rod. He's taken such care of it.'

'I'm very grateful to him.'

They had moved into the hall and were standing at the foot of the stairs when Lindy put her arms tightly round Rod. Now she was with him again, the misery of their parting over, she felt a sudden, overriding passion to be one with him, to have what had been denied to her these past two years, to be married as she should have been. Once she had been afraid of marriage, reluctant to take it on. Now she sought it as her right.

'I don't want to go,' she whispered.

'I don't want you to, but your folks will be wondering where you are.'

'They know I'll be late, coming back with you from London.'

'Still, I don't want them to be worried.'

'I tell you they won't be.'

For some time they gazed into each other's faces, then Lindy turned to look up the staircase.

'We are engaged, Rod.'

'I know,' he said huskily.

'We're as good as married, really. I mean, we might have been married two years already.'

'We'll arrange another wedding, as soon as possible.'

'What I'm saying is . . .' She hesitated. 'Maybe you can guess, eh? What I'm saying?'

'No, Lindy, no. I couldn't ask it.'

'I'm the one who's asking.' She began to draw him up the stairs. 'I know you'd never have asked me, Rod, so it had to be me.' Halting at the top of the stairs, she looked back, her hand on the banister, trembling. 'It will be like the honeymoon we should have had.'

'My room's there,' Rod said, his voice a whisper.

'I know where your room is. You remember, I've been checking the house for you? Yesterday I made your bed.'

Slowly, gently, they moved into his room, not looking at his old books and model ships made long ago, or even the family photographs and one of Lindy herself on his chest of drawers. All that drew them was his bed, so neatly made by Lindy, and it was there that they lay, exchanging long, deep glances before undressing and sinking into each other's arms.

'Oh, Lindy!' Rod gasped. 'Lindy!'

'It's all right, don't worry about me. I told you – this is our honeymoon. The one we should have had.'

And then for a while there was no more talking, and Rod stopped worrying while Lindy gave herself up to the joy that was new, yet all she'd come to imagine.

'It will be better next time,' Rod murmured as later they dressed, eyeing each other as though they'd passed through some something unbelievable. 'That's what's always said.'

'I liked it this time,' she told him. 'I told you no' to worry, didn't I?'

Downstairs, putting on coats, they wonderfully felt themselves to be married, but of course they weren't. Lindy had to go home, tell her folks something of her momentous day, but not all of it. Would they see that she was different? She hoped all they would see was her excitement over Rod's return; after all, that was real enough.

In the car, Rod tried to speak of his feelings, without much success. 'I just feel – hell, I don't know what I feel. Not guilty, anyway, as maybe I should be feeling. Remember how I worried about bringing you to my home alone? And you said I could be trusted?'

'Rod, times have changed. We weren't engaged then. There's nothing to feel guilty about now.'

'OK, I'll believe you. But let's organize our wedding as soon as possible, then I'll feel better.'

'Me, too,' said Lindy.

Outside number nineteen he stopped the car and took her hand. 'It's been wonderful, Lindy, my homecoming,' he told her. 'Better even than I could have imagined, thanks to you. Whatever happens in the future – and it doesn't look promising – we'll be together, won't we? We'll have each other, and that's what matters?'

'All that matters.'

'Wish me luck tomorrow,' he said lightly. 'When I go job hunting at the council.'

'I'll always wish you luck, wherever you go,' she answered seriously. 'Because your luck's my luck.'

'And it will always be good, Lindy. We'll make it so.'

'Do you want to come in and see them?' she asked, after they'd exchanged a long, quiet kiss. 'My folks?'

'Just for a minute. If they'd like to see me.'

'Of course they'd like to see you! They've come round to understanding why you went. I knew they would.'

'All right, then.'

Holding hands, they went together into number nineteen, a place so familiar, with familiar people waiting, yet both feeling ready to face a life that would be new. Full of challenge, maybe, but as they had said, they would face it together. And that was all that mattered.